MW01503497

What White Boyz Fight For

by

Giselle Carmichael

Kelley Nyrae

Pamela Leigh Starr

Eve Vaughn

What White Boyz Fight For

Noire Fever is an imprint of Parker Publishing LLC.

Copyright © 2010 by Giselle Carmichael, Kelley Nyrae, Pamela Leigh
        Starr and Eve Vaughn
Published by Parker Publishing Inc
12523 Limonite Avenue, Suite #440-438
Mira Loma, California 91752
www.parker-publishing.com

ISBN: 978-1-60043-092-3
First Edition

Manufactured in the United States of America
Cover Design by Parker Publishing Inc

A Kiss on the Lips
by
Giselle Carmichael

Chapter One

Marine Staff Sergeant Cree Novak parked his Ford F-150 outside the Landon Key Civic Center and shut off the engine. Picking up the invitation in the passenger seat, he read it again and just like the first time, anger like he had never known overcame him. He leaned back in his seat trying to bring his emotions under control. He allowed his thoughts to wander back to a month ago. He had been notified of his next assignment, one that would guarantee a promotion to Gunnery Sergeant, a big feat for someone twenty-eight. But with one trip to the mailroom everything had changed.

He had sat on his bunk staring at the black script type with disbelief then anger had consumed him at the audacity. Finally he was left to face some real truths about himself and his life. He had convinced himself the Corps was all important and the rest would wait; however, the invitation had placed everything into perspective. He had immediately returned to his office picking up the telephone making a decision. Calling in every favor he had coming, as of yesterday morning, he was honorably discharged from the United States Marine Corps. The sudden decision and the swiftness of his actions had surprised all those who knew him, or thought they knew him. His buddy, Jared Lighthorse had stared with disbelief when he returned from Afghanistan, back to the base and told him of his decision to be released early from his extension.

"Are you sure you want to do this?" Jared had asked. He had stood stiff and a bit pensive.

"Very sure." He had continued to shove the last of his things into his duffle bag. He had glanced around the room of his temporary living quarters one last time and spotted the invitation on the desk. Walking over, he picked up the white envelope.

"Is that it?"

"Yeah."

Jared had pulled the envelope from his fingers. He stood there reading what was printed on the card inside. When he concluded reading, he had looked at him a bit angry and a great deal disappointed. "Do you realize you're throwing away a career not to mention a well deserved promotion?"

Cree turned on him, nailing him with a stare. "I've defended my country honorably for ten years. I went when and where they wanted me, no questions asked, and no thought for anyone else. It's my time now. Time for me to fight for what's important to me. That promotion won't keep me warm at night."

"Is that what you're worried about? I can call up a few ladies to keep your bed warm any night of the week."

Cree rolled his eyes and stomped across the floor to retrieve the envelope. "There's only one woman I want warming my bed."

"Yeah, don't I know, but is she worth you throwing everything away? Hell man, she split right after you left."

"Yes, she's worth it and a great deal more. She is everything to me. I didn't realize that before, but I do now."

It was amazing how clear things became when you were close to losing them. Throwing open the truck door and stepping out he had no intention of losing. One thing the Marine Corps had taught him was how to establish an objective, strategize, prepare, and implement a plan of action, and now was no different. Losing wasn't an option. Closing the door, he easily slipped into fighting mode, the objective front and center in his mind. His emotions were of no use here as they would distract, and cause him to be careless in action. A warrior didn't win by being careless. He had to make every word and action count if his plan was to work.

Walking across the parking lot he was well aware of the numerous cars. The event was obviously well attended and in full swing. He stepped onto the sidewalk realizing this was the most important mission of his life. Pulling open the door, he placed his hat under his arm and followed the sound of music to the open doors of Ballroom One. Taking surveillance of the room, he recognized several familiar faces, a majority of those he called friend. He knew his presence would cause a commotion, but it was unavoidable. He moved through the crowd passing an old classmate. A quick nod in the man's direction and he moved on searching the room. Loud male laughter drew his attention. A quick survey of the professional dressed men, he zeroed in on one in particular, knowing he had identified the enemy. He was the rooster with his chest stuck out. Ignoring his special forces training of taking out the enemy before being detected, he gave the man one final glance before moving on.

A few more casual nods then a familiar sensation similar to radar directed him to the right. Standing with three very familiar faces was the woman he was searching for. His heart did what it always did when she was near. It thumped heavily against his ribs, sending blood rushing to his groin. His nostrils flared as though scenting her, and the room fell away as he stood there looking at her.

She had changed since he had last seen her. The long hair he remembered running his fingers through was gone. A halo of springy auburn curls framed her round dark brown face now, an extreme change that was sexy as well as mature. She had always looked younger than she was and the new style helped her to look her age of twenty-eight. Expressive chocolate brown eyes stared back at him, sparking with a mixture of longing and anger. God, he had missed her. His eyes dropped to her small stubborn mouth painted in a dark cherry lipstick that would stain his cock. The idea had him growing heavy. The square neckline of the cherry-wine dress fell temptingly across the swells of her lush breasts and his mouth watered. He remembered the taste of her small nipples on his tongue. He ran his eyes down the length of her body before returning to her face. It was then he noticed her defiant dimpled chin hike higher. She was pissed, probably had a good reason to be so, but he was overjoyed to be back home. Two solid years in the desert with no leave time was the only thing preventing him from coming back to her, especially after his phone calls went unanswered or returned. His emails were deleted unread and the gifts he had mailed were left at his mother's home. But he was back now and God help anyone that got in his way.

Jaxon Alexander stood in the middle of a sea of well wishers feeling completely alone. It was her engagement party and instead of being overjoyed with happiness, she was terrified she was making the greatest mistake of her life. She loved Drew Joiner that was a fact. He was kind and gentle, dedicated to family, and community. They shared similar likes of books, movies, and political views, but that's where the similarities ended. On the matter of sex, they were miles apart. Not that they had actually made love. Drew had informed her early in their relationship a year ago that he had reclaimed his virginity. Okay, not exactly what a woman with a strong libido wants to hear, but she could wait. Anticipation after all was half the fun. Then he had declared he was a traditionalist and that man was meant to be on top. She could go for that as long as she was on all fours. But a life of tepid kisses and the missionary position he preferred wasn't going to cut it. She wasn't a freak by any stretch of the imagination, but she loved a good hard ride every now and then, and it didn't seem to be in Drew's nature.

God, how could she settle for lackluster chemistry when she knew what it was like to be in a perpetual state of arousal simply because the other person existed? She was haunted by memories of making love to the point of exhaustion. The type of love making that left your hair wild about your head and the sheets stripped from the bed. The uninhibited session of love making that began in one room and ended in another with you crumpled on top of each other in a sated heap. She moaned with longing, just remembering such a time, and felt her body respond to the memory. Her breathing had deepened and if she was right, her panties were a little moist. How the heck was she supposed to do this?

So here she stood pretending to listen as her friends wished her well and told her how lucky she was. She had heard Drew was a great catch; good looking, successful, and from the right family. Lord, she didn't have the heart to tell them the man left her cold. Glancing across the room to where Drew stood with his boys, their eyes connected and although he smiled back, there was no passion in his eyes. No sudden change in his breathing. He merely turned around focusing back of the conversation at hand. She watched his face become expressive while talking to his friends, and realized there was more excitement for them, than her. So why were they having an engagement party, and why had she allowed the relationship to progress to this point?

Then the answer to her question walked in. Clad in the Marine Corps blue uniform with red stripe running down the side of the pants leg, and a chest of colorful medals, Cree Novak was the passion she had been missing. She immediately became aware of her heart thundering wildly in her chest, and her panties were definitely wet now. In the dark of night when she laid alone in bed, it was his hands she'd imagined touching her and his dirty blond head between her legs making her flow like a champagne fountain. And God help her, if the man crooked his finger right now, she would gladly strip butt naked for a round of his marathon love making.

It had always been like that between them. From freshman year in high school, she had known Cree was what she wanted. He had sat in front of her in Algebra, giving her something more to study than the mathematical equation on the board. Then he had turned around smiling and in that single moment, she had lost her heart to him. Sex would come the night before he left for the Marines after years of mounting anticipation, and boy had the wait been worth it. By the time he kissed her good night under the porch light, she knew no man would ever compare to Cree, and unfortunately that was true to this day. However, the one thing Drew possessed that Cree didn't was stability.

She was an adult now and accepted the fact she and Cree weren't meant to be. His love for the special ops missions the Marine Corps sent him on outweighed his love for her. For years she had settled for visits from him and her to him, each a whirlwind of heart-stopping, hot and sweaty sex. She had moved to settle near his base a time or two. With each visit or move she gave him a little more of her heart until there was no more to give. She had finally given him an ultimatum, her or the Marine Corps, and he had chosen her. With his enlistment winding down, they were happy and making plans for a future together then a dangerous, yet an exciting mission came up, one that had him extending in the Corps. That had been two years ago and she had stopped waiting.

She stood now staring into crystal blue eyes becoming keenly aware of them stripping her bare, and although she was mad as hell, she couldn't stop herself from quivering with desire.

"Oh my God, it's Cree," Gaby whispered as though she thought Jaxon didn't see him. "Did you invite him?"

"No! Of course not," Jaxon snapped.

"Then why is he here?" Gaby asked like the attorney she was. Tall and reed thin with a caramel complexion, she was a force to be reckoned with.

"From that come hither look in his eyes, I'd say he was here for you." Tori the reporter tapped Jaxon on the shoulder making sure she knew whom she was referring.

"This can't be good," Jessica the worry wart, warned. Her classic Irish features were strained with apprehension.

"I don't know," Tori spoke up. Her gray eyes, a gift from her Caucasian father sparkled with mischief in her lightly toasted brown face. "The way G.I. Joe is looking at our girl, I'd say she was going to get it real good later."

"Tori, do I have to remind you this is Jaxon's engagement party?" Jessica hissed, appalled.

"Engagements are meant to be broken, and since the ring hasn't been officially placed on her finger, it's a moot point. Besides, I've never seen Drew look at Jaxon like that," Gaby added.

"I have to agree with her," Tori chimed in.

"Oh alright, the man does look a bit randy," Jessica said, giving Jaxon a nudge. "He also looks damn good."

Jaxon hated to agree with her, but when didn't the man look good with his classic features. He was taller than most men at six-four, with a body that made women purr. Broad in the shoulders, narrow in the waist with long, muscular legs, he moved with effortless strength. And damn if he wasn't wearing that uniform. His chiseled jaw ticked with obvious unease as he stared down at her with his perfect straight nose. Her eyes dropped to his wide kissable lips remembering the feel of them taking control of hers. Tired of being analyzed, he jutted out his movie star square chin with arrogance, regaining her full attention.

"Will you three shut up?" Jaxon finally found her voice. Now that the initial shock of seeing him was gone, anger was quickly moving in. She couldn't believe the audacity of the man to show up at her engagement party. "I'll be back." She strutted across the floor aware that all eyes were on her.

"Hi Cree." Jaxon swallowed under the affect of his hypnotic gaze.

"Is that all you have to say to me?" His tone was biting.

"It's probably more than you deserve."

His jaw flexed, signaling she had struck a nerve. "Is there somewhere we can talk in private?" His eyes darkened to a lethal ice blue when they swung from her face to something behind her.

Jaxon didn't need to be told Drew was coming in their direction. She felt her stomach clench with fear because Cree was strung tight and Drew had no idea whom he was dealing with. She spun around cutting him off before he confronted Cree.

"Is everything all right here?" Drew asked, eyeing Cree suspiciously.

"Yes." She flashed a reassuring smile. "Cree and I are going to step out on the patio and talk. I won't be long."

Drew nodded. "Take your time."

Jaxon frowned not sure she liked his response. She watched him walk away a little miffed that he seemed so nonchalant. She heard Cree chuckle as he closed in behind her.

"I sure as hell wouldn't leave you alone to talk to an ex-lover." He walked around her and headed toward the patio.

She followed behind him and knew the moment he spotted their mothers. She recalled the numerous hours they had spent at each other's homes. Her mother and father loved Cree because he was a military man serving his country. His mother loved her because she loved her only son as much as she did. Their mothers had taken their breakup badly as all had expected them to marry. Both women now beamed with happiness on seeing him.

"Mrs. Alexander, how are you?" Cree greeted Jaxon's mother. He drew Amanda Alexander into his arms and pressed an affectionate kiss onto her cheek. To his mother he whispered, "Hi Mom." He picked the petite woman up, hugging her.

"Welcome home, baby," Julia whispered back.

"Good to see you, Cree." Amanda smiled up at the handsome young man who had been a fixture around her home since he and Jaxon were in high school.

"You too." He looked back at Jaxon. "Will you both excuse us? I'll see you later."

Amanda nodded, taking a look at her daughter. "You okay, precious?"

Jaxon rolled her eyes. "What do you think, Mama? I'll see you later." She kissed her mother's cheek and followed behind Cree, missing the high five exchanged between Julia and Amanda. Stepping out onto the large patio she followed Cree away from the door, out of sight from the guests inside. She turned on him unleashing two years of anger. "What the hell do you think you're doing showing up here like this?"

"Why did you send me an invitation if you didn't want me to come?" His eyes were cool and unruffled.

"I didn't send you an invitation. Why would I?"

"Because you know you're making a mistake."

"How, by agreeing to marry a man who wants to be with me?" She stood her ground.

"You don't love him," Cree stated flatly.

"Don't you dare tell me who I love."

"I can show you better than I can tell you."

Cree grabbed her before she knew what was happening and pushed her against the outside wall, crushing his mouth down upon hers. The kiss was brutal. His tongue pushed passed her tight lips to the warm interior of her mouth feeding upon it. His tongue raked against the roof her mouth the way she liked. He sucked her bottom lip into his mouth, teasing it with his tongue. His hands were busy under the silk hem of her dress, bunching it around her waist as he fit his swelling crotch into the seat of her panties. He dry humped her hard the way she liked while devouring her mouth, and when she was on the brink of coming, he released her, allowing her to teeter on her heels confused and dazed.

"Try telling me you love him now." Cree smiled at her discomfort.

Jaxon regained her footing while trying to right her clothing. Her hands trembled, evidence of how shaken she was by the kiss. She felt tears sting the back of her eyes because she would have humped him against that wall until they both came, and knowing he was well aware of her desire for him, only made her feel worse. "There's more to a relationship than sex, Cree." Her voice trembled surrendering.

"I know that, Jax and we have more," he whispered hoarsely with emotion. "Baby, I love you. I missed you." He moved in close, placing kisses over her face. "God, I've missed you."

"But not enough to leave the Marines." Hurt filled eyes met his. She wanted to push him away but couldn't.

"I was wrong, Jax. At the time I thought I was making the right decision for us, but honey, I know now that I was wrong." He kissed her swollen lips. There would be no hiding the fact that she had been thoroughly kissed. "Please don't ruin three lives."

"Drew loves me and wants to build a life with me. That's more than you ever offered," she slung the angry words at him, gaining no pleasure when she saw the look of guilt cloud his eyes.

"I deserved that."

"No you didn't. You made your choices in life and I've accepted them." She tilted her head back to meet his gaze. "Now, I've made mine."

Cree knew he couldn't simply walk in here with a few well placed words and win her back. Jaxon by nature would fight him tooth and nail to prove that she didn't need or love him. If she wanted a fight, he would damn sure give her one. "You're not in love with that guy. You and I both know it, Jax. You've loved me for half of your damn life, as I have you."

"Didn't stop you from extending in the Corps and taking that next mission, did it?"

"Dammit Jaxon, I was wrong! Like a fool I thought you would always be there and when the Corps was behind me, we would get married. I never thought you would hook up with the first guy to come along."

"Don't you dare turn this around on me. You could have married me years ago, but you didn't?" She jabbed him in the chest with an angry finger.

Cree grabbed her finger refusing to let go when she tried to pull away. "The missions I were assigned are known for leaving widows. I didn't want that for you."

"Am I supposed to thank you? It wasn't your decision, Cree, it was mine. Did you think the pain would be less because I wasn't your wife?" She stood there glaring at him. "You're a fool because you let the best thing to happen to you get away. Live with it." She turned on her heels to walk back toward the door.

"No baby, you live with it," Cree, shot back, grabbing her by the arm and yanking her back into his arms. He hauled her once again to the wall pinning her with his larger body. "You live without me kissing you the way you like. Can you live without me sucking on your nipples?" His thumbs stroked the buds poking through the thin fabric of her dress. "How about how I play with you?" He shoved his right hand under her dress to cup her mound. He was pleased she wore no pantyhose. He worked his fingers under the elastic of her panties to stroke her.

"Stop, Cree." Jaxon shoved against his hand.

"Does he touch you like this? Do you get hot for him, baby, cream all over his fingers?"

Jaxon squirmed trying to get away from his talented fingers. "Don't do this, please."

"Oh, I have to because you want it baby. I can see it in your eyes." His fingers found her wet lips. "You're hot, Jax and so damn wet." He pushed his middle finger into her and began fingering her. "Damn you're tight. Doesn't your man fuck you?"

"God, Cree, you've got to stop," she pleaded, but didn't push him away. Her eyes were slightly glazed with desire.

"Ride it, baby." He continued to make love to her with his fingers. "You belong to me, Jax. Your body knows my touch, honey. Feel how it weeps for me." He worked her over good. He watched her eyes close as she gave herself over to the pleasure and stopped fighting him. Her head tilted back as she suddenly came all over his hand. Cree pulled his fingers away and held them before her face. "Look at my fingers, Jax. This is all the proof I need to know you love me."

"It's sex, Cree." She still trembled from his touch. Her face was stricken with embarrassment.

"Sex your man obviously isn't giving you."

Jaxon shoved hard against his chest not wanting to go there with him. She could feel his eyes on her.

"Why haven't you made love with him, Jax? You enjoy sex."

"Who said I haven't?" she responded petulantly.

"You're too tight," he told her crudely. "You humped my fingers like a starving woman." He ran his fingers down the side of her neck. "Don't let stubbornness ruin our lives." He turned her chin bringing her face around to his. "You are my heart, Jaxon." He kissed her sweetly. "We belong together, baby."

"And I'm supposed to rush back inside and tell Drew I can't marry him, because you have finally gotten around to paying attention to me. Go to hell, Cree."

"Without you I am in hell." He took several steps back putting distance between them. Looking down, he noticed for the first time he had dropped his hat in his haste to get at her, an act he had never committed in his entire career. He picked it up and shoved it back under his arm. He wandered the patio trying to gain control. He came back toward her, softening the look in his eyes. "I love you, Jaxon. The thought of you with another man is killing me, and the thought of him touching you, is like shoving a knife into my gut."

"I'm not trying to hurt you." She wanted to run a hand down his chest to comfort him, but didn't trust herself to touch him.

Cree grasped one of her curls, rubbing the strand between his thumb and finger. "I know that, and if you look me in the eyes and tell me you're in love with this guy, I'll walk right out the door never to bother you again." His eyes locked with hers.

"I love Drew."

"That's not what I said. Are you *in* love with him?"

Jaxon tried to look away. She couldn't look into Cree's eyes and lie. "Just go. Please." A single tear ran down her cheek.

His expression was sympathetic. She could see he wasn't enjoying pushing her, but was determined to get her to say what he wanted to hear. He reached into the interior pocket of his jacket and removed an envelope. "This is a ticket for a cruise leaving out tomorrow afternoon. You'll have your own cabin. All I ask of you is that you join me for seven days. Seven days for me to convince you that we belong together."

"I can't."

"Yes, you can."

She resisted taking the envelope. "I don't know, Cree."

"Take it." He placed it into her hand. "Just think about what I've said." He kissed her lightly on the lips. "I'll be on that ship. Either I'll see you tomorrow, or never again." With one final look he turned and walked back through the door leading back into the party.

Jaxon clutched the envelope like a life line while watching him go. There was no time to think. People waited inside. Drew waited inside. Righting her clothing and patting her hair back into place, she wiped at her mouth. She squared her shoulders, pushing away from the wall and headed for the door. Headed back to Drew.

Chapter Two

Cree watched from the Lido deck as the cruise ship pulled away from the dock. He had been on board since twelve thirty when the ship began boarding passengers, most of that time was spent at the railing looking down upon the other cruisers as they came on board. He was searching for Jaxon. He hadn't seen her and didn't know if that meant she wasn't coming or simply he had missed her. Hoping for the later, he continued to search the faces of passing passengers as they took to sea. He fought against the weight of loss trying to swamp him. Perhaps he had come on too strong last evening. He knew how stubborn she could be when pushed, and he had definitely pushed her. He had all but thrown her down on the patio and made love to her. Not that it would have been a bad idea considering last night may have been the last time he would see her.

It had taken everything in him to walk away from her. He loved her and no one else. When he had initially joined the Marines, he'd had every intention of marrying Jaxon, then he had been selected for special ops, and things had changed. They had been warned about the high mortality rate of members as their missions often ventured behind enemy lines. On his second mission the team experienced such a loss. He had been present when the wife had been informed of her husband's death. The sound of her wail had stayed with him for years. He vowed right then never to place Jaxon in that position. At the time it seemed like the right thing to do, but just as she had said last night, she would have mourned his death whether married to him or not because she loved him. So if she loved him so much, where the hell was she and why hadn't she used the ticket?

He was exhausted after weeks of moving mountains and calling in favors to get an early discharge, with nothing to show for it. He was at a loss as to which direction to turn. Pushing away from the railing, he walked over to a chaise lounge stretching out near the pool. He released the buttons on his blue cotton shirt to better feel the pleasant breeze against his skin. Several women clad in barely there bikinis were already in the swimming pool and flashing come-hither looks in his direction. He continued to watch as they jiggled their tits and shook their asses waiting for something to pop out. He thought about hooking up with one or all of them in an effort to get Jaxon out of his system, until he realized his pal down below wasn't responding. He snorted in disgust. A limp pecker would only bring him embarrassment. Damn the woman had ruined him for other women. He closed his eyes trying to banish all thoughts of

Jaxon Alexander.

"A Kiss on the Lips, sir," a male voice said beside him.

Cree's eyes popped open. He turned toward voice with his most lethal expression in place. "Do it and die."

The African waiter chuckled realizing Cree didn't understand. "A drink from the lady at the bar." The waiter handed him a frosted glass containing a fruity looking beverage.

"What's it called?"

"A Kiss on the Lips. From the lady at the bar," the waited repeated, pointing in the direction of the large bar.

"What lady?" Cree asked looking off to the left of the deck where the man indicated. A relieved breath left his body at the sight of her. She had come. A pleased smile stretched across his face at the image of Jaxon sitting on a bar stool. She raised her glass in greeting. Swinging his feet to the deck, he wasted no time in going to her.

"Thanks for the drink." He slid onto the stool beside her. "But I prefer this type of kiss on the lips." He placed his hand to the back of her head, drawing her mouth toward his as he claimed her lips for a deep, thorough kiss. He pulled away meeting her eyes. "I'm glad you came."

"I didn't come for you."

"Then why are you here?" he asked with a raised brow. His piercing eyes were daring her to lie.

"There was no point in allowing a good ticket to go to waste." A teasing smile touched her lips.

"If that's what you have to tell yourself, go ahead. I'm just pleased you're here." He ran a hand down her arm. He admired the short aqua tropical print sundress she wore. Her dark skin glowed against the color and felt just as buttery soft as he remembered. Her fabulous legs that would grip his hips as he drove into her, were crossed before her, and on her feet were a near nothing white thong sandal. "What did you tell *him*?" His eyes swept up to hers.

Jaxon chewed on her bottom lip uncomfortable with the quick shift in topic. "You had nothing to do with my decision," she said quick and up front. "I did what I knew was right."

"You told him you didn't love him."

"I told him I did, but that I wasn't in love with him." She reached over taking Cree's hand. "But, I'm not going backwards either. So if you want me, you're going to have to prove I'm your priority. I won't make it easy for you."

Cree grinned and leaned forward whispering low and seductive in her ear. "You were never easy, but I got you, baby." He watched as a visible tremor went through her body.

"There you go talking about sex again, Cree." She fought back a smile.

"I wasn't talking about sex." He laughed. "Okay, I was, but that's because it was always hot between us."

On that Jaxon took a long sip of her drink. "That was never our problem," she reminded him.

"Have dinner with me tonight and we can talk."

"Don't they seat other people with you?"

"Not in the restaurant," he told her. "I have an eight o'clock reservation."

"I'd love to join you," Jaxon finally agreed.

"Grab your drink. Let's sit at one the tables." He assisted her in getting down from the stool and threaded his fingers through hers. They located a quiet secluded table and turned their chairs so they overlooked the water. Side by side they set for several minutes enjoying the beauty before them. He still held her hand. "I've missed you." He looked over at her.

"Not enough. It took you two years to come after me."

"Is that what you wanted? Me to come after you?"

"It wouldn't have hurt," she admitted, finally looking at him.

"After you rejected my phone calls and gifts, I decided to get over you."

Jaxon swallowed hard. "You mean with other women?" Her eyes roamed over his face and he wondered what she was thinking.

"I've been celibate for two years. Tracking in the mountains of Afghanistan doesn't lend for amorous rendezvous."

Jaxon's eyes flew to his on hearing those words. She could almost feel the heat coming off his skin. A man like Cree needed sex. To be celibate for two years was unthinkable. The unleashing of all that energy was going to be a volcanic eruption of erotic passion. The man was demanding on a woman on a normal day and now after two years, she shivered at the thought of all that energy powering into her. She clamped her legs together to ease the persistent beat between her legs. Closing her eyes, she couldn't allow him to see how hungry she was for his touch.

"Don't be afraid of me, Jax."

She opened her eyes to him unable to hide her desire. "I've never been afraid of you, Cree. I'm not now." She released a sultry laugh. "You might need to be afraid of me."

His eyes crinkled at the corners with humor. "It's been that long for you too?"

"Couldn't you tell? That night in the swimming pool was the last time." She watched as emotions played over his face as he recalled their last time together. They had rented a vacation home in Key West, taking full advantage of the swimming pool. Midnight swims in the nude led to amorous lovemaking until the wee hours of the morning.

"Damn woman you were hot that night." He leaned his head back against the chair. "You know it's not like we don't know each other."

Jaxon's head whipped in his direction. "Are you implying what I think you are?" Her pulse raced at the possibility, while her womb clinched with longing.

"Two years is a long time. We could help each other out."

"Sex buddies?" She saw his nostril flare and knew her words were exactly what he was proposing and to her surprise she actually liked the idea. Two years was a long time to go without the feel of man between her legs.

"Hot sex I can guarantee, but darling, I don't want to be your buddy." He swung his legs around so that he faced her. He trailed his fingers back and forth on her thigh, just under the hem of the short dress. "Come on, baby, let me take the edge off. It'll be good. You know you want it."

And she did, all day and a night until she couldn't move, but she didn't say anything. She concentrated on the feel of his touch on her leg.

"Think about it, the two of us naked; you on all fours the way you like, and me giving it to you from behind. Or if you prefer, I can pleasure you with my mouth. Either way I can get you off."

"Shut up, Cree."

"Just think about my fingers and tongue working you over."

An agonizing groan tore from Jaxon's lips as she suddenly stood up grabbing his hand. "Your room or mine?" She dragged him to his feet. The man had her hot and horny and by damn he was going to put out her fire.

"Oh, definitely, mine darling. I have a balcony cabin with a king size bed." Cree smiled at her like the big bad wolf and led the way to the elevator.

Jaxon stood beside him waiting for the car to arrive while the prospect of being flesh to flesh with Cree heightened her arousal. She felt her cheeks flame when he looked over at her, raking her body with a suggestive glance while dropping his hand to her hip. The heat from his large palm seeped through her dress and undergarments sending warmth to her core. She felt her breasts swell and strain against the fabric of her dress, her nipples hard and pointing. And the longer they waited, the more anticipated her breathing. She wanted him. Rubbing up against him like a cat in heat, she slid her hand slyly over his crotch and smiled when she heard his quick intake of breath.

"Forget the damn elevator," Cree snapped.

She was abruptly tugged behind him as he took to the stairs, eating up the distance to his cabin. They burst onto the next level and were forced apart by a family of four. Going in the opposite directions, they reached for each other and continued rushing down the narrow corridor, then back up another flight of stairs to the deck of suites. She was led to the third door on the right. While Cree removed the key card, she leaned against his back, running her hands down his muscled arms. She stroked his neck with her nose, inhaling his spicy male cologne. When the door opened she was pulled inside and roughly shoved up against the wall. Cree's open mouth came next, his tongue stabbing into her mouth, stoking the flames of her desire. Her arms came up around his neck while she fed on his talented tongue. At the feel of his hands tugging on her panties, she offered a shimmy and sighed with relief when they fell damp around her ankles.

The feel of Cree's insinuating hand between her legs, stole her breath. His long fingers skillfully parted the lips of her sex to rim her opening. She trembled with needed wanting to be filled. She opened her legs wider and when a thick finger pushed into her wet passage her head fell back against the wall while she cried out with pleasure.

"Damn baby, you're hot," he breathed into her mouth as he drilled her with his finger. His movement maddening, working her over good, then he forced another finger into her. They stroked in and out of her until pleasure juice flowed down her legs. Her muscles latched on to his fingers like a baby milking a nipple. "Shit! I've got to get inside you." He tore his fingers away from her body attacking the button on his jeans, and ripping the zipper down to free himself.

Jaxon provided a hand by pulling his shirt off then went for the stiff flesh waiting to be freed. She tugged his swollen member free from the confines of his underwear. She stroked the rock hard appendage making it swell even more. She loved the feel of pulsing cock in her hands, but preferred it in Miss Kitty more. She leaned forward running her tongue over his ear. "Inside, now!" She accepted the condom Cree pulled from his pocket, ripping it open with her teeth then rolled it down his straining penis. She gloried when he raised her leg and pinned her to the wall at the same time, he fed his thickness into her starving core. "Damn that feels goods."

"You have no idea, baby," Cree bit out, his face showing the strain of his resistance to ram into her. The feel of her wrapped around him, hot and pulsing, was obviously a test of his willpower. He grabbed her other leg and opened her further to his probing. Slowly seating himself in her heat, he groaned in response to the velvety softness yielding to him. In a strained voice, he ordered, "Lose the dress."

"You want me completely naked?" Jaxon managed to tease him despite the throbbing flesh between her legs.

"What I want is a tit in my mouth so I can get this party started."

He watched her with hooded lids while Jaxon pulled the dress over her head and tossed it to the floor. He licked his lips when her breasts bounced free before him, the small dark nipples, poking out and begging to be sucked. He licked his lips with anticipation when she grasped a breast and raised it to his hungry lips. He licked the full breast several times before sucking the harden tip into his mouth chewing on the nipple.

"Ooo, that's good."

"But this is better." He pulled back and powered into her causing her to gasp. Over and over he stuffed himself into her until she was singing a tune that chorused to the change in his thrust. It was always good between them, but after two years, this was mind blowing. His fingers dug into her thighs forcing her to take more of his thickness, while a long finger found and stroked the puckered hole of her rear, causing a jolt of pleasure to harden her clit. He shoved hard inside of her, hitting her spot with enough force to elicit a passionate squeal.

"Harder. Give it to me hard."

In answer to her demand, Cree used his shoulders to hold her immobilized against the wall as he slammed into her with enough force to rattle her teeth. Repeatedly he stroked back and forth, and each moment of contact was punctuate by a whimper of delirious zeal. As the building pressure traveled up her legs and down her body to converge in an atomic climactic explosion, she gripped his hips with her legs in a vise like hold while convulsing in his arms, suctioning his cock deeper and into climax. He shot off like a randy teenager coming for the first time, the force of his release sending him to his knees.

Cree took pleasure in the sound of their labored breathing filling the silence of the room. He wrapped his arms around Jaxon's body, loving the feel of her in his arms. Two years away from her was too long. He pressed a kiss into her damp neck. "I didn't hurt you did I?"

"You should hurt me like that again."

His chest rumbled with laughter. That was his girl, no shyness or pretense. "Well let's take it to the bed this time." He pushed to his feet, bringing her with him, then swinging her into his arms, he carried her over to the king size bed. He waited while she tore the covers back then deposited her in the center of the bed. Bending down, he kissed her passionately before pulling away. He removed the used condom, dropping it into the waste basket. He walked over to the balcony doors and pushed them open. The sound of the sea rushed in creating a romantic backdrop for an afternoon of lovemaking.

"I had forgotten how beautiful you are."

He turned at those words to find Jaxon looking at him with a ravenous hunger in her in her eyes. They appeared to be devouring him as they swept across the breadth of his muscled chest and lower. His penis swelled when her eyes skimmed over his groin area, her tongue snaking out to lick her lips.

"You're the beautiful one." He stood there looking down on her stretched out in the center of the bed, the white sheets contrasting her dark skin tone, trying to ignore the tightness of his erection. "I like the short hair."

Her hand flew to her head pulling on one of the soft curls. "I was wondering when you would get around to mentioning it.

"It gives you a feminine maturity."

"You mean it makes me look my age."

"Whatever, you look beautiful." He walked to the foot of the bed folding his arms across his chest. "Why is it you haven't been made love to in two years?" His eyes held hers.

Jaxon pulled her bottom lip into her mouth while glancing past him and out to sea. "Drew reclaimed his virginity and was waiting until we were married," she told him, finally looking at him. She sat up and pulled her legs before her.

"Lucky for him."

Her head tilted to the side. "Lucky for him? What does that mean?"

"Just what I said."

"Oh, I get it." Her head bobbed with resentment. "Mr. Marine is staking a claim, am I right?" She came to her knees.

"Let's drop it."

"No. Don't be shy now. What were you going to do if Drew and I had made love?"

Cree stepped away from the bed not wanting to get into it with her about the guy. It was a dangerous subject and she had no idea how angry he was at her for thinking she could marry some other man and forget him. Yeah, he had been wrong not to marry her, but he hadn't hooked up with the first woman to come along.

"We should really change the subject, Jax."

She flashed him an *I don't think so* smile. "I know you were going to do some of your bad boy moves." She waved her hands before him. "Perhaps punch his lights out."

"He should be so lucky," he muttered under his breath.

She tugged on her earlobe leaning forward. "What was that?" She stepped off the bed to stand in front of him. She shoved his shoulder. "What were you going to do tough guy? A karate chop to the windpipe?"

"Jax you're playing with fire." He stepped back further, glaring down at her.

"Come on Mr. Marine, show me some of your moves," she continued to taunt him.

Cree's jaws tightened with annoyance as he took a step toward her, then in lightening speed slid his arms around her neck, turning her into a choke hole. He pushed her toward the bed, bending her forward. He used his larger body to hold her in place while moving the arm from around her neck to grab a handful of her hair. "I'll show you a move, Jax." He licked the side of her neck and heard her moan with excitement. His hand caressed her bare back and down further over her lush hips. "You want me to show you a move. How about this?" His hand came down on her bare bottom with a smack.

"Ouch!" she yelled, and wiggled her bottom.

"Not exactly what you were looking for?" He whispered into her ear. "Try this one." He pushed his big stiff member deep into her knocking the air out of her. The feel of her tightness so exquisite, he could only lie on top her, savoring the moment. "Damn, woman, you have the best...

"Well do something with it," she croaked in a strained voice, looking back over her shoulder.

"Try this." He smacked her butt once more and pulled out to slam back into her. He rode her hard, knowing how she loved a good ride and he too happy to oblige. He released her hair to grip of hips as he set a punishing rhythm. The sound of flesh smacking flesh competed with their mutual sighs of pleasure. Perspiration soon covered their bodies and he continued to thrust in and out of her sopping wet channel. He concentrated on the spasms of her passage indicating her pending climax and pushed her upper body down to the mattress so that he could go deeper. Bottoming out, he threw his head back stabbing into her until she released a scream he was sure was heard up and down the corridor of the ship. Fueled by her release he hurdled into the dark abyss between life and death erupting like Mt. Vesuvius. He pulled from her body weak and thoroughly exhausted from the earth shattering experience.

He dropped a kiss into the small of her back. He stood up allowing her to move. "That was incredible."

Jaxon pushed to her feet and turned to face him. "You're right it was." She stepped to him, going up on tiptoe, covering his mouth with hers and began making love to his mouth with just as much intensity as he had taken her body. When his penis twitched to life between them, she pulled away leaving him to stand there with an enormous hard on. "Thanks for the pick me up." She smiled like a well serviced woman and walked over collecting her clothes.

"Pick me up!" *Was the woman for real?* "Where are you going?" He watched stupefied while she gathered her clothing and rushed into the bathroom. He heard the lock settle into place. "Jaxon, get your ass out here."

"Patience, Cree."

"Patience my ass." The lock disengaged and the door swung open.

Jaxon strolled out fully dressed. "Now that you've taken the edge off, I'm going to my room to shower and dress for dinner. "I'll see you at eight."

Cree stood there with a hard on and revenge on his mind as Jaxon walked out the door. The woman was going to pay for leaving him with an erection hard enough to drill through the side of the ship. He wobbled over to the shower, his stiff staff making it difficult to walk normally, formulating a plan.

Chapter Three

Jaxon stood under the spray of the shower aware of the delicious soreness between her legs and the back of her thighs where Cree had her bent while taking her from behind. If the man approached his missions with the same focused zeal as he did a woman's body, then the enemy didn't stand a chance. For that matter she knew she didn't stand a chance of walking away from him again, but things had to change. No more would she settle for simply being the woman he loved, left to await his return. It was time for stability and a commitment if there was going to be a relationship.

She stepped out of the shower recalling his expression as she walked out the door. The sight of his alert little head almost caused her to lose *her* head and fall back onto that bed spread eagle in invitation. But like she had told Cree sex wasn't their problem. His love for the excitement of the Marine Corps was and until he put her first, there was no going back for them. In front of the mirror she expertly applied make up, paying special attention to her eyes. She knew how Cree loved it when she did her eyes. Satisfied by the image reflected in the mirror, she reached for the scandalous *La Perla* undergarments. She adjusted the sheer red lace swatch of her thong. The circular lace pattern looked more like a target than underwear. She knew for sure Cree would zero in on the target, and the way the string disappeared between her cheeks, the man would definitely be willing to put his tracking skill to good use. She reached for the matching bustier and cinched herself inside. Going for her shoes by the bed, she returned to the full length mirror on the closet and checked her image. The man didn't stand a chance. She looked smoking hot.

Cree no doubt would be looking for payback after the way she left him earlier, but one look at her in red lace would have him changing his mind. She removed the red beaded gown from the hanger in the closet and stepped into it, as a knock came at the door. She rushed to the door fluffing her hair. The image of him dressed in a navy blue suit that brought out the intense color of his eyes had her standing there with her mouth hanging open. In all the years they had dated, she had never seen him in a suit. As a teen, he had worn shirt, tie, and slacks. Once he joined the Marines, he had opted for his uniform, saying it was appropriate for any occasion, so to say she was shocked to see him in a suit was an understatement.

"Damn, you look good woman," Cree said, coming into the room. The jagged hem of the gown stopped mid-calf. The red beads picked up the light and shimmered with her every movement. The dress had thin beaded straps with a rounded neckline that was provocatively low and displayed the top globes of her breasts. The sight of them straining against the fabric caused him to lick his lips. He grabbed her hand turning her so that he could get a better look. His eyes widened at the sight of the dangerous plunge in the back. "I'm keeping you close tonight."

"I'll be, Cree Novak, every time I turn around these days, you're acting jealous and possessive.

"That's because you're mine, Jaxon Alexander and the sooner you accept the fact, the safer the males of this world will be." He snaked an arm around her waist pulling her into him.

She released an amused laugh. "I don't believe I've agreed to come back to you?"

"You don't have to agree. Your heart will do that for you."

"What kind of sissy talk is that for a Marine?" she responded, teasing him. She slipped from his arms to retrieve her handbag.

"Ex-Marine."

Jaxon's head came up, her eyes connecting with his. She walked back to where he stood, and asked, "What did you say?"

"You heard correct. I'm no longer in the Marine Corps. I was honorably discharged three days ago." He pushed her out the door before she could ask the next question.

She walked beside him with her head swimming with questions. Cree was no longer a Marine. Why had he made the decision to leave the Corps now? Did she dare believe he had done it for her? And what did it mean?" Her heart fluttered with the possibility. She loved him. Had always loved him, but two years ago she made the decision to love herself more. It would serve her well to remember that now.

They arrived at the five-star onboard restaurant and were promptly escorted to their table. Their waiter, Javier, eloquently recited the evening's special, finishing with a dramatic kiss of his the fingers. After reading the menu they decided upon the special of roast duck with apricot sauce. The meal was served with a pinot noir which brought out the flavor of the duck, and wild rice, petite green peas, and onion blend. They ate in silence for several minutes before Jaxon placed her fork down.

"Why did you leave the Corps?"

Cree look across the table at her. "It was no longer the priority in my life." He continued eating.

"You loved the guys of your team and the Marine Corps. I can't believe it no longer matters to you. Did something happen?"

He shook his head smiling at her. "No."

"Cree this makes no sense," Jaxon told him, leaning forward. "You lived to be a Marine."

He shook his head, his blue eyes holding hers. "No. I lived to be with you."

Those words continued to reverberate inside her mind. She had allowed them to hang between them without comment. She didn't know how to respond. She had become choked with emotion. Cree had said he loved her numerous times, but never had he expressed his feelings for her so movingly and she feared it was an act to suck her back in to their old way of doing things. But he hadn't pushed the subject further. He had actually changed the direction of the conversation to what was happening back home. Now as they strolled on the deck enjoying the moonlight, they continued to talk.

"How is the business?" Cree asked guiding her to a secluded area.

"Business is great. I've actually taken on a part-time employee."

"Really?"

"Yeah, one of the kids from the local college. He's a website master and very creative. He talked me into designing social sites for our clients as well which have gone over better than I could have imagined. I'm thinking about making him a partner in the business when he graduates. As I see it, it's best to have him for a partner than a competitor." She appreciated his interest in her business. She had studied and worked hard to build her advertisement and web design business. Even when friends and family had expressed their doubts about her working for herself, Cree had been her champion. He had told her she could do anything she set her mind to do. To prove his faith in her, he had loaned her the start up money, dipping into his savings. The day she had paid him back with interest was one of the happiest days of her life.

"Do you have room for another client?"

Her eyes widened. "You?"

"Yeah, me," Cree responded laughing. He leaned back against the railing grinning. "So what do you say?"

She didn't know what to say. Of course she would take him on as a client, but first she needed some answers. "What type of business are you interested in?"

"Actually it's already established. Once I made the decision not to reenlist, I went to work setting things up. I called a few of my buddies that were no longer in the military and together we've partnered a business. We even have a few clients. An official website and proper advertisement can only boost business."

"Wow, I never truly gave thought to what you would do when you left the military."

Cree shifted uncomfortably. He turned his head slightly to the right to look at her. "Two years ago, you never believed I would leave the Corps, did you? Even when we were making plans, you had no faith in me."

She cringed on hearing the way he had put it. She looked at his handsome face, seeing a real change in him. "I wanted to believe you because I loved you." She dropped her head for a moment then looked back at him. "I wasn't surprised when you didn't return home after your enlistment was due to expire. I was hurt, but I was also prepared to get on with my life."

He placed his hand into her hair, grabbing the back of her head, and turning her to face him. "Did you honestly believe you could move on without me?"

"I did move on. I had no choice."

"You could have taken my calls."

"For what, Cree? So you could make more promises?" She stared at him not hiding her pain. "I believed in your promises for ten years."

"So you tried to forget me with another man?" he snapped with anger.

"No, I didn't. I knew that wasn't possible. I did; however, try to find someone who would place me first," she didn't hesitate to tell him. She watched as the color of his eyes changed from crystal clear to dark and moody. She knew her words had stung, but he had to know what he was up against. All the wining and dining in the world wouldn't win her back without some real changes.

Cree recalled her voicing her desire to be first in his life the night she issued the ultimatum. They had hurt then and they hurt now. Obviously he had done a poor job of letting her know how very important she was to him. Not anymore. He never wanted her to feel second to anyone or anything, because to him she was his everything. He had told her over dinner that he lived for her, and he had. Whenever he found himself in a tough firefight or up against challenging odds, he fought with renewed energy because he knew he had a reason to live. Jaxon. He had spotted her on the first day of high school and knew he had to meet her. Taking the desk in front of her had been the wisest decision he had made. Now he was making another wise decision by fighting not only for her love, but faith in him to always put her before all else.

"You were always first, Jax." He pulled her into his arms. Her head rested against his chest, over his heart. "I'm sorry for not making you feel that way." They stood in the quiet of the evening for several minutes before Jaxon pulled away looking at him.

"You never said what type of business you're in."

"Security."

"Like in the mall?" She laughed with amusement.

"No." He shook his head, joining her in laughter. "We conduct site inspections and make security recommendations, body guard, and escort duties." He noticed her expression became guarded. "What's the matter?"

Jaxon shrugged, not meeting his eyes. She leaned against the rail looking out over the water. "So there's traveling involved. I should have known." Unshed tears shimmered in her eyes.

"No." He pulled her around to face him. "I'm management. Snake and Cutter will be the field guys and anyone else I can recruit." He brushed his lips against hers. "I'm not going anywhere, honey, except where you are."

Those words had seemed to do the trick. He had watched her tears disappear to be replaced with cautiousness. Now on the crowded dance floor of the ship's nightclub, she had chosen to shelve their conversation, opting instead to enjoy the rest of their evening. Cree was having the time of his life dancing with the woman he loved. He watched the way the beaded red dress moved with Jaxon's sensual gyrations. Forced in close by the sea of bodies, she brushed up against him, stroking all the right spots. He slid his arms around her waist moving in time to the music with her. He could tell Jaxon was feeling no pain. The wine at dinner and two Kiss on the Lips in the club had her smiling broadly and giggling like a schoolgirl. But there was nothing girl-like about her sexy bump and grind. He looked into her smiling eyes well aware she knew what she was doing to him. Sucking in a breath when she turned brushing her sweet backside against him, rocking her hips, he fought against the monstrous hard on raging inside his slacks.

"What's the matter, Cree?" she asked over her shoulder. She wore a devilish little smile on her face that lit her eyes with mischief.

"You want to play games, sweetheart?" He pulled her in tight so she could get a good feel for what she had done.

"Someone has a big problem?" She giggled and slipped from his arms turning to face him.

Cree joined her in laughter. "As I recall you're a great problem solver?"

Jaxon threw her head back laughing. She leaned in close pretending to whisper. "I have just what you need under this dress." Her eyes held a promise.

His eyes dropped to her dress trying to imagine what the hell the woman was wearing. As hot as the sex was between them in the past, she had never truly invested in a great deal of lingerie, opting to wear coordinated bra and panty sets, but now with the haircut and a maturity that she wore so well came a sensuality, and he had no idea what she could be wearing. "Let's get out of here."

"No. Not yet," she purred as the music slowed to a sensual ballad.

Cree pulled Jaxon into his arms giving into her wishes. He groaned when she wrapped her arms around his neck, flattening her breasts against the wall of his chest. The woman was blessed with a great pair. He breathed in her fragrance and felt his arousal increase. Jaxon was perfect for him. She was five feet eight inches in height barefoot and with the three inch heels she now wore, the peaks and valley of her body fit to his in all the right places. Her hips were lush and bowed just right for hanging on to. As the singer's words spoke of making love, he didn't know how much longer he could wait before rushing her to the nearest bed.

"Let's go to your room," Jaxon whispered in his ear, rubbing against him like a cat in heat.

"Right behind you."

They made their way out the club and up one deck. Cree entered the keycard and the door of his suite opened. He stepped aside, allowing her to enter before him. He raked his eyes down her feminine form when she walked past. He closed the door and followed her in taking a seat on the bed. This was her party and he was waiting to see what she had in store for the night. "Did you have a good time tonight?"

Jaxon opened the balcony door. She looked up at the stars and closed her eyes as though making a wish. After a while, she opened them and turned looking at him. "I had a wonderful time," she replied with slightly slurred speech. She stared at him sitting on the bed. "God, you look good enough to eat."

Cree smiled to himself, well aware that she advanced toward him on unsteady legs. One too many of those fruity drinks had given her an obvious buzz. Her eyes were a bit unfocused. She came to stand between his spread thighs, forcing him to look up at her. She buried a hand into his hair gently massaging his scalp. The sensation was sensual and played havoc with his libido. He closed his eyes enjoying the attention until it stopped. When he opened his eyes, he was stunned to find Jaxon on bended knees before him. He swallowed hard at the picture she presented.

"What are you doing?" he asked with mounting excitement.

She smiled saucily, dropping her hands to his muscular thighs. "I think you know." Her tongue snaked out to lick her lips while a hand slid to cover his crotch.

"Not tonight Jax." He was trying to be honorable. He suspected the alcohol was responsible for her amorous advances.

"I want you, Cree" she whispered before her hands began attacking the button and zipper of his slacks.

"Jax, are you sure about this?" He knew the alcohol was talking, but damn, he was only a man. He hissed when her delicate fingers wrapped around his penis, removing it from the briefs. He protested and tried to ease her away, but determined to have her way with him, she came to her feet, silencing his protest with a kiss. She forced him flat onto his back and he allowed her to have her way, unable or unwilling to fight her any longer. The feel of her wiggling body straddling him made promises he sure hoped she would keep. Her lips pried his apart and went to work seducing his tongue into responding for several heady moments in an intimate dance that had him primed and ready to get the night started. He grabbed the sides of her hips forcing her down upon him while returning the kiss until it registered she no longer participated, and her body had gone limp above him.

"Jax?"

His answer was a very unladylike snore. He lay there in disbelief, penned beneath her unconscious body with a hard on from hell. Her snore grew louder sending him into a fit of laughter as the reality of the situation registered. She had passed out. He rolled her gently to the mattress then came to his feet. He glanced down to his now deflating member and gently tucked it back into his briefs, zipping up his slacks. He ran a shaky hand over his face and glanced down upon his sleeping beauty. Licking his lips, he could still taste and feel the pressure of her mouth. The heat of her body had burned into his. And the feel of her fingers wrapped around him still had him aching.

"Damn Jaxon, what am I going to do with you?" He ran his fingers through his short hair. She was still dressed in her gown and shoes. He couldn't allow her to sleep as she was, but damn, he didn't know if he had the strength to remove her clothes.

He scooped her sleeping form up into his arms and placed her more comfortably in bed. He knew she couldn't sleep in the beaded dress and proceeded to remove a red sandal, admiring her red painted toenails. He ran a hand over her toned calf before going for the other shoe. The thin straps of the dress slipped off her shoulders easily. Gently rolling her onto her belly, he went for the zipper, which didn't go down easily. It snagged on the beaded material several times before it glided down to reveal the smoking-hot bustier. The sight of the red whale tail caused sweat to pop out on his forehead. The woman wore a thong. God, did she have to pass out before he got to see it? Determined to see his mission to fruition, he rolled her onto her back then grabbed her legs, raising her hips. There the perfect plan went to hell when he pulled the dress off leaving Jaxon in bustier and thong.

"Damn!"

The front of his slacks immediately tightened. What man didn't love a thong? And the lacy target pointing out the promise land only made matters worse. He wiped more beads of sweat from his brow as he tried to ignore the pulsing of his penis and her long pretty legs. He collapsed onto the floor beside the bed exhausted. The dress lay across his lap as a reminder that Jaxon was damn near naked in bed beside him. He raised the dress to his nose inhaling her scent. The years of celibacy had heightened his male senses which were now on high alert. He needed a cold shower. By the time he reached the bathroom he was nude.

Chapter Four

The aroma of bacon teased her senses. Rolling onto her side she inhaled deeply and the scent of fresh brewed coffee greeted her. She slowly opened her eyes looking around. It took a moment for her to get her bearings. This was Cree's cabin. She recalled the previous evening. Cree had planned a romantic evening for them. Dinner had been delicious, and followed by a stroll on the deck. She replayed their conversation about his new business wanting to believe he wouldn't be traveling any more, but the man she loved, thrived on excitement. Pushing the nagging doubts and questions to the side, she continued thinking about the prior evening. She remembered their dancing together last night. They had laughed like they used to. That's what she had missed most, well after the sex, but it was definitely missed. The man knew how to have fun. He had the ability to pull her out of her comfort zone and introduce her to new things. Stretching, she recalled she had been wearing a red beaded dress. It was gone and she didn't remember removing it.

Jumping up as an image of her on her knees between Cree's thighs flashed in her head, she rose to her feet, alarmed. She couldn't remember anything past that point. What had happened? She glanced around the room looking for the one person who had the answer. The balcony door was open. "Cree?" She padded toward the door.

"Sleeping beauty is awake," Cree said appearing in the door. "I took the liberty of collecting your luggage."

She glanced down at herself. "Thanks. I should probably get dressed."

"You don't have to on my account."

Jaxon laughed. "What happened last night? Did I make a fool of myself?" She chewed on her lower lip concerned.

"You could never make a fool of yourself with me." He came fully into the room, but stopped short of reaching her.

"That sounds like a yes." She ran her fingers through her hair. "I must look a fright."

"That I can definitely say you don't." His eyes raked down the length of her. He licked his lips with a sexual hunger that was reflected in his eyes.

"So what happened? Did I pass out?"

"You did, but it was adorable," he rushed to say with a laugh.

She covered her face with her hands. "How embarrassing? I had too much to drink. You know I don't usually drink more than one glass of wine."

"I know." He came to stand in front of her. "That drink you've fallen in love with may look and taste fruity, but it's loaded with alcohol and packs one hell of a wallop."

"Obviously." She frowned.

"How are you feeling? Do you have a hangover?" He trailed gentle fingers across her brow.

She shook her head, no. "I want a shower then food." She turned spotting her luggage sitting outside the bathroom door and walked over unmindful of her state of undress.

"Damn, baby, please hurry up and get dressed."

She glanced down at herself and realized she still wore the bustier and thong. She'd had plans for this little getup. Halting in her tracks to glance back at him, her expression was flirtatious. "Got a problem?"

"If you don't cover that fine ass of yours, you're going to have a ten inch problem."

She released a sultry laugh that brightened her dark eyes. "Is that supposed to be a threat?" She knew she was playing with fire, but couldn't resist.

Cree backed toward the bed. His answering laughter was laden with lust. He stretched out in the space she had vacated, folding his arms behind his head. "Get dressed woman. I have plans for us in port."

"You do?" She looked at him with interest. "How should I dress?"

"Shorts, and did you bring a pair of sneakers?"

"I did." She stood there with a puzzled expression trying to figure out what he had planned for them in port. Coming up blank, she closed the door to the bathroom ready to get the day started.

Jaxon stood in front of the majestic Mayan ruins in awe. The cruise ship had docked early that morning in Cozumel. After a quick breakfast on the balcony of Cree's suite, they had boarded a bus for the ride to the ruins. Their guide had given an informative tour around the ancient kingdom detailing the history of the people. She and Cree had followed in line holding hands along the way looking very much like two people in love. She was falling under his spell again and was helpless to fight against his charismatic pull. She was well aware he had chosen this excursion because of their shared love of history. Looking over at him snapping pictures, she admired his handsome good looks. Dressed today in camouflage baggy shorts that emphasized his long legs and muscled calves, with an olive green T-shirt that formed to his rock solid chest, the man stole her breath away. Spotting two women with their heads together while admiring Cree, she realized that she wasn't the only one affected by his male beauty. She smiled with pride knowing for the moment, Cree Novak was hers.

They wandered freely around the grounds on their own. Several pictures of the empire had been taken. A few pictures of each other in front of the site, and with the kindness of fellow passengers they had managed to get several pictures of them together. She paused taking in the beauty of the surrounding countryside. She smiled when she felt Cree's arm encircle her waist. She leaned back against him savoring the moment. She loved it when they were quiet like this, expressing their feelings through simple touch. The day had been perfect and she had Cree to thank.

"I'll never forget this day," she told him over her shoulder. "Thank you for bringing me here."

He caressed his cheek against hers. "I've been all over the world and never got to share any of it with you, so beginning with this trip, I want to change that." He brushed his lips across her ear. "I want us to explore the world together."

"You're moving a bit too fast, besides are you really going to be around?" She turned within his arms to face him.

"I'll be around for our next trip, and the one after that. I'm not going anywhere, Jax." He covered her lips for a kiss. Pulling back he looked into her eyes. "I want to be where you are."

Jaxon smiled, pleased by what she was hearing. "Why now?"

"You've followed me from city to city because you loved me and wanted to be where I was." He brushed a stray curl of her hair back into place. "Now it's my turn." His arms tightened. "I'm following you to where you are because I love you and want to be with you. And to prove my commitment to you and our relationship, I recently purchased the old Tolliver place."

Her mouth fell open like a trap door. Surprise and utter amazement was stamped on her face as she struggled for words. "You did? I noticed they had put the place up for sale, but how did you know?"

"I told my Dad if it ever came for sale to let me know, and he did."

"I love that old house," she expressed with heartfelt sentiment."

"Don't I know? How many days did we take the long way home so you could walk by that house?"

"I'm sorry if you were bored."

Cree laughed. "Being with you is never boring."

"Right."

"Seriously, I purchased the place because I know how much you love it." He beamed with happiness. "It needs some work to bring it up to date, but it holds great possibilities. There's even room behind the house to run both our businesses. It's important to me to keep business separate from the home."

She stood there absorbing all that he was telling her. He was actually moving back home. He had purchased a grand Victorian home because she had fallen in love with the place as a teenager. "So your coming home to stay is real?"

"As real as it gets." He pulled her in close and took her mouth once more. He slipped his tongue past her lips for a quick lick against the roof of her mouth before pulling away. "Now that it has been established that I'm back and making a home for us, where would you like to go next?" He sat on the ground and pulled Jaxon onto his lap.

"You keep saying us? What does that mean?"

He hugged her to him, running a gentle hand up and down her back. "I'm renovating the old house for us to live in. I know you aren't ready to make a home with me, but when you come to realize you are my priority, and that you can trust me with your heart, I'll be there," he said a bit unsure of himself.

Jaxon hated to see him so uncertain of his next move. It wasn't his style. Cree Novak had always been confident in himself and his abilities. She could give him that confidence back by agreeing to move in with him, right then and there, but she couldn't. She trusted him with her body, because he had always been protective and careful with it. Her heart was another matter and she wasn't prepared to place it in his trust again.

"I know your heart is in the right place, and that you love me," she whispered with emotion, the enormous gift filling her heart to overflowing. "I wish I could say yes."

"But, you're unsure of my intentions." He touched her cheek.

She shook her head in disagreement. "No, not your intentions, but your priorities. Like I told you before, I need to know I'm your top priority. This cruise has been a wonderful start, and the house, I don't even know how to express what I'm feeling." She leaned forward pressing her lips to his. She hugged him for several emotion-filled moments before releasing him. When she looked into his face, disappointment dimmed the brightness of his eyes as he forced an understanding smile.

"You are my top priority, but I'm willing to table the discussion for the moment. Now select our next destination."

"No. I know better than to make plans with you. I get my hopes set on something only to have them dashed."

"Select our next destination," he ordered. "I'll be around to take that trip. It will have to be after the renovations are complete, but we're definitely going away together." His hand gently stroked her cheek.

She gave the question some thought. "Anyplace you haven't been. I want it to be a new experience for us both."

"I like that idea." He too gave their next destination some thought. "How about Singapore? I haven't been there, but I hear it's beautiful. Getting around is easy since the working or common language is English. What do you think?"

"I love the idea." A wide excited smile painted her lips. She locked her fingers around his neck truly happy.

"Perhaps we can rent a car and take our time exploring."

"Really? What about your business?"

"My business like yours can be run with a computer and cell phone, at least for a while."

"Singapore it is then."

Cree kissed the top of Jaxon's sleeping head as they rode back on the bus headed to the cruise ship. Today's excursion had been everything he dreamed. He knew Jaxon enjoyed history as much as he did and the Mayan ruins were the ultimate historical subject. She had listened intently to the guide and smiled over at him with excitement as the wonders of the ancient structure were revealed. He had felt close to her as he had in the past. He couldn't wait to get home and print off the pictures of them. He had the perfect place in his new home for them. He brushed his lips against her hair once more savory the moment.

He had definitely surprised her with news of his purchase of the Tolliver house. He knew it was a bold move considering the state of their relationship, but he was a man on a mission and he wouldn't be denied. The old house was the perfect place for them to begin their life as a couple. It provided private space to the rear of the property for their businesses and enough room in the house for expansion. He glanced down at her more determined than ever to win her back. He knew he had her love, even if she wasn't ready to admit it, but her trust was another matter. She had given him ten years of love without asking anything in return, and the one time she had asked that he choose her over the Marine Corps, he had ultimately chosen the Corps. What a fool he had been. No adrenaline high could compare to the euphoric feeling he experienced being back in her arms. He had taken her love for granted, but never again. All he wanted out of life was Jaxon Alexander.

He had selected this cruise with all the things she loved to do or wanted to do in mind. He couldn't wait for the next port. It was going to be another event filled day. He glanced down once more to where she rested in his arms. Their fingers where still joined as they had been most of the day. It was such a simple thing, but the familiar touch of her hand his was emotionally heavy. It broadcasted to the world that she was with

What White Boyz Fight For

him. He squeezed her fingers then glanced out of the window. Why was he only now realizing what a treasure she was? The thought of some other man kissing her, touching her, made him nauseous, but thank God no man had ever touched her intimately. Jaxon's passion was his.

"You're thinking too loudly," her voice broke into his thoughts.

"That's what happens when I'm thinking about you." He raised her hand to his lips.

"Good thoughts I hope."

"Any thought of you is a good one."

"More sweet talk. I think I could get used to this." She laughed looking up at him.

"I intend to spoil you every day."

"I don't need to be spoiled, Cree. I only need to know that you're mine." She covered their joined hands with her free hand. "I want to know when I need you that you're only a phone call away, or better yet, just in the next room."

He sat their quietly processing her words. There was so much conveyed in the few words. She wanted to know if the car broke down, he would be there to help. Or perhaps when a part on an appliance gave out that he would be there to repair it. He understood her need wasn't a necessity because she had been taking care of herself all this time without him. This need had more to do with having that special someone to lean on, who helped to ease your burden. She hadn't had that because he was always gone taking care of other people or countries, seeing to their defense and well being. It was time for him to see to Jaxon's needs.

"If you moved into the Tolliver house with me, I would be beside you when needed."

Brown eyes studied him for a long silent moment before dropping to their joined hands. "You have no idea how badly I want to say yes."

"Then do. You won't be sorry, baby."

"I've never been sorry about one moment with you." She looked back at him. "I don't want you to do something that you'll later regret. Your happiness is important to me as well."

He nodded, touched by the depth of her love. She had made her needs clear and yet, she held off accepting what he was willing to offer because she worried about his happiness. "In that case I would really like for you to give serious consideration about a life with me in the Tolliver house."

"Have *you* seriously considered what a life with me in the Tolliver house would look like?"

"Of course I have," he piped up. "Me chasing you around the house trying to get you naked." He laughed, kissing her temple.

Jaxon elbowed him. "I'm serious. There will be mundane chores to perform, lawns to mow, gutters to be cleaned, and trash to be taken out. Can you see yourself having the same routine week after week with no adrenaline rushing missions?"

"I can and I'm looking forward to those days. But can you see yourself chasing up behind few hard-headed Novak's?" he tossed out, catching her by complete surprise.

"Children?" Her eyes went wide with wonderment.

"Of course and a dog too." He grinned, knowing she wasn't expecting those words. They had never talked about children because he hadn't planned on marrying her until after the Marine Corps. That time was now and he knew Jaxon wanted children as much as he did. He watched her chew on her bottom lip fighting her fears. "Before you ask, yes, I'm ready for it all."

"Well then, I'll definitely have to think on that."

Two days at sea followed. They busied themselves at the swimming pool playing water volleyball, over indulging on the abundance of none stop food, and hours of people watching on deck. After a leisurely nap in the afternoon, they dinned in the formal dining room then made their way to the lounge for the evening show. Late night partying on the Lido deck under the stars was the perfect finish to the evening before returning to their separate cabins. The third morning the ship docked in Costa Rica. The couple ate a hearty breakfast that would have to carrying them to late afternoon then left the ship for the next planned excursion by Cree.

Jaxon hiked behind him an hour later on the steep yet narrow Costa Rican path of the rain forest. Brilliant shades of green, yellow, and vibrant red surrounded them. As she followed their winding trek, her eyes kept returning to Cree's effortless movements. The man was definitely in shape. Although she was in good physical condition, by way of her local fitness center, Cree's conditioning came from a life of tracking the enemy across rough, hostile terrain. The man didn't even break a sweat. She noticed the manner in which he scanned their surroundings. She realized he was oblivious to doing so, but understood his life and that of his team counted on his being on high alert. This hike was supposed to be fun, and although she and the rest of their group seemed to be having a good time, Cree moved like a Marine on a mission. She wondered if the man knew how to truly let his guard down.

"Are you okay back there?" Cree's voice broke into her thoughts. He glanced over his shoulder checking on her.

"I'm good, but do you know how to relax and have fun." She continued up the path. She dodged a deep rut in the worn path.

"I am having fun." He waited for her to join him.

She looked at him and laughed. "Cree, you've been searching the area all the way up here. Are you expecting bad guys?"

He stared at her with a frown on his face. "I guess old habits die hard. I'm sorry, sweetheart, am I ruining things for you?" Blue eyes turned to her.

"Of course not." She flashed him a brilliant smile, leaning into him. "It's absolutely beautiful out here. The colors are so vibrant. I'm having a really good time."

"I thought you would enjoy it. I know how much you enjoy the outdoors." He moved in front of her to take the lead again.

She stared at his back touched by his thoughtfulness. Her eyes slid across his wide broad shoulders down his back to narrow hips and lower to his tight behind, filling out a pair of pockets. She licked her lips remembering the feel of his hips in her hands as he drove into her. She wiped her brow with the back of her hand as it suddenly got hot.

Continuing behind Cree, she tried to concentrate on the beauty around them, but her eyes kept being drawn back to the man in front of her. Their conversation from the bus was never too far from her mind. Her heart fluttered at the thought of making a baby with him. She admired the way he wore the long khaki safari styled shorts with pockets on the legs. His muscled thighs flexed against the fabric as he climbed and the large calf muscles contracted and relaxed deliciously before her eyes with his sure-footed movements. She accepted his bent arm in climbing up the next slope, mindful of the strength he possessed, as he effortlessly pulled her up. And when he flashed his toothpaste white smile, she wanted to tackle him to the ground and have her wonton way with him.

They finally came to a stop high above the floor of the rain forest. A wooden deck with seating offered a dramatic few of the foliage below and off in the distance, the ocean beyond. She removed her camera from the small pouch fastened around her waist and began snapping pictures.

"Here, drink this," Cree ordered, coming to stand beside her.

Glancing over, she accepted the bottle of water. She screwed off the cap and drank deeply. She hadn't realized how thirsty she was.

"Look over there," he said pointing to a colorful bird.

"It's beautiful. Can you believe the brilliance of the colors out here?"

"When I returned from the desert, it was like everything was extremely bright. You don't realize how much you miss color."

Jaxon looked at him. "Is it really as brown and dry as it looks on television?"

"For the most part yes. There are a few blooming plants, but nothing like here or what we have at home."

"You've done it again."

"What?" He stared at her.

"Planned another wonderful day. I haven't been trail hiking in years."

"I'd do anything to make you happy." His hand caressed her cheek. "But this isn't the end of the trail." He smiled boyishly. He pointed in the direction of the guide behind them.

Turning around to look behind her, Jaxon spotted the short, boxy man removing some type of gear from a large wooden storage box on the deck. "What is he doing?"

"Keep watching."

Annoyed by his answer, she glared at him. When a harness appeared and the man worked off to the side of the deck, she made her way over with mounting anticipation. "Is it what I think?" She leaned on the railing spotting the black cable suspended above the tree tops and leading down between the trees to the floor of the forest. "It's a zip line," she squealed with excitement. She turned back to Cree who was now standing behind her. "Why didn't you tell me we would be taking the zip line back down?"

"I wanted it to be a surprise." He laughed, when she launched herself into his arms.

"Thank you, thank you, thank you." She could barely contain her excitement as she returned to watching the guide. "I've always wanted to do this."

"I know. I recall you saying so when we were watching one of those reality shows," Cree answered, trapping her between his arms when he too leaned against the railing. "I told you, I live to make you happy." He pressed a kiss to her temple.

The guide quickly assembled everyone around and instructed them on the process. He counted off the first five people then one by one sent them on their way. Jaxon and Cree were in the next group. As they lined up and secured their belongings as instructed, the line came to a halt as the last woman of the previous group to go down refused. She stood on the platform breathing deeply and terrorized. Her husband had gone before her and had no idea that she was stuck white-knuckling the harness. It was left to the guide and other hikers to convince her into finally going down.

Chapter Five

"Do you want me to go first?" Cree asked moving around Jaxon to the head of the line. They had waited several tense filled minutes while the woman finally talked herself into leaping off the platform. Her frightened screams pierced the air all the way down, sending monkeys and birds running for cover.

"No! Get behind me buddy," Jaxon snapped. She bumped him out of the way to reclaim her place in line.

He stepped aside gladly pleased to see she was still gung ho. His chest swelled with pride as she grabbed the harness and went through the proper safety checks and then strapped in for the trip down. She waved him over and planted a whopper of a kiss on his lips.

"See you down below," she yelled, then jumped from the platform with a, "Weeee".

He stood there grinning with pride at her courage. She was fearless as she zipped through the air tucked perfectly for top momentum. Her excited laughter floated up to him when she disappeared into the canopy of the trees below. What a woman?

When the harness returned it was it turn to make the trip down. He quickly went through the safety check and strapped himself in. He gave the guide a thumbs up right before stepping off the platform for the ride down. He caught a quick glimpse of the beach, their next destination as he sailed through the beautiful trees. Birds flutter off to the right of him while native wildlife kept up a noisy ruckus at having their territory invaded. He finally broke through the canopy of trees and immediately made out Jaxon down below waving at him. He lowered his legs to slow his descent.

"Missed me?" He removed the harness, stepping off the platform and wrapped Jaxon within his arms.

"Of course." She planted a series of kisses on his lips. "That was the most exhilarating thing I've ever done," she said smiling at him. The rush of the ride was still reflected in her wide sparkling eyes.

Cree feigned insult, giving a pout. "I'm not sure I like the sound of that."

"Oh, please." She swatted his chest. "Nothing compares to making love with you," she whispered.

"That's what I wanted to hear." He grinned. "Come on let's head down to the beach. We have an hour before the bus returns to take us back to the ship." He laced his fingers through Jaxon's and followed the clearly marked path which led to the pristine white sand beach.

"I didn't realize how close we were to the beach."

"That's the design of this excursion. The forest in this area runs right to the beach. A hike takes you up into the hills to explore the beauty of the countryside, and the zip line brings you down to the beach for a bit of relaxation." They cleared the line of foliage and stood awestruck, staring at the turquoise water of the Caribbean lapping at the beach. "Wow!"

"Wow is right."

"Let's take our shoes off." He sat down in the sand and pulled Jaxon beside him. Grabbing her legs, he pulled them across his thigh untying her shoe strings. He removed her shoes and tied the strings of her shoes together then removed his own. He rose to his feet and reached out a hand to her. Slinging their shoes across his left shoulder, he walked with her toward the water's edge.

"This is a perfect ending to another fantastic day," Jaxon told him. She released his hand and took off running into the water. She splashed and kicked up water like a child. "The water feels great. Come on in, Cree."

Dropping their shoes onto the sand he followed her in. Soon the splashing turned into an outright water fight. Cree swiped water from his face, launched by a right kick delivered by Jaxon. In return he caught her around the waist with his left arm and tilted her head first toward the waves. "You have to pay for that."

"Cree, you wouldn't," Jaxon giggled, then yelled when he faked dipping her.

"Apologize."

"No."

"Okay." He tilted her once more, this time allowing her to slip a fraction.

"Don't!"

Cree laughed listening to her girlish shrieks. "I'm sorry, Cree."

Jaxon continued to laugh while clutching his leg. "You love me, remember."

"You're right I do." He swung her up so that she faced him. "But payback trumps love."

Jaxon fell into the water, seat first. She sputtered and cursed revenge while struggling to get to her feet. Cree saw the determination in her eyes and turned to run, but the wet weight on his back, drove him to the ground. He splashed face first into the waves. He spun sending Jaxon right in next to him. By the time their energy waned and they returned to the sand, both were soaking wet. "Look what you did?"

"Me?" Jaxon wailed. "You're the one who dumped me in the water." She squeezed the water from her clothes.

"But you kicked water into my face."

"It was just a little water." She grinned. "At least it's nice and hot."

Cree squeezed the water from his shorts then pulled his shirt over his head, wringing it out."

"That's not fair," Jaxon said with a scowl.

"Hey, you can take your shirt off anytime you want." He sat down on the sand and leaned back to soak up the sun. His eyes widened when she suddenly grabbed the tail of her shirt, pulling it over her head. She stood before him in a navy blue bra that was pretty enough to pass for swimwear. She collapsed onto the sand beside him with a satisfied grin. "Trying to give me a heart attack?"

"Of course not." She laughed, and leaned over to kiss him. "Just want to insure I have your undivided attention."

He fisted her hair in his hand, halting her actions. "You have that and my heart." He pulled her forward, covering her mouth with his. The intensity of his love for her was expressed in the passionate nature in which he fed from her lips. When he had temporarily satiated his hunger for her, he drew away, holding her close, and looked into her moody brown eyes. "I'm going to ask you to marry me before this cruise is over and I'd like for you to consider your response."

Jaxon sat back on the sand with a stunned expression on her face. It was clear she hadn't been expecting his words. She cocked her head staring at him. "I can't believe you said that. Why did you say it? Why now?" Her eyes roamed over his face.

"Because I've wasted too much time already. I love you, Jaxon and I want you to be my wife. So I want you to give marrying me serious consideration. Now come over here and enjoy the view with me." He opened his arms to her. He knew he had surprised her. In a way he had surprised himself, and yet the moment had felt right. Their horsing around had been reminiscent of the old days and when he had looked into her eyes, all he saw in their depths was his future. He held his breath while Jaxon seemed to consider his request. Her eyes locked with his as though searching for what was in his heart. He sighed with contentment when she settled between his legs, giving him her weight. This was what he wanted out of life and was fighting so hard to win.

Jaxon couldn't believe he had finally said the word wife. Her heart was beating rapidly with the desire to say yes. Taking several deep breaths she brought it back into rhythm as logic took control. She thought about the careful planning that had gone into the cruise to make it a trip to remember. Each excursion had been planned with thoughts of her. Their numerous conversations spoke to his maturity and personal growth. The man had even purchased an old house because she loved it. And to prove she came first in his life, he had pulled strings for an early release from the Marine Corps. Then there was the basic foundation of their relationship. Their friendship.

She wrapped his arms around her and took a trip down memory lane. Cree knew her better than anyone. He had sensed her timid nature as a teen and encouraged her to speak up and step out. His words of encouragement had convinced her she could do anything, and before she knew it she was taking chances. Her biggest chance had been following him to his next assignment so they could be together which had led to several more moves. Now as she thought about it, she had to accept her role in the state of their relationship. She should have spoken up and out when she grew tired of simply being his girlfriend. By the time she did voice her opinion on the matter, he was so confident of her love that he had taken it for granted. So here she sat wrapped in the arms of the man she loved contemplating her next move.

She turned facing him and reached for his hands. She turned them over, running her fingers over the prominent veins. His hands were large and held great strength and power, and yet when they caressed her body, they were the most gentle. "I care about you."

"Bullshit, you love me," he fired at her, dropping his hands to his raised knees. Just because you're too afraid to invest in me again doesn't change the fact."

"Your right."

"And you're afraid to commit yourself to me again." His blue eyes were direct.

She pursed her lips, nodding. She looked deep into his eyes, unwavering. "You're right I am afraid to commit, but you're also right about my loving you. I have always loved you and because I do, I need to think things through. I owe it to us both to make the right decision.

"The right decision is to marry me."

Jaxon smiled. "I promise to seriously consider marrying you."

"That's all I ask."

The bus stopped at the port. Jaxon retrieved her boarding pass and passport then followed Cree off the bus and into the line for boarding. She stood in the circle of his arms while they waited. She closed her eyes, soaking in the feel and warmth of his embrace, his masculine scent comforting to her soul. Her eyes opened as the line moved forward. Finally making it to the front, she handed the purser her identification, and after being verified, she was waved forward. She waited to the side for Cree.

"Mr. Novak," the purser said looking at Cree's identification with interest. "You're wanted in the Captain's office. Purser Lanoi will escort you." The olive complexion man finally looked up. His dark eyes were all business as he gave a curt nod.

Jaxon glanced at Cree, concerned. She prayed there wasn't bad news waiting for him. She accepted his offered hand, falling in step beside him and behind the attractive Asian purser who stepped forward to escort them to the Captain's office. The woman's dark silky hair was neatly knotted in the back. Her quiet professional demeanor did nothing to ease Jaxon's tension. They were led to the elevator and up several decks. A door marked crew only was opened for them and another corridor appeared. They took the second door on the right where they came to a waiting room.

"Do you have any idea what this could be about?" Jaxon whispered to Cree when the woman knocked on the door, and disappeared into the office.

"Stop worrying." He pulled her in close, kissing her head, for reassurance.

The door opened and the woman waved them in. A distinguished gentleman in his early fifties walked forward with an outstretched hand. His steely gray eyes seized upon Cree with great curiosity. "Staff Sergeant Novak, I'm Captain Jean Gutier. I hope you and the lady are enjoying the cruise."

"We're having a wonderful time," Cree responded, shaking the man's offered hand. "May I introduce my fiancée, Jaxon Alexander."

A surge of excitement rushed through Jaxon's system on hearing Cree introduce her as his fiancée, but the knowledge that the Captain had addressed Cree as SSgt Novak, quickly doused the feeling.

"Ms. Alexander," Captain Gutier addressed her.

"Captain." Jaxon studied the man closely, and wonder what bad news he was about to deliver. She tightened her hold on Cree's hand.

"SSgt Novak, a Sergeant Major Robins contacted the ship earlier and asked that you return his call when you returned on board. I've taken the liberty of calling him back for you. Line two." He pointed to the telephone on his desk then left the two of them alone in his office which overlooked the navigation deck.

Jaxon released Cree's hand. The Marine Corps was calling and that could only mean one thing. They wanted their man back. She wandered over to the large window that looked into the navigation area, holding her breath. She listened as Cree took the call. When she heard the voice on the other end, she knew Cree had placed the telephone on speaker.

"Tracker you're needed back in theater. Magician has been spotted in the area and only you can track him," the authoritative, deep voice stated over the telephone.

"Why me?" Cree asked with an eye on Jaxon. Her stiff spine indicated that she was definitely focused on the conversation despite pretending interest in the crew sailing the ship. "Apache could lead."

"Yes he could if he wasn't tracking elsewhere. You know the interest level," Sergeant Major Robins said, pushing the issue.

Cree scratched his head, hunching his shoulders. "Sir, I'm no longer in the Corps."

"Mere technicality that with a phone call and a flick of an ink pen, you're back in. I wouldn't contact you if you weren't needed."

Jaxon's head snapped around on hearing those words. Her chest tightened with fear at the thought of her future with Cree taking the backseat yet again. Tears threatened, but she fought them back. She watched him. His whole demeanor had changed. He was pumped with adrenaline that had him now pacing the floor. He was firing questions and making suggestions that were all being shot down. When he glanced in her direction she could see in his blue eyes he was torn between going back and staying with her. Unwilling to stand in his way any longer because she did love him, she walked over, and kissed him. Without a word being spoken, she gave him back to the Marine Corps and left the office.

Each step that she took away from Cree was agonizing and slow. Her chest was tight at the prospect of returning home and having to watch him leave once again. She had come close this time to her dream. He had actually said he was going to ask her to marry him. She found herself back at her cabin, yet unable to stay there and wait for him to come to her with an excuse, she left the room and headed for the top deck. She ordered her new favorite drink and found herself a quiet spot to sulk.

Fifteen minutes into her pity party a shadow fell over her. Ignoring it, she prayed whomever it belonged to would go away.

"Hey beautiful, mind if I join you."

Jaxon frowned realizing that her visitor wasn't getting the message. She turned glaring at the intruder on her misery. At any other time she would have appreciated the man's good looks, but not today. She'd had enough of men, hers in particular, and wasn't interested in another. Although how long the one she had would be around was unclear. She prepared to deliver a saccharine sweet reply that would send him away when she was interrupted.

"I mind." Cree stood behind the man looking lethal and daring him to object. He flashed an annoyed glance in her direction to which she swiftly returned. The guy backed away with an apology.

"Already trying to replace me?"

"I wouldn't have to if you were around." She took a sip of her drink then placed the glass on the table. "So when do you leave?" she asked not looking at him. She folded her arms across her chest and her right leg over her left, swinging to a pissed rhythm. She heard him take the chair beside her.

"I'm not leaving."

She stopped swinging her leg and turned looking at him. She searched his face for a sign of deceit. "You said *no* to the Marine Corps?" Her expression was one of disbelief.

"That's right I did."

Jaxon shook her head of curls. "You should have told him you'll do it, because I not marry you." She jumped up needing to get away from him.

"Wait a minute, Jax." Cree's hand whipped out grabbing her. "I told Sergeant Major Robins *no* because you said you would consider marrying me."

"This time you said no, but what happens the next time he contacts you? I don't want to plan a wedding and the groom not be there."

"That's not going to happen. I love you." Cree tried to pull her into the circle of his arms.

Jax resisted his efforts not wanting to be consoled. "You always love me, Cree, right before you leave again." She saw him flinch from the harsh words, but couldn't feel sorry for speaking the truth. "Why don't we leave our relationship as is? We love each other, we have great sex, and then you leave. This way I don't get my hopes up and they don't get trampled on your way out the door."

"I've said this before and I'm really getting fed up with your not believing me, but I'm not going anywhere." He tugged her into his arms, not being denied her closeness. He wrapped an auburn curl around his finger. "My place is with you."

She really didn't want to fight with him. The day had been too enjoyable to end it on such a bad note. She draped her arms around his neck, meeting his gaze. "I know a part of you wants to go after this guy."

"You're right there is." He kissed her sweetly on the lips. "But the part of me here." He tapped the place over his heart. "Only wants to be with you. This time I'm fighting for myself and what I want."

"And that's me?"

"It's always been you, baby, and I need you to have faith in me."

"I don't know if I can do this again." Her heart was filled with dread.

"Look at me, Jax." He waited patiently for her to meet his gaze. "The only adrenaline high I want is from making love with you. I want a home and family, but I can't do that without you."

"And I don't want to any of that without you, but I don't know if it's written in the stars for us to have a future."

"If it's not written, we'll write it, because you are my future."

She looked deeply into his eyes seeing his sincerity, but hadn't he been sincere all the other times. "Here's the deal. I'll move into the house with you, but I can't marry you."

Cree looked like he wanted to shake her until her teeth rattled. "You can be so damn stubborn, even when it's causing you pain. Your indecisiveness has to end here. You were right when you said things had to change. I'm not looking for a lover or girlfriend. You either have faith in my love for you and my commitment to our relationship by marrying me, or we're finished."

Jaxon stood pondering his words. She thought to dig her heels in with stubbornness, but she was frightened. Cree didn't make idle threats that he wasn't willing to carry out. Was his desire to marry her truly that great, or was he giving her the hard push she needed to see that her future was with him?

"Yes," she suddenly said, not willing to risk losing him.

"What?" Cree stared into her upturned face. He had been holding his breath waiting for her response.

Jaxon lips curled into a brilliant smile that made her eyes sparkle. She knew what she was doing was right. She had tried to make a life with another man and failed miserably. She had never truly loved Drew the way he deserved, or the way she loved Cree. If and when the Marine Corps called him back, she vowed to be supportive because no matter what, Cree was the only man she loved. Her happiness was at his side. "I said yes. I'll marry you."

"It's about damn time," he growled, lifting her into his arms. He kissed her deeply then pulled back smiling at her.

"You, jerk. You kept me waiting for ten years."

"Well you're stuck with me now."

"Not yet, but I planned to be in about five minutes," she purred into his ear.

"You naughty girl. What a mouth you have?" Cree said laughing. He lowered her to the deck.

"Last time I checked you liked my mouth." She licked her lips.

"I've got something to silence you."

And he did, but damn if Jaxon wasn't making him howl with pleasure. The sight of her dark curls shielding his crotch as she engulfed his stiff flesh added to the eroticism. He leaned his head against the headboard with his hands buried in her hair as she bobbed up and down on him. The shy girl he had loved was now a woman with skill, and still the love of his life.

"Shit!" he hissed at the feel of her teeth lightly grazing him. He couldn't take any more. "My turn." He pulled her away and rolled, changing their positions. He slid to the floor, draping her legs over his shoulders.

"No fair...Oh!

Cree silenced Jaxon's words with a hard pull on her hidden nub. He went to work stoking a fire, licking, nibbling, and sucking her off. He stayed her thrashings hips with an arm against her hips while his face was buried deep. An image of the guy earlier flashed in his mind and he grew angry. Jaxon was his woman and he would be the only man to give her pleasure.

He slid a finger inside her already wet passage and stroked her hard and fast. Her delirious moans only fueled his actions, but enough of this, he needed to get inside of her. Pulling away, he reached for a condom making quick work of sheathing himself. He sat on the bed and pulled Jaxon to straddle his hips. He eased her down onto him with one final push to seat himself to the hilt. Her delicate hands gripped his shoulders as he began to establish a demanding pace. He guided her hips up and down on him. The sound of flesh slapping flesh reached their ears. The tempo escalated at lightning speed. Their bodies glistened with perspiration. Jaxon slung her head back thrusting her breasts forward. Unable to ignore the temptation, he leaned forward taking a dark nipple between his lips, sucking it into his mouth. Jaxon tightened around him in response to the hard pull on her nipple. Her fingers moved to his hair, gripping in a frantic grasp when he began rocking hard and fast into her. She dropped her head on top of his enjoying the ride.

"I love you, Cree," she whispered softly, taking his next thrust.

Her softly spoken words penetrated his thoughts. She had spoken the words he wanted to hear, outright with no hint of fear in her voice. She loved him.

He gripped her around the waist. Maintaining their connection, he rose, turning and placed her on the bed. He leaned over her not moving. "Look at me, baby." He wanted her to see in his eyes what was in his heart. When her eyes finally rose to meet his, he surged forward. "You are my heart, Jaxon Alexander, and I can't wait to make you my wife." He pulled out and stroked back in holding her gaze. Over and over again he took her. She began to shake with a shattering climax and he was still looking into her eyes, and when his world spun out of control, it was Jaxon's brown eyes which grounded him.

Chapter Six

Nassau was their last port of call before heading home. The ship would stay in port for twenty four hours so they had the entire day to explore. Jaxon and Cree sat on the Lido deck enjoying breakfast and the view of the city as the cruise ship sailed into port. They were anxious to go into the city after spending two days of sailing. Jaxon was anxious to see what Cree had planned for the day.

"Will we be climbing, swimming, or swinging through the trees today?" she asked with a smile. She speared a strawberry waiting for his response.

Cree raised his head from his overflowing plate with a frown. "Would you be disappointed if we simply toured the city and a bit of shopping?"

"Of course not? What woman do you know doesn't enjoying shopping?"

"You're not most women, sweetheart." He winked.

"You're right I'm not." She studied him closely. "You're up to something."

His brows rose in surprise. "Me?" He shook his blond head. "I'm afraid to disappoint you, but there's no plan." He forked a slice of French toast into his mouth.

Perhaps she was wrong. She studied him for a moment in silence then relinquished the thought. "That's okay. I'm looking forward to touring the island. Do you think we can go over to the Atlantis?"

"I believe they have an all day excursion which includes the pools and beach." He flipped through the pages of the cruise excursion booklet lying beside his plate.

Jaxon placed a hand over his. "I like your original idea of no plans. Let's wing it."

"Sounds good to me. I was reading in here they have some wonderful shops." He continued to eat. He suddenly placed his fork down, looking over at her. "So when do you want to get married?"

Her fork stopped in midair. "We've waited long enough," she answered honestly, holding his gaze. "I want to become your wife as soon as possible." She hoped she didn't sound desperate, but heck she was. She didn't see any point in waiting. There was a house to renovated, wasted years to make up, and children yet to be born. No, she wanted to become Mrs. Novak as soon as she could, and get their life together back on track.

"Good, because I can't wait to make you Mrs. Novak." He reached for her hand and brought it to his mouth.

"Perhaps we can find a few special pieces for our new place." She sat back staring at him. "I still can't believe you purchased the Tolliver place."

Cree's mouth turned up in a proud smile, while his eyes sparkled with happiness. "It's the Novak's place, and it's going to be beautiful when I complete the renovations." He went into details telling her about the kitchen wall that he would be removing. "With all the tearing down and wall moving, we'll still end up with four bedrooms and a large master suite."

"Four bedrooms?" Her brows hiked with interest. "What are we to do with four bedrooms?"

"I was thinking we try to fill them with babies." His eyes dropped to her breasts with a seductive sweep. The pretty dress she wore was cut low and gave a generous view of cleavage.

She suddenly got hot from the heat in his gaze. The way they practically attacked each other whenever they fell into bed, it would take them no time to fill each room. "Let's start with two and see how it goes."

"Three and we keep one for a guestroom." He leaned across looking into her amused eyes.

"Three ah? I guess I can do three."

"We, Jaxon, can do three." He stretched across the table to kiss her. "I can't wait to get started."

Jaxon laughed. She should have known all the man was thinking about was the sex it would take to create their children. Heck, with the intensity of their lovemaking, she couldn't wait to get started either because when they came together it was explosive.

"You're thinking about my making love to you," Cree whispered, with a knowing grin.

"I am not."

"Jaxon Alexander, you have become such a little liar," Cree taunted her.

She rolled her eyes pushing away her plate. "I wasn't the only one thinking about sex."

"Baby, when I'm around you, getting inside of you is all I think about."

Her body instantly responded to his provocative words by getting damp and throbbing in anticipation. She crossed her legs under the table to ease the ache.

Cree placed his napkin across his plate, indicating he was finished. Pushing his chair back, he assisted Jaxon with hers. "I can take care of that ached for you," he whispered against her ear.

"No, Cree." She practically ran to the stairs. She met his hungry gaze knowing that if they fell into bed now, they would miss Nassau altogether. She avoided his arm when he tried to slide it around her waist. One caress up against his hard body and she would find herself butt naked with him buried deep inside of her. "You promised to show me Nassau."

"I can show you the heavens if you let me." He chuckled, stalking behind her.

Jaxon raced ahead of him to wait at the cabin door. Her heart was filled with love for the man. Cree held her heart and the magic touch which made her body sing with pleasure. She turned her head in his direction when he rounded the corner. His gait was carefree and sexy as hell. He looked like an island stud in white linen shirt, blue jeans, and leather sandals. Only his military haircut messed up the illusion. Licking her lips as he grew near, she knew it would be awhile before they made it ashore. She waited with anticipation for him to unlock the door. The muffled click of the lock, signaled time to get the party started.

She entered the cabin in front of Cree. Reaching under her buttery eyelet sundress, she pulled her panties down, stepping out of them, all while Cree watched, and worked himself free. Perching on the room desk, she hiked her skirt up to receive him.

Two hours later they sat in an air conditioned minivan for a tour of the island. Their guide, Shaun was a caramel colored man with a slight island accent, muted from his university days in Atlanta. He proudly wore his Morehouse t-shirt while keeping up a steady stream of conversation, interspersed with facts about Nassau, the city and New Providence, the island. He drove the narrow roadways with skill, on the right side of the road. It was a new experience for Jaxon and Cree found humor in her antics every time it looked as though Shaun was going to run into another car. He had been to several places in the world where they drove on the right side of the road. Hell, he had been places where there weren't any roads at all, and yet people drove. He sat with his arms draped around Jaxon's neck taking in the surrounding beauty. Although a crowed city with areas of poverty like any other, it was the bright colors of the plants and buildings that added to its unique beauty. The police station as Shaun pointed out was painted and island pastel green and white.

Their first stop was the highest point on New Providence, Fort Fincastle, reached by climbing the Queen's Staircase. Cree and Jaxon exited the van to explore the area's stone creations. At the top of the staircase, they listened as the old story-teller recounted the oral history of the slaves who labored from dusk to dawn, chipping away at the rock formation to create an escape route to the sea for Lord Dunmore. From the observation floor of the fort they took in the majestic view of the ocean beyond.

"It takes your breath way, doesn't it," Cree commented, close to Jaxon's ear. He stood with her in the circle of his arms taking in the view.

"It does. Too bad slave labor had to create it."

He kissed her head lovingly, while remaining silent about the modern day slavery he had witness on his missions. The cruel injustices and the safety of their country are what had kept him serving his country and apart from her. They snapped a few pictures then moved on to see more of the island.

Around three o'clock they were finally returned to Rawson Square where Jaxon began her shopping. Cree held her purchases while she ventured from store to store. He waited near the entrance to a home décor shop realizing he was getting a glimpse of their life together, and he liked what he saw and how he felt even more. Watching Jaxon move through the store, he questioned all the wasted years keeping their relationship on hold. He had thought he was happy when tracking through the mountains of foreign countries with his team. But now, standing here watching the woman he loved do something as simple as shopping, he knew being with her made him the happiest. He checked his watch for the time. He had a surprise for Jaxon and needed to get moving.

"Why did you rush me out of there?" She clutched her ceramic chicken like a prize possession. She had been making plans to redecorate her kitchen and was looking for a few special pieces, like this chicken, but now her decorating would take place in their new home. The large colorful chicken would be a part of their new beginning.

"I too have a few stops I would like to make," he told her, holding her hand.

"Oh, why didn't you say so?"

"How could I with you're running here and there. I swear, how many handbags do you need?"

Jaxon bumped him with her hip. "Those were genuine designer handbags, and at these prices, I can afford to splurge a bit."

"A bit? You purchased three."

"Yes, I did and they were worth every penny." She smiled proud of her purchases.

Cree turned back out onto the crowded sidewalk of Bay Street anticipating her reaction to his surprise. Spotting his destination, he tightened his grip on Jaxon's hand while trying to maintain his excitement. At the entrance to the jewelry store, she halted in her tracks, tugging on his hand. He swung back to see what was the problem.

"What are we doing here?" Her eyes roamed the window displays of stunning jewelry.

"What do you think?" Cree asked with wide stupid grin. He pulled her behind him as he went inside. No sooner did they enter before a clerk came to assist them.

"May I be of service?" the forty-something woman asked. Her dark eyes swung between them with eagerness.

Cree glanced over at Jaxon still smiling. "Yes, we would like to see your selection of engagement rings." He felt Jaxon's fingers flex against his hand. This time when he looked at her, she too was beaming with excitement. He leaned over kissing her quickly, unable to resist her smiling lips.

"I can't believe you're doing this."

"We can't be officially engaged without a ring."

"You won't hear any complaints from me," she giggled.

The woman waved them back to a counter with several trays for their viewing. Together they narrowed their choice down two, but after trying them on, the decision was made. The two caret cushion cut diamond in a platinum setting. The fit was surprisingly perfect. Cree paid for the ring while Jaxon held her hand out before her.

"Thank you, I love it," she whispered on their way out of the store.

"And I love you."

The happy couple slowly made their way back to the ship. They returned to his cabin and set out on the balcony enjoying the sunset over Nassau. Cree held Jaxon in his arms knowing that this city would always hold a special place in their hearts.

"I'd like to come back here one day," he told her.

"Me too. Perhaps an anniversary."

He smiled to himself pleased there was no more doubt in her voice. "Know that I'll always love you, Jax."

She turned in his arms to study his face. She traced his eyes, then his nose, and finally his mouth with gentle fingers. She leaned forward pressing her mouth ever so gently to his. "I have no doubt."

"We're going to grow old together." He studied her face trying to imagine it lined by the passage of time. He thought of her mother's aging beauty and knew Jaxon would age gracefully as well. "I'll still be chasing behind even into our eighties."

She giggled at his silliness and leaned forward hugging him. "I'll still allow you to catch me."

His hand caressed the center of her back in slow loving strokes. "I'll always love you, Jax."

She squeezed his shoulders filled with emotion. "I know, baby."

And deep in her heart she did.

Jaxon rolled over the next morning with the intention of snuggling with Cree, but he wasn't there. The sheets were cold indicating he had left the bed quite some time ago. She pushed into a sitting a position, glancing at the bedside clock which read nine o'clock in the morning. She groaned with disappointment on having missed the ship sailing out of port. Running her fingers through her hair, she left the bed to check the balcony, but discovered it empty. She shrugged her shoulders with disappointment. *Oh well, I'll be dressed by the time he gets back.*

She retraced her steps back to the bed, and removed her toiletries bag from the side table then went to the closet for shower shoes. Pulling the door open she reached for her shoes and stopped. Panic washed over her as she realized there was only one piece of luggage in the closet. Hers. Since agreeing to marry Cree, she had moved into his much larger cabin suite. She raced to the bathroom, hoping, praying she would find his luggage sitting on the floor, but she didn't. Her heart was beating so fast now, pumping blood through her veins that she could hear the roar of it in her ears. "He wouldn't do this to me. Not again," she voiced out loud, opening the closet once more. Her eyes landed to the small walkway between the bed and the wall. Crawling across the bed, she prayed, *let it be there, let it be there.* But it wasn't. She sat in the middle of the bed noticing for the first time that all signs of his having been in the cabin were gone.

His wooden hairbrush had sat on the bedside table since they had arrived. His cruise ship tickets had been on the small desk along with the excursion guide he had planned their adventures. No black flip flops in the corner or coins from his pocket on the side table. She also noticed there wasn't a note. But what did catch her attention on the bedside table was the gorgeous engagement ring he had purchased for her yesterday. She picked it up with shaky fingers unable to put it on. It didn't make sense.

She grabbed the pillow he had slept on bringing it to her nose. She could smell his fresh scented soap and woodsy aftershave. She filled her lungs with the scent, not ready to accept that he had left her once again. She replayed their time together and the effort he had put in to making this trip special. He had even said he purchased the Tolliver house back home. Spoke of the renovations he had planned. Shaking her head, she knew there had to be a logical explanation for his disappearance. She left the bed determined to get some answers, but first she had to get dressed. She returned the ring to the table.

Leaving the bathroom several minutes later, fear and

disappointment was settling in. No matter how she wanted to believe in him and his love for her, his disappearance was making that difficult. She opened the closet to place her things away. Grabbing her luggage, she spotted a folded sheet of paper, and reached for it. She unfolded the neat little square and discovered it was a message with instructions to contact Sergeant Major Robins, dated yesterday. Cree hadn't mentioned receiving the message. Rolling her eyes heavenward, she recalled his words about always loving her. Had he been telling her in his way that he was returning to the Marine Corps? She folded the message back and slid it into the side pocket of her luggage followed by her night clothes.

The diamond sparkled in her peripheral vision causing her to stare at it. It was a gift from Cree. One she knew deep in her soul he enjoyed giving to her. She placed it back on her finger also knowing that in his way, he truly loved her. The question she was forced to ask herself was his love enough? She released a frustrated laugh, knowing that it would have to be. She had already tried to love another man and failed. There was no other man for her. There was only Cree Novak.

A knock at the cabin door pulled her away from her pity party. Opening the door, she was surprised to see the female purser from the other day.

"I have a message for you, ma'am."

Jaxon stared at the white envelope that was held out to her. It didn't take a genius to know the envelope was from Cree. He was always good about expressing his reason for leaving on paper. Obviously now was no different. She took the note with a whispered thank you and shoved it into the back pocket of her jeans. Halting the woman's retreat with a hand to her arms, she had to ask, "When did Mr. Novak give you the note?"

"Right before we pulled out of port this morning."

Jaxon strolled out of the cruise ship terminal rolling her luggage behind her the next morning. It had taken nearly three hours before her section was allowed to disembark. The check through customs hadn't taken long at all. Now it was a little before eleven, and all she had to do was locate a taxi for the hour long drive back to her small home town. Approaching the taxi lane she noticed there were several taxis lined up waiting for passengers. As she headed off to the left, a white limousine pulled into the pickup lane, and the doors were thrown open.

"Jaxon!"

Hearing her name being called, she halted turning back around, searching through the numerous faces. She spotted Gaby waving frantically at her. She rushed in her friend's direction as she stepped fully out of the limousine. Jaxon came to a screeching halt, taking in Gaby's appearance.

"What the hell?"

Tori suddenly appeared climbing out the limousine, followed by Jessica. All were dressed in the pale lavender bride's maid dresses she had decided upon for her wedding to Drew.

"Okay, who's sick joke was it to buy these dresses and pick me up at the port?" Jaxon's furious gaze swung from one woman to the next. "Jessica, was this your idea? I know you didn't approve of my breaking things off with Drew and coming on this cruise with Cree, but this is too much." She was building up steam, and taking out her disappointment with Cree on her friends. "And before you ask where he is, he left again. There, now you know. Now is someone going to tell me why you're standing here dressed for a wedding?"

"We can speak now?" Gaby, snapped. Her well sculptured brows raised in question.

Jaxon rolled her eyes not in the mood for this. "Yes, Gaby."

"Well, now that we have been allowed to speak, you might find what we have to say of interest."

"If you ever get to it," Jaxon mumbled, cocking her hip with impatience.

"Just tell her," Jessica practically shouted.

"Jessie, you're no fun," Gaby, complained.

Tori pushed forward cutting Gaby with annoyed stare. "You do love to hear yourself speak. She turned back to Jaxon grinning. "We're dressed for your wedding."

"Mine?"

This time Jessica spoke up. "Cree came home early from the cruise and told your mother and his that he wanted to plan a wedding for you both by the time the ship docked," Jessica recited without taking a breath.

"Cree came home?" Jaxon felt the cloud of depression that had been following her take flight at the news of a wedding. Hers. Theirs. Tears blurred her vision at the thought of the maneuvering it must have taken for him to catch a flight from Nassau, and back home in time for a wedding. "I can't believe he did this."

"Believe it girl," Tori said with a smile. "Your mother called us and announced we were having a wedding."

"I don't have anything to wear," Jaxon cried, remembering the fact.

"The man thought of everything. Get in." Gaby waved her forward. The other women followed. When the driver pulled away from the curb, the bride's maid went to work transforming Jaxon into a stunning bride.

An hour later the car stopped at Cree's parent's home. Jaxon stared out the window noting the dead end street was lined with cars. She giggled with excitement, just imaging her mother and Cree's on the telephone alerting family and friends to their sudden wedding. She knew they both had been disappointed when she had returned home without him two years ago. Her heart beat with excitement at the prospect of seeing him. She stole a moment while her friends slid out, taking time to thank God for allowing this day to happen. Her hands ran nervously over the delicate fabric of her wedding gown. It was a beautiful strapless white gown with straight neckline, perfect for a backyard wedding. Taking a deep breath, she stepped from the limousine and was met by both their parents.

"Julia and I have to tell you something," her mother rushed to say.

Jaxon looked from one woman to the other. They stood with their arms linked and a serious expression on their faces. "Don't tell me he's gone," she said alarmed.

"No, no," Julia said, taking her hands. "Nothing in the world could keep him away from this wedding." She glanced at Amanda. "We sent Cree the invitation to the engagement party."

Jaxon looked at both women and broke into laughter. "I should have known." She drew them both into an embrace. "Thank you for sending him back to me."

Epilogue

Cree stood in the doorway of their newly renovated home filled with pride. He watched Jaxon trying to decide where to place her treasured chicken. They had completely gutted the old kitchen. New maple cabinets provided an abundance of storage. Stainless steel appliances sparkled with cleanliness. The stools at the breakfast bar were from his old place and fit the space nicely. The granite countertops had taken longer to select, but once they spotted the white granite with specks of brown and yellow quartz, they knew they had to have it. Jaxon also had to have the large center island and double ovens, but knowing of her great cooking ability, he was all for it.

"What do you think?" Jaxon looked at him waiting for a response. She had finally decided to place the chicken on the island off to the right.

"It looks perfect."

"The house looks great, Cree." She walked over wrapping her arms around his waist. "I can't believe you got all the work done in less than a year."

"It was tough, but definitely worth it." He checked his watched for the time. "The movers should here any moment."

"I can't wait to have the rest of the house furnished." Jaxon walked into the living room, one of the few rooms in their home completed. They had decided her traditional furniture worked well in the room.

Cree looked around very pleased with the way they had blended their things together to create a warm inviting home. Their marriage had been just as smooth and easy. The surprise wedding had been a collaborative effort of their friends and families, each assigned a task. The wide smile on Jaxon's face as she had walked down the aisle toward him had been worth all the running around. He had wanted to make the day special for her. He realized not for the first time that he had been a fool to wait in making her his wife. Life with Jaxon by his side was so much more meaningful.

The honeymoon night had been just as momentous. He recalled that night with a wistful smile, still moved by the tenderness they had shared.

Admit it, you thought I had left." Cree toyed with the silky ties of her negligee. The bodice was made like a corset and was driving him crazy. Her lush brown globes were cinched in, sitting high, and inviting. He ran the end of the ties over the swells of them.

Jaxon lay sprawled on top of her husband, deliriously happy. They were spending their honeymoon in their new house, on the new sleigh bed Cree had purchased for their special night. She dropped her eyes briefly to her chest, watching his movements. She glanced back at him. "I had faith in you."

"You are a liar, Jaxon Novak." Cree laughed.

"I like the sound of that."

"That you're a liar or the Novak part?" He laughed harder when Jaxon swatted his chest.

"Jaxon Novak."

"I like the sound of it too." He leaned forward and kissed her.

"I found the second message from Sergeant Robins," she told him.

"And?"

"Of course I thought you had left, but I decided that I would accept our relationship as is, because I loved you."

Cree narrowed his eyes. "Had you been drinking?"

Jaxon giggled because she'd definitely had a few of her favorite new drink after he left the ship.

"I hope my surprise made up for the disappointment I caused."

"Our wedding was perfect."

"You were a stunning bride."

"Thank you." She caressed his lips. "Thank you for giving me the wedding I'd always dreamed of having."

"You deserved a big church wedding." He released the first row of silk.

"I never wanted one. All I wanted was you, me, and our families and friends." She sat up releasing the next row of silk. Her hands shook slightly and Cree steadied them with his.

"Tonight is different isn't it?" He held her gaze knowing exactly how she felt. For all the times they had made love, tonight was special because it would be their first time as man and wife.

"Yes."

"There's no rush. We'll take it slow."

The doorbell chimed taking him away from the memory. He glanced around suddenly aware that Jaxon was on the upstairs landing. He would oversee the unloading and make sure all the furniture purchased had been delivered. He went to the door to let the delivery men in. A clipboard with the listed delivery items was thrust into his hands. Standing back as they hauled furniture in, he checked off the items, then pointed them in his wife's direction. She would tell them where she wanted it.

So far so good he thought when the weathered leather sofa was carried in. He was excited about the attic game room Jaxon had given him free rein to decorate. The pool table was next, followed by the large plasma television.

"Hold it," Cree ordered, the burly guy at the door. "That's not ours."

"It's on that list in your hand. I double checked the load myself," the delivery man responded.

"I don't care," Cree challenged him. "Jaxon, get down here."

"What's the problem?" She came to the top of the stairs.

He held up the clipboard. "They have a nursery suite on here. Tell this guy we didn't order it."

"Don't you think our baby is going to need somewhere to sleep?"

Cree's head whipped around. His astonished eyes found her with a wide expectant smile plastered on her face. He forgot about the guys carrying the crib and bound up the stairs to his lovely wife. "You're pregnant?"

"I didn't do this by myself. We're pregnant. Six weeks," she teased him, and was immediately swept up into his arms.

"We're having a baby," Cree shouted down to the movers. "Bring that crib up here. Our baby needs someplace to sleep." He turned back to his wife grinning like a fool. "I love you."

"I love you too."

"This moment calls for a kiss on the lips," Cree said, lowering his lips to hers.

Jaxon giggled at his play on words. "I couldn't agree more."

About The Author

My military upbringing introduced me to different people and cultures, but it would be my parents who taught me what true love was. The secretive glances, shared laughs, whispered conversations, and loving touches, exemplified the beauty of their relationship. You'll discover that same beauty and passion as my heroes and heroines navigate the course of true love. That belief in happily ever after and my military childhood would also fuel my overactive imagination. No wonder I developed this crazy notion of one day being published. However, it would be years later, while at home with my daughter, that I began writing seriously.

Fight for Me
By
Kelley Nyrae

Chapter One

"So, the ball buster strikes again, huh?" Kellan Travers leaned against the wood bar chair and shot the sexy woman sitting across the table from him a grin. Everyone sitting with them chuckled as he goaded his best friend, Alana Mitchell, again. "Poor guy probably didn't know he never stood a chance with you, Lana."

Just like he knew she would, she ruffled her short, black hair and narrowed her brown eyes, which were the same color as the whiskey in both their glasses.

"You better be careful before I decide to bust yours, Travers." She swirled the liquid around in her glass before downing the rest.

Damn the woman was sexy.

Their friends all oohed and aahed at them acknowledging the challenge she'd just issued him. Kellan never backed down from a challenge and he never backed down from something he wanted. He wanted Alana. He wasn't sure when things changed for him; when he started seeing her as more than just a friend, but his eyes were open now.

The only thing he had to do now is open hers.

Alana belonged to him. She didn't know it yet, but she would. Soon. He was damn tired of waiting for her to figure it out on her own. "I'm offended. You'd break my heart just like one of those schmoes you usually got out with?"

"First of all, I'm not *that* bad. You're blowing it out of proportion and second, I doubt any woman could break your heart, Travers. Especially me."

In the background the band switched from the loud, bass-filled tune to a slow song. This was his chance to get his arms around her, to hold her tight and start to make his move.

Kellan ignored the snicker coming from one of his friends who sat next to him and stood up. He slipped around the square table and pulled

Alana to her feet. "Come on, Lana. We're dancing."

"I'm dizzy and drunk. What if I don't feel like dancing?" She may have argued with him, but she still followed. They were always like that. With both of them being lawyers, they enjoyed a little friendly argument. It kept their relationship fresh, new.

"Then I'll make you." He winked at her earning a glowing smile from her plump, kissable lips. "Besides, it's your birthday." They stepped to the side of the dance floor and he scooped her into his arms.

"And what, getting to dance with the great Kellan Travers is my birthday present?"

"Yep." He held her tightly against him, her soft, curvy body molding perfectly against his own. Damn he couldn't wait to have this woman. If he had it his way, which he usually did, it would be soon.

Alana laughed, her eyes dancing with mischief. "You're such an ass, do you know that?"

"Yep," he answered simply again. "Did you have a different gift in mind?" He sure as hell did, but because of all the alcohol she drank tonight, he wouldn't be getting any.

A deep breath seeped from her lungs as she leaned forward to lay her head against his chest. Kellan just held her tight, knowing what was coming. She always did this. Always second guessed herself when what she really needed to do is open her eyes and see what was right in front of her.

"I'm thirty today, Kell. I'm old, and drunk, and getting a pity dance from my best friend."

He laughed, knowing it was what she needed right now. "You're not old." Her soft chuckle socked him in the chest. He loved hearing it, loved giving it to her, and just plain loved knowing she was happy.

"So, I am drunk and this is a pity dance?"

"You're drunk as a skunk and you know it, but no, it's not a pity dance. Like I said, I didn't have time to get you a gift…"

"I'd be careful if I were you. My knee is in perfect position for a very important part of your body."

"I don't think you want to do that, Lana." Kellan pulled her closer and let her feel the ridge of his erection. She gasped at the contact, but didn't pull away. He let his hands travel up and down her back, taking in the feminine arch at the base of her spine. "So where's all this talk coming from?"

Alana leaned forward and let her head rest on his shoulders. Kellan held her, letting her take her time to tell him whatever she needed to say. She always opened up to him, always in her own time. She was cautious. You wouldn't always know it from her hard, sarcastic exterior, but inside she was hurting. She'd always been hurting, but never admitted it.

"I'm just tired, Kell, tired of being alone, but too scared to do anything about it." Her voice had gone from playful to sad, hurt.

"He wasn't good enough for you. There's nothing wrong with not accepting anything less than what you deserve. That's one of the things I respect about you the most."

Her arms wrapped around his neck tighter. The tips of her fingernails played with the hairs at the nape of his neck. Fuck, he had it bad for her. It took everything he had in him not to take her right here and now in the middle of the dance floor. He had to work her into this slow. Lana would run if he didn't, because as strong and confident as she was, she didn't trust herself. He may be a cocky ass, but when it came to her, he knew his shit. She wanted him just as badly as he wanted her, she was just scared.

"You're picking losers on purpose, Lana, because they're safe. You know you'll always leave them before they have the chance to leave you."

Kellan tightened his hold on her, so she wouldn't try to pull away. He had to take things semi-slow with her, but he was also tired of waiting to claim her as his own.

"What are you a psychologist now?" She tried to hide the fact that he was right.

"No, just a man, a smart man who knows you." Bending his head, he let his lips skim her ears. "You want to know why none of those men are good enough for you? Want to know why you keep picking men you'll never want to risk a chance with?"

"Yes."

"Because, they're not me, Lana. They're safe." The song ended, but he continued to hold her, to rock with her. "No man will ever know you the way I do. They'll never be able to give you what I can."

She gasped, but didn't pull away. Not that he would have let her anyway. "And what is that, Kellan? What can you give me?"

It was the alcohol talking and he knew it. Alana wasn't one to mix words, but also would have been too shocked right now to say a word if it wasn't for all the liquid courage floating around in her system. "Everything."

As if she just realized what he said, she tried to pull out of his arms. Kellan just held her tighter, and continued to skate his fingers up and down her back. "Don't run, Lana. I'm not pushing. Not tonight at least, but tomorrow, the fight begins. Your mine, Alana, and it's time I take what belongs to me."

Alana awoke with a jackhammer, pounding her brain. She drank way too much last night. She threw the first couple back when the holy-shit-I'm-thirty-and-alone syndrome first wormed its way into what should have been a great party with Kellan and a group of co-workers. Feeling her buzz, she kind of let the entire semi-midlife crisis stuff float out the window, determined to have a good time.

Then she danced with Kellan.

Holy shit.

Did that really happen?

The bed dipped, except it wasn't her. Alana opened one eye, slowly tilted her head to the side and was met with the back of a blond head. *Crap.* It really had happened. Well not sex, but something.

Slowly, as if searching its way through the fog, her memories began to resurface. Dancing with Kellan. Letting her hands skim his hard, masculine body. Feeling the comfort of having him there. Last night, like always, he was there for her. Any time she needed him, any time she needed anything, Kellan always came through for her.

But then he dropped the bomb. He wanted her. In some ways she shouldn't be surprised, because Kellan wanted most of the female variety. The part that scared her is he always got what he wanted and no matter how many times she might have wondered what it would be like to give into those urges she felt, it would be a mistake.

Because sex would never be enough for her, not like it was with the other guys she dated. And she couldn't lose Kellan. She lost everyone in her life: her mother, foster parents who didn't care enough to fight for her or who shipped her away themselves. Everyone. Since college, he was her constant and it would be a cold day in hell before she lost the one person who was always there for her.

So she'd downed another shot. Then another, and another and the next thing she knew he was carrying her out of the bar, and driving her home. And now he was sleeping in her bed with her like he owned the damn place. If she didn't feel like her head would combust with the slightest movements, she'd shove him out of her bed and give him a piece of her mind.

Not that he'd listen. That was Kellan, strong, confident, pigheaded—but also caring, loyal, and the best friend she had. Oh God, what was she going to do? Just thinking about it made her brain start to pound again. If she was smart, she wouldn't have drunk the bar dry last night. She would have talked to Kellan right then and there and found out exactly what the hell he was thinking.

A quick roll in the sack? As much as her body zinged at the thought; her mind, which is what she always relied on, knew better. It would never end there for her and Kellan, he would never want more. Even if he thought he might, she knew better. He was a fly by the seat of your pants kind of guy. And she knew, sooner or later, like everyone else in her life, he would fly away.

Chapter Two

Kellan lay on his side waiting for Alana to try and make her move. It was coming soon. She'd laid there thinking for a good ten minutes now. Sooner or later she'd think she had everything sorted out in her mind and then she'd try to make her escape. He wouldn't be letting her go.

The bed moved slightly. If he wasn't paying attention, he wouldn't have noticed. A second later it shifted again. He didn't need to open his eyes to know she inched closer and closer to the edge of the bed. She thought he was still asleep. Yeah, right. He knew her better than to let himself get any real shut-eye last night. She'd try and run from him and he'd tie her to the damn bed before he let that happen.

"Where ya going?" he asked when he felt the bed dip more and figured she was trying to stand up.

"Geez! You scared the crap out of me, Kell." She fell against the bed with a humph. "Shouldn't I be the one asking the questions here? What the hell are you doing in my bed?"

"Well, I *was* trying to get some sleep."

She sat up; fully dressed in the pajamas he'd worked like hell to get her into the night before. "Funny. Why are you sleeping in my bed?"

"Because, it's just right."

"Good one, Goldie Locks." She tried to jump to her feet, but swayed a bit and fell back onto the bed. "God, my head is killing me."

Kellan sat up and rubbed his bare chest. "Lie down, Lana. I'll get you some Aspirin and a glass of water."

"I don't want to lie down," she pouted at him, but leaned back on her bed anyway. Yeah, right, she didn't want to lie down. He'd never seen her as drunk as she got last night. She had to be feeling pretty shitty today.

Kellan walked into the kitchen, started a pot of coffee, and grabbed a glass of ice water. On the way back to her bedroom, he stopped off in the bathroom for the Aspirin. "Take these." He handed her the medicine and the water. Surprisingly, she didn't put up a fight. She really must be feeling pretty badly if she wasn't arguing with him. "I'm going to get you a bath going, get some caffeine in you, and then we're going to talk."

"I'm not helpless, you know. I can start a bath."

"Yeah, and so can I."

Kellan turned to the bathroom in her bedroom. He made it about halfway there when she called to him. "Kell."

He turned toward her. "Yeah?"

"We do need to talk. I mean…about last night…I…"

"Shh. Bath, caffeine, then talking." Kellan headed into her second bathroom and closed the door behind him so she wouldn't have the chance to argue with him. No matter how hard she fought him over this, he'd fight harder. This would be a battle, but one he planned to win.

After starting her bath water he poured some fruity, bubble crap he found on the counter into the water. He'd never get why women used all this stuff, but he knew she loved it and right now he needed to score all the points he could. "Come on, Lana. Bath time." Kellan bent down to pick her up. She smacked his arms away.

"I can walk, Travers."

"I can carry you, too." Kellan lifted her into his arms and carried her to the bathroom.

"Fine, just don't think I'm getting undressed in front of you."

"Nothing I haven't seen before." He winked at her, set her to her feet, and left her in the bathroom to do her business.

Alana moaned in delight the second her body dropped into the warm, bubble bath. If she didn't feel so crappy, she'd be kicking Kellan's butt right now. The man was so presumptuous, and bossy, and… "What the hell are you doing in here?"

"Bringing you coffee," he told her with his cocky smile.

"Um, hello? I'm in the bathtub. Ever heard of boundaries?"

"Aw, come one, Lana; don't tell me you're going to get shy on me. Like I said, it's nothing I haven't seen before."

Of course he had to keep reminding her of that. There had been one little incident between the two of them in college when things got a little out of control. Luckily they'd both come to their senses before things went too far, but he had seen her naked. And he had done a bit of playing in the process. "That was years ago. Oh shit. How did I get into my pajamas last night?"

He had the nerve to laugh at her. "Come on. You know me better than that. I don't have to sneak a peek. You changed. I helped because you could hardly stand, but I was the perfect gentleman."

"You? A gentleman? Ha!" She teased him. As grumpy and confused as she was this morning this is one of the things she loved most about their relationship: the ribbing and the teasing.

"I think I'm being pretty damn gentlemanly right now, wouldn't you say? Water, coffee, a bath, when what I really want to do right now is see you naked again."

His hand scratched his bare, muscled chest. Good Lord the man had a nice body. She'd always been a sucker for bare, strong chests and a pair of blue jeans. The jerk. He probably did that on purpose. She probably told him that one day and now it was coming back to haunt her. "Kellan…"

He held up his hands. "Not right now. Take your bath. Do whatever you need to do and when you're done, I'll be waiting for you. We are going to talk today, Lana. I'm tired of waiting for you to come around. It's time you and I get a few things out in the open."

Gulp. *Holy shit.* She was so in for it. Talking is one thing she didn't do well. Talking about her feelings at least. Otherwise, she could talk her way out of anything. And maybe that's just what she'd have to do today, too.

She took what had to be the longest damn bath in history. Kellan looked at his watch. Five minutes. If she wasn't out in five minutes he was going in after her and this time he wouldn't be the gentleman he was the last time. A man could only be so strong and he'd left that limit in the dust.

Four minutes and counting. To keep himself busy, Kellan poured another cup of coffee for both of them. He set them both on the small, circular table in her kitchen right when he heard the door open. About damn time. "Sit down, Lana."

She gave him a dirty look that made him smile. "It is my house, you know? I'll sit down if I want to."

He tried not to let his smile widen when she took a seat at the table. She did it with a huff so classically Alana that he couldn't help but laugh.

"Don't laugh at me. I'm hung-over and a big, hulking jerk has taken over my house." She gave him a half smile.

"You know you love me, Lana."

"I can't for the life of me figure out why." She took a sip of her coffee. "We do need to talk, Kell. I'm…I'm a little confused right now."

Kellan sat down across from her. "I'll talk. You listen. I want you, Alana. I've wanted you for years and I'm tired of waiting. If you stop fighting me for just a minute, I think you'll realize you feel the same way."

"I don't think it's a good idea."

He noticed she didn't deny wanting him. That gave him the green light as far as he was concerned. Kellan got up and moved to stand behind her and kneaded the muscles in her neck. A soft whimper, whispered past her lips giving him an instant hard-on. She didn't think this was a good idea? Yeah, right. He couldn't wait to call her his.

Kellan leaned down, letting his lips brush her ear. That scent of the fruity shit he'd poured in the tub attacked his senses. "Mm, you smell good, Lana." He didn't let his mouth touch her, just whispered against her ear. "You don't think this is a good idea? Are you sure about that?" She shuddered, egging him on more. "I think it's a very good idea. We'd be great together, Lana. You know I'd treat you right."

"Yes…" she gasped between deep breaths. Kellan chuckled knowing victory was within his grasp. "But then what would happen when you got bored? We've been friends too long to let our libido mess it up. I don't want to add you to the list of people who've walked out of my life."

Fuck. He should have known this wouldn't be easy. Not with Lana. She was different which is exactly why he wanted more with her, more than he gave other women and he wanted more in return than she gave other men. He wanted her. All of her. Forever. "Who said anything about being quick?" Kellan kneaded the muscles of her neck. "And I can promise you it sure as hell won't be boring."

He ran the tips of his fingers over the smooth skin of her neck. Damn she was soft. Like fine silk he wanted to wrap himself in. She breathed deep, heavy breaths showing him she felt it just as much as he did. The physical draw between them was too strong, unfucking breakable. "We fit, Lana. You know it. I know it. Why don't you stop lying to yourself? Stop being afraid. Stop wasting your time when what you need is right in front of you. You know I can make you feel good, baby."

Her feminine hand grabbed his, first softly, and then she pulled his hand from her neck. "Sex, Kell. Yeah the sex would be good, but like I said, I'm not willing to throw our friendship away for sex."

She pushed away from him, stood, and crossed the hardwood floors of her kitchen. She wasn't getting this right. Hell, maybe he wasn't telling her right. "I'm not just talking about sex, Lana."

"Sure sounded like that to me."

"I'm a guy. I probably always sound like I'm talking about sex. I mean, I do want to take you to bed, and I will, but I want *you*. All of you."

She laughed. Hard. What was so damn funny he didn't know, but he intended to find out. "What the hell are you laughing at?" She held up her hand like she was asking for a minute and kept up her sexy, contagious laughter. "So much for a headache," he mumbled to himself getting more frustrated by the second. Here he was trying to open his damn heart to her and she couldn't stop laughing at him.

Finally, she settled down enough to speak. "You don't want any woman for more than sex, Kellan. In all the years I've known you, you've always said you'd never settle down. You're a compulsive dater, and have left at least double the quote, unquote, broken hearts that I have. You'd get bored like you always do and then our friendship would be screwed and I'd be alone."

Her last words broke his heart. She was so scared of being alone that her fear kept her from the person who always wanted to be there for her. "Don't be scared, Lana. Don't run from me. You know I'd never leave you alone."

She crossed her arms over her chest. "I'm not running, Kellan, but you're right, I am scared. I'm scared of losing what we have!"

Kellan took a couple steps toward her, but stopped. "We won't be losing anything. You know I'd never do anything to hurt what we have." He let out a frustrated sigh. Why the hell didn't she get it?

"You may not mean to, but in the end, you will. Most people don't set out to hurt someone else, but that doesn't stop it from happening and instead of some random date, it would be our best friend who we hurt. You don't want me, Kellan. Not really."

Fuck that. He'd had enough. He'd show her exactly how much he wanted her. Kellan stalked toward her. Before she had the chance to argue he pulled her against him. "I'm not going to back away like the guys you date, Lana. I know what I want and when I find it, I fight for it. I want you, and I know you want me, too. Tell me you'd get bored of this."

Kellan crushed her mouth beneath his.

Chapter Three

Tingles formed in the pit of her belly with the first touch of Kellan's lips. The kiss was hard, urgent, and when his tongue slipped into her mouth for an erotic mating the tingles shot through her body landing at the apex of her thighs. Kellan could kiss. Damn the man could kiss. As much as she knew she shouldn't, she pushed her way into his mouth, wanting to taste him. Coffee and man met her tongue.

Their tongues tangled before Kellan eased the possession of her mouth to kiss a wet trail down her neck. He took her earlobe between his teeth for a gentle bite. Her mind no longer had control of her body. The evil, horny devil on her shoulder made her drop her head back to give him better access. Alana gripped the taut muscles of his back, feeling them tense beneath her eager fingers.

He felt good. Hard. The damn devil enticed her, urged Alana to grip him tighter. To push her fingernails into his back.

"Shit, Lana. You feel so damn good."

His hands moved to her breasts kneading them, pinching her tender nipples. *This is Kellan. What are you doing? You're going to regret this.* Logical Alana tried to convince herself.

But the devil, his voice was louder, more convincing. *Mm, doesn't this feel good? Keep going. Take what you need from him.* And she did need him. She'd always needed him, but she never wanted to admit it. His mouth skated back up her throat. Kellan nibbled at her lips. "Kell…"

"Not bored now are you, baby?" he snickered against her lips and then damn him. The jerk pulled away; a cocky grin on his face. "There's too much fire between us for anyone to get bored. We're combustible."

Logical Alana took over again. "I didn't mean bored with the sex and you know it."

"We've been friends for years and we've never gotten bored with each other. The sex will just add to what we already have." Kellan adjusted the front of his pants. She shouldn't, but Alana couldn't help but take a peek. Oh yeah, he was hard alright. The man had a bulge like she'd never seen straining inside his blue jeans. "We'll get to that part later, baby, I promise."

He tilted her face up to look at him. "You can think what you want about me, but you know when I set my mind to something, I get it. I want you, Lana. I've always wanted you. We're meant for each other and you know it. Why do you think none of our other relationships ever worked?"

Alana let her eyes drift closed, exhaled a deep breath, and then opened them again. What he said sounded so right, but she knew better. Thinking they could be together was crazy. Thinking he would want to stay with her, when no one who meant anything to her ever did, was crazy. "Because we both have shitty luck?" She tried to offer him a smile.

"Nice try, Lana." Kellan dropped a series of soft, angel kisses to her lips. "No one knows you like I do." One of his hands went to her breast again. "No one knows you're all steel on the outside, but soft on the inside." His thumb circled her nipple. Waves of his electricity washed over her, making her shudder. "No one knows you love to have control, because you had so little of it growing up."

Alana bit her bottom lip. Good God, why was he doing this to her? Her resistance weakened with each of his statements. Kellan ran his thumb over her bottom lip, making her let out a groan.

"No one knows you bite this sexy lip when you're nervous. No one knows your worst pet peeve is people who are late and that you sing at the top of your lungs when you drive in the car by yourself." A whimper escaped her mouth when he bent forward and touched his lips to hers again. "Just me, Lana. Now I want to know what you sound like when you come. That one time all those years ago wasn't enough for me."

Alana's breath hitched. God help her, but she wanted that, too.

"I want to know what you taste like, how you feel beneath me. I want to wake up with you every morning, baby, and I plan to."

"Kellan... I..." Thank God he cut her off; because she almost told him she wanted that, too.

"I have a few things I need to take care of today. Think about what I said, Lana. I'll be back around six with dinner. Maybe we'll watch a movie or something."

They were best friends. They spent a lot of time together, but what he just said sounded so different...so intimate that it scared her. When she was scared, she fought. She'd always been that way. Probably always would be. "What if I don't want to see you again tonight?"

"We both know that's not true, so why even discuss it?"

The man drove her crazy, especially considering he was right.

"No matter how hard you fight, I'll fight harder, Lana."

And he would. She knew Kellan. The man wouldn't give up, until he got his way. She used to respect that about him. Today, it pissed her off. "What are you doing, Kell?" Why did he have to make things difficult between them? She loved that things had always been easy with Kellan. She had enough hard in her life. That's the last thing she wanted from the one person she could always count on.

Kellan leaned down and pressed a soft kiss to her lips. "I'm showing you what it will be like when we're together, Lana. And we will be together." He winked at her. "See you tonight."

Without another word, Kellan turned and walked out of her kitchen.

Kellan grabbed his shirt, shoes, and socks, dressed and then let himself out of Alana's apartment. She needed a little space and he had a few things he wanted to get together for tonight anyway. Right now she probably sat in the kitchen simmering, wanting to come out and give him a piece of her mind, but she wouldn't. She knew if she did, it would be even longer until he left and like he said, she needed a little space.

Actually, he did, too. If he'd stayed much longer, he wouldn't have been able to hold himself back from kissing her again. This time, he wouldn't be able to stop himself. God damn the woman had tasted just as fucking sweet as he'd known she would. Sweet and spicy. Apples and cinnamon. *His.* "Fuck," Kellan laughed, shaking his head. He was in deep and he couldn't be happier about it. Cheesy as it sounded, he wasn't joking when he told her he wanted to wake up with her every day. Took him a while to realize it, but he did.

He opened the door to his car and got in. His mom would have a field day with this when she found out. She'd always loved, Lana. From the first time he brought her home, when she had nowhere else to go on Thanksgiving, their freshman year. His mom had this senile little Shit tzu. The dog hated everyone except his mom. He snapped at anyone new who came to the house, so they had to keep him locked in the bedroom any time someone came over. When Lana got there, the dog accidentally got out. Everyone freaked out when she unknowingly reached her hand down to pet him.

The dog fucking kissed her. He'd never even licked Kellan's hand and he'd grown up with the damn thing. Reggie followed Alana around like a lovesick puppy all night. When she left, his mom told him she was the girl he would marry. At the time he thought she was crazy. Looks like his mom, and even the damn dog were right. For once, Kellan could understand where that crazy dog was coming from, because now he was a lovesick pup, too.

Thirty was too young to have a midlife crisis. If this were midlife, that would only put her living to sixty. She planned to live a whole hell of a lot longer than that. Damn Kellan for putting her through a midlife crisis when she was too damn young! What was he thinking with all this, I want you, we belong together mumbo-jumbo? And why the hell did she get butterflies in her stomach just thinking those words?

Because secretly, buried so deep that she rarely even admitted it to herself, she'd always wanted Kellan. Who wouldn't? He was every woman's dream: strong, confident, funny, and loyal all wrapped up into one delicious package of muscles, blond hair and blue eyes. Yeah, to say she wanted him was a bit of an understatement, but wanting something, and taking it, were two different things.

When push came to shove, they didn't have much of a chance to make it. She never kept a man longer than a few weeks and he was just as bad. Even if he wouldn't let himself think clearly enough to see that right now, she would. She'd been too much of a dreamer when she was younger and that got her into trouble.

She got taken away from her mom when she was five and always believed she'd come back for her. Each foster home she went to she believed, hoped that this one would last. They never did. She'd never known consistency. She'd never known unconditional love. Freshman year she'd met Kellan.

He was the only one who knew what she'd been through. He knew how much pain she'd been put through, so why he would pull this stunt, she didn't know. This wasn't a smart decision. Not if she wanted to keep him in her life and she did. More than anything. Every man she went out with was a smart choice, a safe choice. Kellan wasn't safe. Not to her heart.

When he came over tonight she'd have to make him understand. Kellan always had an angle and if she could figure out where he was coming from, she'd know how to show him this whole thing was a crazy idea. If she didn't, she'd be in trouble. If Kellan wanted a fight, she'd give him one. She'd never been one to roll over and give in easily. She could debate with the best of them. Hell, that's what she did. She'd use their situation just like a case; argue her point until the other side saw that she was right. She was after all.

This would work. It had to, because honestly, she didn't know how many more of his kisses…of his touches she could take before she threw in the towel.

Chapter Four

A loud knock sounded from her living room at six twenty. The jerk. So much for showing up at six. *Yeah, like that's what's pissing you off. You're really mad at yourself for being so damn anxious for him to show.* Alana eased her feet into her fluffy, green slippers and went to the door. There was no reason to try and keep the big bad wolf out. He would find his way inside no matter what. Kellan would huff and puff until he eventually blew his way inside. That's just the way he worked. "Hey." Alana closed the door behind him.

"Don't sound too enthused there, Lana." Kellan bent over and kissed her forehead. This is what she was used to. This camaraderie they'd always had. He always kissed her on the forehead. That she could handle. It's when his lips touched hers that he sent her over the edge into La La Land.

"Just tired and hungry. I had some big oaf at my house this morning that wouldn't stop harassing me," she said with a smile. "And then he gave himself an invitation to come over again tonight when all I really want to do is relax alone. Oh, and did I mention he showed up late?" She was determined to make this just like any other night for them. She would forget his kisses. Forget his touches and forget his ludicrous promises this morning. Tonight was just Alana and Kellan: friends, colleagues.

And if that didn't work, then she'd pull out the big guns and hold on tight. She could argue with the best of them and Kellan sat at the top of that list.

"An oaf, huh? That's not what I heard. Word on the street is some smart, gorgeous guy brought you home last night, took care of you this morning, and then generously came over tonight with your favorite takeout. I'm thinking god might be a better description than oaf."

Alana shot him her don't go there look. "Chinese from Mr. Chens? You don't play fair." Her stomach rumbled. Mr. Chens was her favorite restaurant.

"I never promised to, Lana."

She ignored his wink and reached for his shoulder. Stupid move. A zing traveled up her arm at the contact making her pull away sharply. "Just dinner, Kell. No funny business. Tonight is just like any other night for us." She needed him to understand that before they went any further.

In classic Kellan style he gave her a cocky grin, showcasing those dimples that made all the women go wild. "Whatever you need to tell yourself."

"I'm serious."

"Me, too, Lana. When it comes to you, I'm serious as a fucking heart attack. Now come on. Let's eat."

Like a puppet, Alana let Kellan pull her strings and followed him to her kitchen.

"How's your case going, counselor?" he asked when they sat at her small table to eat.

"Good, actually. The evidence is all circumstantial. He's a good kid. Was just in the wrong place at the wrong time. It's going to feel good to help him walk away from this." Alana took a bite of her Moo Goo Gai Pan. When the savory spices hit her tongue she let out a moan. "Damn, that's good."

"Actually, I'm good. If it weren't for me, you'd be eating Cheerios for dinner tonight. What are you going to do to repay me?"

Alana picked up a pea from her fried rice and chucked it at him. "I'd have you know, it's Honey Nut Cheerios."

Kellan laughed. "Seriously. When's the last time you went shopping, Lana? I couldn't find anything but coffee and cereal this morning."

"I happen to like coffee and cereal. You have a problem with that?" Alana took another bite of her food, and then pointed her fork at Kellan. "And if you hadn't been peeking around in my kitchen this morning, you wouldn't have seen my bare cabinets anyway, Nosey."

"Hey, I'm not nosey. If you remember correctly, I was taking care of my hung over best friend."

"You're *best friend*," she stressed the words, "can take care of herself." She wasn't really talking about bare cabinets anymore. She needed him to know she was fine on her own. Happy. Things were perfect between them the way they already were.

"I know that, but I can take care of her, too. That's what two people who care about each other do and no matter how much she wants to deny it, I know it feels good once in a while having someone take care of her. And I *know* she cares about me just as much as I care about her. She just needs to get off her high horse and admit it."

It did feel good. She'd never had anyone take care of her before Kellan came into her life. He was always there for her, always giving her what she needed which is exactly why she couldn't risk losing him. "There's nothing to admit, Kell. I love you. You're my best friend and you always will be. Anything else would be a mistake."

"Says you." His crystal blue eyes bore into her with an intensity that made it impossible for her to turn away from him.

"Yes, says me. Give it a week and you'll agree with me."

Kellan pushed away from the table, his chair hitting the floor. "Don't tell me how I feel, Alana. Maybe if you weren't so damn closed off, you'd see what's sitting right in front of you. Push me away all you want, but I'm not going anywhere."

His words slapped her. Was she really closed off? No. How could he say that? He knew everything about her. She opened up to him in ways she'd never opened up to anyone else. How did that make her closed off to him? Maybe other people, but never Kellan. *Exactly. Never with Kellan, because he's different and you know it.* Alana shoved those thoughts to the back of her mind.

"It's late, Kell. Maybe you should go." She stood up.

"It's six forty-five. It's not late and like I told you, I'm not going anywhere. You can fight me all you want, Alana, but I'm not letting you push me away. I know you're scared, darlin', and I'm not going anywhere until I show you there's nothing to fear. You're mine and I take care of what's mine."

Kellan watched the lump slide down Lana's slender throat. Yeah, that's what he thought. She was afraid, but eager, as well. A light flashed in her eyes when he called her his. She'd probably never felt like she belonged anywhere before. She belonged with him and nothing she could say would make him believe otherwise.

"So you're just going to push your way into my home, whether I want you here or not?" Her voice shook.

Kellan walked over to her and cupped her cheek. "Can you honestly tell me you don't want me here, Lana?" He rubbed his finger in circles on her cheek. An inner-war raged in her stormy brown eyes. She was at war with herself just as he was at war with her. Because of her past, she was scared. He got that, but couldn't she see he was different?

Kellan would never leave her. They'd been best friends for years and now the natural progression of their relationship needed to come to pass. If she were honest with herself she'd admit they'd always been more than best friends. Kellan was ready to make it official.

"That's not fair, Kell. You know I'd never kick you out. You're my best friend."

"All's fair in love and war, Lana. I'm fighting for your heart. You better believe I'm going to win by whatever means necessary."

"This isn't a war and I'm not a case for you to win."

"I beg to differ." Kellan twisted a strand of her hair with his finger. "You're making this a fight, Lana, because you won't give it a chance." He touched her temple. "Because you won't use the brain in that pretty head of yours. You're too scared to see how much this makes sense." Kellan slid his hand down and placed it on her chest. Lana gasped, her eyes widening. "Because you're scared to listen to what your heart tells you. It beats for me, Lana, just like mine beats for you. We're in tune to each other. Always have been and now it's time to take our relationship to the next level."

She looked up at him, her eyes big and sad. "What makes you think you know me better than I know myself? How do you know I feel more than just friendship for you? Maybe you're deluding yourself."

"Because, I know you." She tried to pull away from him, but he didn't let her. She needed to hear him, really hear him with no walls between them. "No, don't pull away from me. I've known you for ten years. I've paid attention. I know when you get that far off look in your eyes your running away from something. I see the way the pulse in your throat beats rapidly when I walk into a room. I've never seen that happen to you with another man."

Her breath came out in short pants. Her eyes clouded over with the familiar haze of lust. "Physical. It's strictly physical. Any woman would be crazy not to find you attractive, Kellan."

Another lie. Not only to him, but to herself, as well. But still…it just might work in his favor. He wasn't kidding when he said all's fair in love and war, he would win Alana's heart by any means necessary.

"You admit you're attracted to me?" Alana fought to hold on to her resolve. Her insides screamed at her to kiss him, to melt into his arms and tell him she wanted to try and see where this could go. That he was right, she did know that he knew her better than anyone ever would. That she did feel more for him than the friendship they'd had for all these years.

But she couldn't.

But she also wanted him.

Sex she could handle, well, hopefully. She was always detached when she had sex with a man. Usually she didn't have to try like she would with Kellan, but the other men she'd been with…well…they'd been there to scratch an itch. Kellan was so much more, but if she treated him like just another guy, then maybe she could make it through this in one piece.

Because no matter what Kellan told her, she knew he'd eventually lose interest with her just like he did with all the other women he dated. No one else in her life had wanted her, so why would he? Even though she'd let a few men scratch her itch in the past, she'd always wanted it to be Kellan.

Alana let out the deep breath she hadn't realized she'd been holding. She could do this. She could be with Kellan, but keep her emotions in check. "You're gorgeous and you know it, Kell. Like I said, a woman would have to be crazy not to find you attractive."

"I don't give a shit about other women. Only you. Tell me you're attracted to me."

"I'm attracted to you." The words slipped out of her mouth, surprisingly effortlessly.

"Do you want me?"

He traced her lips with his thumb. Alana held back the urge to suck his finger into her mouth. She did want him. She wanted to be with him. To feel him love her in a way she could never let him do completely. "I want to have sex with you."

Kellan chuckled. "I'd love to make love to you, baby."

"Sex."

"Whatever you have to tell yourself, Lana," he whispered before his lips crushed hers.

Chapter Five

Waves of desire swam over her like the beach at high tide washing away any will she might have had to change her mind. Alana wrapped her arms around Kellan's neck, losing herself in the sensations coursing through her body. This was Kellan, her best friend, the only person in the world she could always depend on kissing her senseless. This kiss was different than the one this morning, deeper, slower, more passionate. Like a preview of the delicious torture he would bestow upon her tonight.

His mouth was warm. He tasted of peppermint despite the dinner they'd just shared. Alana took advantage while she could, slipping her tongue deeper into his mouth savoring his distinct taste. Kellan pulled her tighter against him, each inch of his hard body molded to hers. The man was on fire and everywhere he touched her, her body scorched with heat, as well.

"Bedroom," Kellan ordered against her mouth.

"Can't wait." And she couldn't. Her body was on edge for him, pulsing with need.

"You have sex in a kitchen, baby. I told you I'm going to make love to you. I'm taking you in a bed."

Alana tried to block his words from her mind when Kellan picked her up. She wrapped her legs around his waist as he carried her to her bedroom. Kellan's tongue traced the seam of her lips before dipping inside. Alana didn't try to fight him anymore. She willingly, no eagerly, opened her mouth to let him inside.

Their tongues danced and mated erotically, twining together before parting again for a little game of tag. He set her on her bed, his body resting between her thighs as he took the kiss deeper.

"You're so fucking hot, Lana. I could eat at your mouth all day."

She couldn't reply with words. She tried to tell him how she felt with a moan, with the way her fingers clutched the tight muscles of his back. His mouth now teased her neck, her ear, the base of her throat. Kellan alternated between nips, kisses and licks, each one building the pressure inside her.

She ached. "Kell...please..."

"What, baby? What do you need?" His hand cupped her center through her sweats making another moan ripped from her throat.

"You need me here? Is this what you want?"

"Yes. Please." The words came out choppy. Alana had to fight to contain herself when he dipped his fingers below the elastic of her sweat pants to touch her tender core. "Kellan."

"Yeah, baby. It's me. Always me. Say my name again."

"Kellan. Kellan." She couldn't stop calling his name, unable to believe this was him, her best friend treating her to this overwhelming pleasure.

"I'm right here. Damn your wet." He pushed a finger between her throbbing lips, and inside her. "Sweet God in heaven, you're tight."

She couldn't think. She couldn't reply besides to rock her hips toward his hand. Kellan caught her hint. He started to pump his finger. Alana rode it, thrust for thrust. She jerked when he pushed another finger inside her. His other hand pushed up her shirt and freed one breast. "Such pretty little nipples, Lana. I need to taste them."

And taste them he did. Alana bucked when his mouth covered her tender nipple and sucked. "Kellan!" She grabbed a hold of his blond curls, running her fingers through their soft strands. Kellan looked up at her and smiled that knockout smile before flicking her nipple with his tongue again.

Over and over he lashed her pebbled peaks, his fingers working magic beneath her sweats. "Come, baby." He whispered against her breast. His thumb found her nub, pushing lightly against it, then harder. Alana couldn't hold back anymore. The pressure inside her surged and exploded as she shattered into a million pieces calling Kellan's name.

Holy shit. No, that didn't even begin to explain what he was feeling. Holy fucking shit came closer, but still nowhere near the pure bliss bouncing around inside him right now. And this was only his finger inside her. Only his mouth on her breast. He still didn't even have her naked. He hadn't tasted her. Hadn't been inside her. His throbbing cock pulsed in his jeans at just the thought.

"Time to get you naked, Lana." Kellan hooked his fingers in her fuzzy sweats and pulled them and her panties down. "These are sexy."

"They're sweatpants, Kellan."

"So. They're hot on you. They hug your sweet, little ass just perfectly. I've wanted to spank it all night. Kellan threw her pants to the floor, not letting his line of vision near the apex of her thighs. If he did, he'd never get her naked. He'd play, and touch, and worship the second he saw her and he wanted her completely bare to him before he started any of that.

"Sit up a little, baby." She obeyed. Kellan pulled each of her arms out and then slipped the shirt over her head. Leaning forward, he took her mouth with gentle, sucking kisses while his arms reached behind her to unhook her bra. One flick of his wrist and the latches came free. He kissed her once more before sitting up and tossing the bra with the rest of her clothes.

God she was so beautiful his breath hitched: smooth, creamy skin, firm, high breasts. His eyes took her in, the lustful look in her eyes, the slight curve of her lips, her long, slender neck. He kept going, getting his hand involved now. Kellan let his fingers slowly drift down her body; touching her everywhere while his eyes did the same. He circled her breasts, traced the curve beneath them before his fingers drifted down her flat stomach.

His finger dipped into her belly button, danced along her hips, then finally, traveling between her thighs. "You're so beautiful, Lana. You have no idea how many nights I've dreamed about this, about touching you, taking you over and over, each time, my name on your lips when you came."

"Kellan…don't…I…"

He touched her lips with one hand while his other parted the ones at the apex of her thighs. "Yes you can. Don't fight this. Don't fight us. Let me love you the way you were meant to be loved." He pushed two fingers inside her before he replaced his first hand, with his lips, kissing her, showing her how well they worked together. Alana didn't hold back, she kissed him with equal fervor. Another shot of desire erupted inside of him.

He kissed his way down her body, every couple of inches licking her skin. She writhed beneath him, the farther down he went, the more urgent her movements. Finally, Kellan was where he wanted to be. With one hand he parted her. "Fucking beautiful." And then he licked immediately becoming intoxicated with her sweet, feminine taste.

She fisted his hair, urging him on. Kellan licked, tasted, and teased her feminine folds. Each moan, each gasp, each tug of his hair fueled the fire roaring inside him. He lapped at her; then pushed his tongue inside.

"Kellan…Oh God…"

"Mmm, baby. You're so perfect. I want to do this every day for the rest of my life." He was pushing, but he didn't care. He'd meant to ease her into this. He did know how hard this was for her, how scared she was, but like he said, he was tired of waiting. They belonged together and he knew he could make her happy, give her all the things she wanted, but was too scared to admit, even to herself.

Her hips started to move. They pushed against his mouth. She was close, so ready to come. Kellan replaced his tongue with two fingers. He pumped them in and out of her, his tongue flicking her clit. Her grip in his hair tightened. He loved her swollen nub again and then sucked it into his mouth.

Her whole body tensed, tightened and she came for the second time in one night, calling his name.

A twofer. She almost never had a twofer, but under Kellan's expert touch her body wanted more. No, needed more. And he would give it to her. That much she knew. Pleasure she could handle from him. It was all the other stuff that got her all muddled up. His words played through her head. Words she reveled in, but also feared more than anything.

No one in her life had ever wanted her. At least not for the long haul. She'd dealt with it though. Closed herself off, so she didn't feel the pain. With Kellan, there was no closing herself off. He was like a part of her and sooner or later when he decided he no longer wanted her, it would kill her.

"Stop thinking, Lana. Just feel. Feel me. Kellan. Have I ever let you down?"

"No." That was true. He'd never let her down but that wasn't what she feared. "But that doesn't mean I won't let you down." She had to be honest with him. This was about her just as much as, if not more than, it was about him. Something she did chased everyone away from her.

"Not possible, Lana." He ripped his shirt over his head, stood on his knees and unbuttoned and unzipped his pants. Kellan kissed her before getting off the bed to take off his pants. He stood in front of her, gloriously naked, and so gorgeous he stole her breath. "You like what you see?" He smiled at her.

"You're so conceited." Alana tried for nonchalance. She didn't want him to know how much he affected her.

"No, I just know the look of an ogling woman when I see one. You, Alana, are ogling." There he went with that cocky grin again. Alana picked up a pillow and threw it at him.

"Hurry up with the damn condom and get over here."

Kellan winked at her. "Yes, ma'am." He reached into the pocket of his jeans and pulled out a condom. With hurried movements he ripped open the silver package with his teeth and sheathed himself. He pushed himself between her legs, teasing her. "I can't believe I'm here with you, Lana. My Lana."

The sincerity in his eyes scorched her. Without giving her the chance to reply, to tell him she wasn't his, Kellan eased inside her in one thrust. "Oh, God!" Alana called out. At the same time, Kellan cursed, "Fuck." And then he was moving inside her. Thrusting in and out, stroke after delicious stroke. She felt full, stretched in the most erotic way.

The muscles in Kellan's arms and chest flexed as he held himself above her. Each pump flooded her with more pleasure. Alana gripped his rear, digging her fingernails into his flesh.

"Damn, Lana, you feel so fucking good, like your body was custom-made to wrap around mine."

Oh, God, he was right. She'd had sex before. Bad sex and good sex, but nothing compared to Kellan filling her. "Keep going, Kell. I'm so close."

His thrusts came harder, faster. Alana held on while he took her for the ride of her life. Kellan leaned forward, his tongue pushing its way into her mouth. For the third time tonight, orgasm washed over her, this one more potent than the other two combined. She wouldn't have thought it possible.

He was right behind her. Kellan growled, as he came, and then dropped to the mattress next to her. "You can't tell me we'd ever get bored of that."

No, she couldn't, but she didn't tell him that. "Sex isn't everything, Kellan."

He rolled over, pulled off the condom and tossed it into the trash can beside her bed. "I know. It's the icing on the cake. I already can't get enough of you; this just confirms I'm never letting you go."

Alana tried to sit up. She didn't get far. Kellan's strong grasp pulled her back into the bed, and into his arms.

"I don't think so, Lana. You're sleeping right here in my arms all night."

She hadn't seen that one coming. She should have, but didn't. They'd slept in the same bed before, but not after sex. She'd never lain in his arms, felt his heart beat against her cheek like she did right now. "You know I don't spend the night with a guy after sex, Kellan."

She felt him smile. "Then I guess I better be glad what we did wasn't just sex. I told you I planned to make love to you and that's exactly what I did. Don't try and tell me you didn't feel it, too."

She had felt it. Wetness pooled in her eyes. Alana fought not to let them fall. She loved him, always had, but for her that didn't make a difference. Everyone she'd ever loved walked out on her. It would only be a matter of time before the same thing happened with Kellan.

She lay there, holding him until his breathing evened to long, steady breaths of deep sleep. When she knew he was out for the count, she slipped out of her own bed, dressed and went out to spend the night on the couch.

Chapter Six

Kellan stretched, and then rolled over to pull Alana into his arms, only she wasn't there. He slept like the dead, always had. She knew that. He could almost guarantee she'd waited for him to pass out last night before going into the other room to sleep. Anger pummeled him. Why couldn't she trust him? Why couldn't she give this a chance? She knew him, knew everything about him. How could she not know he'd never hurt her? He'd do anything for her. It had been like that since the first day they met. Why would anything change now?

Maybe he was pushing too hard. Maybe he read the signs wrong and she didn't feel the same way he did. Deep down, he knew she did. Her walls were just too high, too thick to fall down overnight. No matter how long it took, he would break those walls down. Kellan didn't give up. Especially when it came to Alana. He'd never give up on her.

He pushed from the bed, didn't bother with his clothes and stalked into her living room. "Wake up, sunshine. I have a bone to pick with you."

Alana rolled over to face him. "I'm not asleep—good God, could you put some clothes on?"

"Why? Does my being naked bother you? I'm up for another round if you are; I just need to get something off my chest first."

"Don't be a jerk, Kellan." She sat up on the couch.

He was being a jerk. Kellan paced the room a couple times before plopping down on the couch beside her. "Shit, Lana, I know I'm being a jerk, but I'm pissed off right now. I hate to think of you out here on the couch last night because I chased you out of your own bed."

Sure he was pushing. He knew she would be nervous about the whole sleeping in the same bed after sex thing, but he thought she'd get over it. Thought she'd relax against him and let him hold her, protect her. Instead she'd run away from him. But still, he couldn't give up. Not on her.

"It's not your fault, Kell. It's my hang-up. Any woman would love to share a bed with you."

"I don't care about just any woman. I only care about you. I want you to want to share my bed."

She looked up at him, the pain in her eyes spearing his heart. "It's not that simple. I wish it was. There's just too much here. Too much between us." She glanced down at him. "You really need to get some clothes on."

He'd almost forgotten he was naked. "There's not too much

between us. It's still just me and you, same as always, Lana. I'm just tired of hiding what's always been there." Kellan stood up. "Come on. We both need to get ready. My mom's got a birthday party planned for you and we don't want to be late."

Alana nearly gave herself whiplash when she snapped her head up to look at Kellan. "What?"

"You heard me correctly. It's supposed to be a surprise, so I need you to act shocked when you come in. My whole family will be there. They've been planning it for months now."

"No, no, no. Why would they do this? I can't go to a party with your whole family!"

"Yeah you can. You've been around my whole family hundreds of times."

"That was before," she waved her hands between the two of them. "Before we...before this...oh you know what I'm talking about."

Kellan looked at her, so lost she wanted smack him. It was so unfair that men could be so clueless sometimes. "What the hell does that have to do with anything? It's not as if they're going to know what happened last night, Lana, and even if they did, they'd be ecstatic. You're the only one who doesn't seem to realize we're supposed to be together."

Alana let that one slide because honestly, she just didn't have the strength to fight him right now. "But why would they throw me a surprise birthday party?" Sure she knew his whole family. They'd spent a few holidays together over the years and she attended some of their family parties when Kellan drug her along, but she didn't get why they were throwing *her* a birthday party.

Kellan, in all his naked glory walked back over to her. He held out his hand and for some reason, she placed hers inside and he pulled her to her feet. Kellan didn't just stop there. He pulled her into his arms, holding her tightly. God it felt so good to be held by him. She could curl up in his arms and live there for days, surviving off his warmth.

"Because, you're part of the family, Lana. They love you." Then as if he hadn't just filled her heart in a way she'd never experienced before, he touched the tip of her nose and said, "Plus, it's not every day a woman turns thirty." Kellan kissed her quickly, and then drug her to her room. "Come on, Lana. We have a party to attend."

A few months before, his mom and sisters told him they wanted to throw a party for Alana. They knew she had no family and according to them, a woman needed a little extra love on her thirtieth birthday.

Apparently, that was a big milestone for women. Why he didn't know, but he trusted the women in his family.

And he also knew Lana needed this. She needed to enjoy herself. She needed to see he wasn't the only person who loved her. She had a whole family within her grasp if she would just reach out and grab them. Or, knowing the Travers family, they'd do it for her. He wasn't the only determined one in his family, another reason, Lana fit right in with them.

Much to his frustration, they took separate showers. While Lana took hers, he ran down to his car and grabbed the overnight bag he'd packed. Yeah, he'd been pretty damn confident he'd spend the night, so shoot him. He knew better than to bring it up with him the night before. That would have earned him a swift kick out the door. An hour later they were both ready, just in time to make the drive out to Newport Beach, where his family lived.

"I feel so bad that your family went through all this trouble for me, Kellan. You should have told them not to." She told him when they exited the freeway.

"Ha, you know my mom better than that. If I'd have told her no, she just would have done it anyway. That's how us Travers work. Plus, it's not trouble, Lana. Like it or not you're a part of my family. You have been since that first Thanksgiving dinner ten years ago." Kellan pulled up to his parents' house.

"Now remember, this is a surprise. My sisters will kick my butt if they know I told you." She gave him a small smile then reached for the handle on the door. Kellan grabbed her hand and stopped her before she could get out. "And have fun, Lana. I'm not the only person you mean a lot to. You have a whole group of people in there who love you and that will never change. Once a Travers, always a Travers. You're stuck with us now."

He wanted her to know that no matter what, they'd never walk away from her. *He* would never walk away from her. He wasn't like her parents, or the foster families she'd had over the years. He was here to stay.

Alana tried to mean the smile she plastered on her face for Kellan's sake. The truth is she was scared to death. She'd gone out with friends for her birthdays, she'd spent them with random boyfriends in the past, but this was different. This was Kellan's family. This was the one thing she wanted, but feared she'd never have. Her last foster parents told her on her sixteenth birthday that they were having a baby and that she'd be going back into the system.

Ever since then, she'd kind of tuned them out. I mean, yeah she celebrated them, but she never let them mean anything to her. Spending the day with Kellan *and* his family would definitely mean something to her.

"Promise me," Kellan told her, as they approached the front door. "Promise me you'll try and have a good time."

Alana looked up at him, and smiled. "I will." And she meant it. Today she wanted to just relax and pretend to be part of a family for the first time in her life.

"Surprise!" Everyone one yelled when they walked in the door. Alana found she didn't have to pretend too hard to be surprised. She jumped, at the sound of the booming laughter and cheers from Kellan's family. She looked around the room. Everyone was there. His parents were both smiling widely along with his three sisters, their spouses and his nieces and nephews.

Real, joyful laughter bubbled inside her. "Oh, my gosh. I can't believe you guys threw me a party." And she really couldn't. Even though she knew about it, she still couldn't believe they thought of her like that.

"It's not every day a girl turns thirty." His mom, Emily, said from across the room.

"Ugh! Don't remind me," Alana replied. As the words slipped from her mouth, she felt Kellan's arms snake around her from behind.

"Don't you start. You're gorgeous. Nothing wrong with turning thirty."

The whole room went silent. Everyone had their eyes on Alana and Kellan. She shifted, trying to move his arms without making it too obvious. Typical Kellan, he wouldn't budge. Heat flamed her cheeks. What the heck was he doing? He'd said himself no one would know what they did last night and here he was making it look like they were a couple.

Then, as if his mom realized they were all staring at the two of them, slack-jawed, she said, "Kellan's right you know, dear. I hear thirty is the new twenty-five anyway." Emily winked at her. "Alright, everyone. What are we doing standing around. This is supposed to be a party." Just like that, the whole group started chatting away; hugging and wishing her a happy birthday just like she was part of the family.

Kellan sat at the picnic table in his family's backyard, watching Lana. She was over talking with all three of his sisters. All four girls gabbed a hundred miles an hour, their hands flailing around in the air as they went. Whatever they were talking about, it was something good. Lana dropped her head backwards and let out a full-fledged, belly laugh.

God, she was beautiful. Her graceful hand covered her mouth like she meant to mute the sound, like she couldn't believe it had come from her. His sister, Molly, grabbed her arm and the two of them continued laughing together. Kellan couldn't turn away. How could she not see she belonged with his family? That she belonged with *him*? Everything about them fit. They knew each other in every way possible. There wasn't anything about him she didn't know and he doubted there was much about her he didn't know, as well.

And he loved every part of her. Probably always had.

"I recognize that look in your eyes, son. Finally realize she's the one?" His mom sat down next to him.

"Yep. I've known for a while, Mom. Hell, I've probably known almost as long as you have."

"What took you so long?"

Hell if he knew. "She wasn't ready, Mom."

"Well I'm glad you're going for it now. You guys are perfect together. We've all known it. I'm glad to see the two of you are finally opening your eyes."

Kellan exhaled a frustrated breath, and turned to look at his mom. "I have my eyes wide open. It's her I'm trying to convince."

"She knows it, Kell. She's just scared. She's been through a lot in her life. I'm sure more than you or I know. Just don't give up. Prove to her that you love her and that you'll always be there for her. She'll come around."

"I know, Mom." She grabbed his hand.

"Have you told her exactly how you feel yet?"

Kellan turned back toward Lana, watching her continue to talk with his sisters. "Pretty much. I haven't come out and told her I love her yet, but I've made it pretty clear."

"Men!" his mom mumbled. "That's not good enough. You want Lana? You have to fight for her. Prove to her that you deserve her heart. That you won't ever give it back to her. I have a feeling she's had it thrown in her face a few times in her life."

Molly tilted her head his way and said something to Lana. She shook her head, her body visibly stiffening. "You're right, Mom. I'm going to go save Lana and then we're going to get out of here."

He stood and started to walk away. His mom's voice stopped him, "When you're ready, I have the ring." Kellan laughed and made his way to Lana. Whatever his sister said had made her uncomfortable. Not that Molly would have meant to, but she probably mentioned something about the two of them and Lana froze. Still, he wasn't going to let up on her. Not completely. Kellan wrapped an arm around Alana and pulled her against him. "Are you giving the birthday girl a hard time, Molls?"

"Who? Me? I'd do no such thing."

"Yeah, right." He laughed at his sister and then turned to Alana.

"You ready to go? It's getting pretty late?"

"Yeah. I've had a pretty long weekend." She looked at Molly. "Thanks for everything."

Catching the hint, Molly hugged them both goodbye. A few minutes later, after a barrage of hugs and goodbyes they were in his car, driving away.

Chapter Seven

They were silent almost the whole way home. Alana's head swam with memories from the afternoon, while Kellan gave her the space she needed. They were always like that. They could sense what one another needed. Right now, she needed time to sort through her thoughts. Today had been...well great. She'd felt like a part of his family. They'd laughed, talked, ate. Kellan's mom brought up memories of the first time they met and how her crazy little dog took to her so much.

It was almost like they were a real family. Like she belonged with them. God, she wanted that. She wanted them. She wanted Kellan. Alana glanced over, taking him in. His boyish, yet masculine, good looks. He had slight stubble on his jaw since he hadn't taken the time to shave this morning. He was right. Things with him were so easy. They fit. Being with him was natural: the meal they'd shared last night, making love, their talks, their arguments, and his family. It all fit.

And it would break her heart if she ever lost that. It would kill her if she ever lost Kellan. Given both their track records, given the fact that everyone she'd ever loved had walked away from her, things didn't look too good for her. But she wanted to believe. God, she wanted to believe. Even if just for one night.

They pulled up in front of her apartment. They both got out of the car and walked inside. "Did you have a good time today?"

Alana smiled at him. "I did. Thank you, Kell. I know I gave you a hard time earlier, but I really needed this. I'm glad you drug me along."

He stepped forward, wrapping his arms around her just like he would if they really were a couple. "Am I hearing this right, counselor? Are you admitting you were wrong and I was right?"

Fear skittered up her spine. For once, she pushed it back. She was tired of being afraid. Right now she just wanted to feel. "Yes, there's a first time for everything, you know?" Alana let her hands drift up and down his back, an open invitation to touch her as well. Kellan followed her lead. His fingers floated up her back, danced across the bare skin of her neck.

She felt him everywhere, from the tips of her toes to the top of her head. One of his hands grabbed her waist and pulled her tightly against him. The other hand tilted her face up to look at him. He was so insanely gorgeous, her breath caught. Kellan smiled; then teased her lips with quick, succulent kisses. One after another he kissed her, sucking at her bottom lip, before kissing her again.

"You're so beautiful, Lana. You're mine. Do you finally see that?"

He didn't let her reply, which honestly, she probably couldn't have anyway, before he kissed her again. This time, his tongue licked the seam of her lips, his hand slipped under her shirt as he caressed her back. God, he tasted so good. So Kellan. So hers that her heart ached with the fear she wouldn't be brave enough to risk giving herself to him the way he seemed to want.

Kellan pulled away just enough to pull her shirt over her head before his mouth fused with hers again. He kissed her deep while his hand skated all over her back and shoulders. Her whole body buzzed, eager and hungry to have him again. One flick of his wrist and her bra was unlatched and his hand replaced one of the cups. Needing to feel him, too, she pushed her hands under his shirt and found the thick, hard muscles of his back.

Kellan was all man.

Alana's feet were suddenly off the floor as he picked her up to carry her to her bedroom.

"If we don't get to your bed now, I'll be taking you on your living room floor." Kellan placed her on her bed just like he had the night before. Was it only last night? It felt like days…weeks ago since she last felt him on top of her. Bra and shirt already disposed of in the living room he reached for her pants. Slowly, teasingly, he slipped her pants and panties down her legs as if unwrapping a fragile package.

Then he stared. His intense gaze raked her up and down before his eyes landed on hers. He didn't move. Didn't speak. Didn't look away. God, she loved him and she wanted him so badly. Not just for tonight, but forever. An inkling of fear began to nudge its way to the forefront. She needed to lighten the mood. Like now. "You have too many clothes on." She reached for the button on his jeans, but he stopped her.

"Don't do that, Lana. Don't run away from me." Kellan jerked his shirt over his head and tossed it to the floor. "You have to know I'm not like them." He unbuttoned and unzipped his jeans. "I'd never walk away from you. I'd never leave you. I've been here for ten years. Why would I walk away now?"

Her mouth went sticky and dry. Words were lodged in her throat. She couldn't swallow them, yet couldn't spit them out either. She wanted to tell him he was right. That she knew he'd stay there for her, but she couldn't.

Kellan's jeans dropped to the floor, followed by his black boxer-briefs. "I'm yours, Lana. I'm here. I'm fighting for you. I won't give you up."

Alana gasped. She'd always wanted to be loved like that, always wanted someone willing to fight for her. No one had ever fought for her in her life. That's part of the reason she became a defense attorney. She wanted to fight for others the way no one ever fought for her.

Kellan lay beside her on the bed and touched her. His finger slid up her arm, over her shoulder. He touched her neck, her chest, cupped her breasts, slid over her belly. Her heart rate lurched to high speed like a racecar when the driver gunned it. "Let me love you, Lana. Let me be there for you. I promise you, once you give me your heart, I'll always treasure it."

A tear leaked from her eye. She didn't try to fight it. She wanted to give Kellan her heart, wanted to trust him with it, but she didn't know if she could. He leaned forward, and kissed her tear away. His hand cupped her cheek, heat radiating off his skin and warming her. And then his lips were on hers again, kissing her fiercely.

Alana succumbed, letting herself get lost in the pleasure, lost to Kellan. She went easily when he rolled to his back, taking her with him so she lay atop his long, hard body. He snaked his arms around her, cupping her rear and delivering kisses that touched her soul.

"No thinking tonight, baby. Just feel me. Feel what I do to you." He rubbed his pulsing erection against her. "Feel what you do to me. Feel how fucking perfect we are together. Just us." He gave her a quick kiss. "You never have to be alone again." Another quick kiss, that only accelerated her already wildly thumping heart. "We could be a family. You'd have the family you always wanted." A third kiss. "You've never ran your whole life, baby. Don't start now. I'm giving you my heart. Don't throw it back at me."

Finally, his kiss deepened, blocking the jumble of thoughts crowding her brain. Alana melted against him like honey on a hot biscuit. They touched from head to toe, rubbing, touching and kissing. This is what life was supposed to be about. This is what she wanted, but could she reach out and take it?

Kellan rolled again, pinning her beneath him. Her lips immediately ached for his when he ceased his kissing, but the feeling was replaced with pleasure when he latched onto one of her nipples instead.

"Oh, God. Kellan."

He parted the lips of her aching sex and sank his fingers inside. The tingles of orgasm already began to bubble and fizz inside her. Her whole body was sensitive to his every touch, his every lick, every plunge of his fingers.

"Me and you, Lana. You know me. I'd never hurt you."

She'd never trusted another soul the way she trusted Kellan. She wanted nothing more than to give him that same confidence now, but she didn't know if she could.

All thoughts of trust or fear were replaced by pleasure when Kellan flicked his thumb over her clitoris. Alana lurched, passion and pleasure exploding within her. "Kellan. Oh...Yes."

He groaned, leaving her breasts to give her his mouth again. His tongue plunged inside the cavern of her mouth right as her orgasm washed over her.

He didn't give her time to recover. Before she had the chance to catch her breath he had a condom pulled out of his wallet, his erection sheathed and he was pushing his massively hard erection inside her. "Kell...wait...Oh, God." She wanted to tell him she needed a few minutes, but once he buried himself to the hilt, all she could think about was the satisfying fullness; the heat from his body on top of hers.

He flexed his hips forward, slowly. With the same pace, Kellan pulled out, before easing himself between her thighs again. "Are you sure about that, baby?" With a long, drawn out movement, he pumped his cock in and out again. "Are you sure you want me to stop?"

Hell, she wasn't sure of anything anymore. Her brain was a jumbled mess of contradictions. "Yes...I mean no...please no."

In typical Kellan fashion, he chuckled. In the next breath his smile was replaced with an intense, consuming stare.

For the life of her, she couldn't turn away.

Neither one broke their eye contact as he pumped. Alana wrapped her legs around his hips, letting out a moan with the depth of his strokes. He touched her womb and her heart all in one delicious motion. She met him thrust for thrust. Her eyes started to drift closed.

"No, Lana. Look at me."

She obeyed, unable to deny him at this moment. She bit her lip, savoring this moment, this joining of more than just bodies. Damn he felt so good, so right inside her. She fit with him. She was made for him.

"You feel so good, Lana. So right. Just like you were made for me."

Alana gasped. His words mirrored her thoughts. "Kell..."

"Shh." He kissed her quiet. She should be glad because she would have just told him something she might regret: that cared about him, too. The heat of the moment wasn't the time for opening your heart to someone. She tried that and just like with every other important relationship in her past, it came back to bite her.

Alana lost herself to him, to his kisses, his delicious thrusts; until orgasm started to bloom again. As if he sensed she was close, Kellan picked up the pace, moved his lips to her neck, biting and whispering against her.

Alana let loose. For the second time tonight she came. Kellan was right behind her. Within seconds he had the condom disposed of, her wrapped in his arms and for the first time, she didn't fight him and drifted off to sleep.

Chapter Eight

A strip of sunlight peaked through the blinds in Alana's bedroom. Kellan wasn't sleeping. He'd been awake for about an hour, holding Lana and watching the little strip of light. He still hadn't told her he loved her. In all ways except actually saying the words he had, but part of him feared, once he told her, she'd run. He couldn't put it off any longer. He didn't want to put it off any longer.

Alana needed to open her eyes and face him, face the truth. "Lana, wake up, baby." He whispered in her ear. She stirred, stretched, and then opened her eyes to look at him.

"Hi." She tensed, but he didn't let that deter him. Kellan continued to hold her, looking at her, and stroking her smooth, bare skin.

"We need to talk, counselor." He smiled at her, trying to lighten the heavy air around them.

"I suppose we do." She gave him a weak smile in return that didn't quite reach her eyes.

"How long have we known each other, Lana?"

"Ten years."

"And in that time have I ever done anything to make you think I'd ever hurt you? Have I ever given you a reason to doubt me?" He knew how to question people. It's what he did and right now he needed to go with what worked for him.

"Your inner lawyer is showing, Kellan. I'm not a witness."

Kellan laughed. "I know, but I'm pretty damn good at what I do and I have a feeling I'm going to need it with you."

"I'm good at what I do, too." A spark went off in her eyes. She enjoyed a little competition just like he did.

"May the best man win. Or if I get my way, we'll both walk away from this one a winner, Lana. Now, answer my question."

She sat up in the bed and wrapped herself in the sheet. Kellan joined her, but didn't bother to cover up. Like he said, he needed to go with what worked for him and it was pretty obvious his body had an effect on her.

"No."

She answered just as he expected. Short, and simple, not giving him the chance to mix up any of her words to use against her. "Do you trust me?" he asked softly, coaxing her out of her tough shell.

"You know I do, Kellan."

"Do you love me?"

Her eyes drifted closed. Her chest rose and fell with a heavy breath before she opened them again. "I plead the fifth."

"You don't play fair."

"Wasn't it you who said all is fair in love and war?"

She had him there. He laughed. "Yeah, I guess I did." Kellan reached out and touched her cheek. She sighed obviously pleased with the contact whether she would ever admit it to him or not. "Do you need me to go first? I can tell you right now that I love you, Lana. I love everything about you, even when you're being damn stubborn like you are now."

Her eyes widened into wet pools of brown. Her breathing sped, the pulse in the base of her throat beat rapidly. "I've heard that before, Kell. It never lasts."

Kellan pulled his hand back, frustrated. "I'm not them, Lana. Jesus," He ran a hand through his hair. "You just told me you trusted me. If I was going to bail, don't you think I would have done it ten fucking years ago?"

"That was different! You didn't have any ties to me then, you'd never made me any promises. That's when everything changes. You know I had three different foster families over the years. Everything was fine until it came around to making things permanent and that's when they always realized that I wasn't what they really wanted!" Tears spilled from her eyes, running down her face. "Hell, my own mom didn't want me, Kellan. What makes me think anyone else will either?"

She tried to crawl off the bed, but he grabbed her, pulling her toward him. "I want you, Lana. Fuck all them. They're losers if they couldn't see how amazing you are. You've got to put this shit behind you. I can't keep fighting for you, for *us*, if you aren't willing to fight, too."

Quietly, almost to the point where he couldn't hear her, she whispered, "I can't lose you, Kellan."

"Then stop pushing me away, baby. I'm fighting for you but you have to give in a little, too." He nuzzled her neck, kissing her and taking in her scent. "Tell me you love me, counselor."

She sighed, dropping her head back. "Objection. You're badgering the witness."

Kellan pulled his lips away from her throat. "That's because I'm not giving up on you. Isn't that what you want? It sure would be easier if you didn't give up on me."

As if admitting defeat, her eyes drifted closed. "I'm not giving up on you, Kellan. I already gave up on me. I think...I think I need you to go."

Fuck he hated this, but he couldn't be the only one pulling for them. She had to open her eyes. She had to love him enough to get over her past. Kellan kissed her. "I love you. I'll be here when you're ready, when you realize nothing in life is a guarantee and we're both worth it."

He left her sitting in the middle of the bed, dressed and walked out of the apartment.

Kellan's voice spoke to her, in her head as she heard the front door close. *That's because I'm not giving up on you. Isn't that what you want? It sure would be easier if you didn't give up on me.*

She was giving up on him. She was doing the one thing that had been done to her, the one thing that hurt her most in the world to the only person who had never hurt her. To the one person she loved, who had proven time and time again that he loved her, too. Alana thought about his parents, his sisters. They loved her, too. If she hadn't known it before, which honestly she had, she saw it yesterday.

She loved them, too. They'd been like the parents she'd never had. His sisters were like the siblings she never had. He was offering her everything she ever wanted and she just let him walk out of her apartment. No, she pushed him out.

I love you. I'll be here when you're ready, when you realize nothing in life is a guarantee and we're both worth it. There were no guarantees. She'd learned that time and time again, but damn, he was worth it. She was worth it.

Have I ever done anything to make you think I'd ever hurt you? Have I ever given you a reason to doubt me?

He was the one person she knew she could always count on. How many times had she said it herself?

I want you, Lana. Fuck all them. They're losers if they couldn't see how amazing you are. You've got to put this shit behind you. I can't keep fighting for you, for us, if you aren't willing to fight, too.

He was fighting for her. He'd always fought for her. He hadn't put drugs above her like her mother had. He hadn't let someone else push her away like her first foster mother had. All he'd ever done is love her, care for her, even though she wasn't doing the same. Even though she pushed and pushed him away.

She was willing to fight for him. She loved him more for fighting for her and now it's time she fought for herself, for them, just like he said. Alana jumped up, and threw on a pair of sweats and a t-shirt. She didn't bother with a bra or panties. Slipped her feet into her flip-flops and ran to the door. If she hurried, maybe she could catch him before he made it too far. Her heart thudded in her ears.

Was she really doing this? Yep, she was. Alana jerked open the door and ran out only to be stopped by a hard, shirt covered wall. "Umpf." She pulled away. "Kellan?" He had that cocky grin on his face, all smile, blue eyes and dimples.

"I told you I'm not giving up on you. Did you really think I'd walk away that easily?"

Alana ignored the giddy excitement in her belly. She ignored her fear. "I have a confession to make, counselor."

"I can't divulge anything you tell me. I'm here for you. Whatever you tell me is in complete confidence."

She ignored the fact that they were standing in the middle of her hallway. Not much privacy that way, but right now she didn't care. She just wanted him to know how she felt. She wanted to be honest and give him everything he'd given to her. "I love you. I was stupid and scared. I still am, but you are worth it. We're worth it. You've been everything to me for ten years, Kellan, and I'm not letting you walk away without a fight."

Warmth snaked over her skin when he pulled her into his arms. "I'm not going anywhere. Not now. Not ever."

"Thank you, Kellan. Thank you for fighting for me. I love you so damn much and I'm so sorry I've been too scared to admit it."

He cupped her cheeks. "You're admitting it now and that's all that matters. I love you, too, Lana." He dropped his lips to hers, and kissed her. "Now get back in that apartment. I'm going to make love to you at least a dozen more times today and then we're going to get my mom's ring. She's been waiting for years to give it to you. She reminded me it was waiting just yesterday at your party."

Alana's heart almost burst from her chest, but she held firm to the ground. "Um, ring? I don't recall agreeing to that," she said with a smile.

"You'd really disappoint my whole family that way?" He winked at her.

"You still don't play fair."

"You know what they say."

"All is fair in love and war."

"I love you, counselor."

"I love you, too." This time it was her who kissed him senseless.

About The Author

Kelley has been writing for as long as she can remember. Life got in the way and she wasn't able to work on accomplishing her goal of becoming a published writer until 2005. When she became a stay at home mom for the first time she decided to start working on her dream again. Since she's always been a romantic at heart she took her two passions, romance and writing and started her very first romance novel. Her life hasn't been the same since. Life couldn't be more wonderful. She has a job she loves, two beautiful little girls who always bring a smile to her face and her husband and soul mate Dominic who supports her beyond belief.

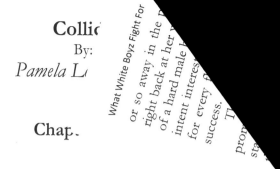

The nut was hers!

That thought sunk deep and hard in Ambria Soublet's mind as she watched the Mardi Gras float drift past her and down the center of Jackson Avenue.

Twelve Mardi Gras floats decked out in traditional Zulu African style had already cruised by at a snail's pace. While ideal for coconut catching, it brought her absolutely no success in snagging the coveted prize.

She was going to get her Zulu coconut from the next float even if it killed her. Better yet, even if it killed—well, maybe not *killed*—but seriously damaged a couple of fellow parade goers. Mainly, Mr. NBA Player outfitted as a basketball star, his costume complete with a rigged up version of a basketball goal doubling as a catch-all effectively kept any potential nuts from her grasp. She hadn't even been able to intercept one as it came through the hoop simply because one never did. The lack of a natural opening at the end of the tightly cinched net allowed him to steal away every beautiful glittery, decorated trademark coconut from each and every float rider who had meant to gift her with such an iconic prize.

Well most of them. If she was completely honest with herself, four of the dozen or so had been meant for her, so she was justified in feeling four times offended by the greedy player towering above her.

Then there was the masked Zorro impersonator who Ambria would bet her soon to be caught coconut, to be the pseudo-athlete's accomplice. Every maneuver she made—an *unintentional* bump into the tall costumed basketball player or shift to the left meant to connect her elbow into his lanky midsection met only air as Mr. Zorro intercepted each move; and not even for his own benefit. He had in his possession as many Zulu coconuts as she had.

Zero.

As a matter of fact there was an "I-couldn't-care-less-if-I-got-a-coconut" attitude surrounding him. As far as she was concerned, that meant that he had no business thwarting her efforts.

She glared at Zorro standing just to the right of her, less than a foot

ressing crowd waiting for the next float. He stared
ith a dark unwavering intensity that sent an awareness
ody under mysterious black cover shooting a message of
. The same message he'd sent at least twelve times before
oat that passed, just before he'd gotten in the way of her

is was getting ridiculous. She had a quest, a noble cause, a
ise to keep and no man, be he basketball player or Zorro would
nd in her way. She gave Zorro guy a nasty stare, a nonverbal warning
that she wasn't putting up with his interference any longer. He
disregarded the threat with a lift of a shoulder bringing her attention to
the solid chest encased in black, immediately causing her to lift her eyes
to his masked face. She couldn't see his eyes but got the impression that
they were as dark as the mask he wore. Add the firm seductive mouth
and chin, and she found herself more intrigued than she should have
been as she stared, mesmerized by the brief lift at the corners of his lips
as his face seemed to soften for a second before turning hard and direct,
his mouth straightening into a firm line as if he suddenly remembered
that he wasn't supposed to smile.

She had a feeling that he had been laughing at her until he
remembered himself. This was no laughing matter. Ambria took two
steps to the left and leaned toward him to warn, "Stay out of my way.
The next one's mine!" she muttered.

"Think so?" he asked, his deep voice sent a vibrating timber
through her as a sudden stillness between them forced her to take
another long, steady, appreciative look that held until he gave a slight
shake of his head, reminding her that he had upset her efforts for the last
time.

Her head jerked back to his face, with an "I-know-so" glare relaying
exactly how mistaken he was until she found herself focusing on his
mysteriously sexy half veiled face yet again. Sexy! Shifting the nod into a
shake to clear her head Ambria glanced back down the street to see the
tail end of the last float finally moving and the next one just a few feet
away slowly making its way toward them, the crowd cheered now that
the floats were in motion again. The riders, roused by the excited crowds
began tossing beads, doubloons, trinkets and the treasured Zulu coconut.

Well, coconuts weren't exactly tossed. They were gently lowered
into outstretched hands, riders having long ago been forbidden to throw
them due to a multitude of lawsuits. Ambria's hands itched to have one
gently laid into her own palms. It was her turn and nobody was going to
stop her.

Having already issued her warning to Zorro she dismissed him and
turned to Mr. NBA, tapped him on his back and looked up at him in all

his way over six feet wonder to say, "Stop being a coconut hog!"

He stared down at her to snarl, "Shut up!" before peering down the street as if the oncoming float signified the second coming.

It was on! Ambria didn't just want the coconut, she needed it. Not just for her niece Ashlyn. Her pride was now at stake.

The next few seconds was a blur of action that she was barely able to remember when she would recount the story to her sister and niece.

Here it came. Float number thirteen, for her, lucky number thirteen. The float riders wearing blackface and grass skirts were tossing beads and trinkets like crazy. A few were waving coconuts above their heads in a teasing manner. Ambria was beyond tolerating this blatant taunting.

. One of the riders handed one nut then another to a couple of gyrating teenagers dressed as rock stars. Another rider continued flaunting the prizes, one in each hand pretending to hand one to someone in the crowd only to pull back with a malicious kind of shimmy dance. Wanting to hop onto the float and give him a shimmy herself Ambria stared at him in disgust until she realized that the dance he was doing was as much of tease as it was a search. He was looking for someone. His eyes seemed to land on her.

She'd been right, this was her lucky float. Not one but both of those coconuts were hers. Ashlyn was going to be twice as happy and she was going to laugh her head off when Auntie Bri told her the story of how she snatched the coconuts because Ambria just realized that the gyrating rider wasn't looking at her but the overly tall, rude NBA star. As the float inched closer she did what any fed up aunt who promised a Zulu coconut to a sick niece stuck in the hospital on Mardi Gras day could do. She bided her time and the exact moment the dancing rider stretched hands toward the makeshift goal she pretended to trip and fell onto the basketball player who landed on the ground, at the same time kicking Zorro just shy of his most precious manly parts and caught both coconuts before they hit the sidewalk.

"What the f---?" NBA star grabbed one of her wrist with a violent twist, his expression frightening her to the point that she dropped a coconut, the black one with gold lettering and glittering eyes. It landed right into his lap.

Realizing his reaction was too extreme for the loss of a trinket, even a coveted one, Ambria decided to get some distance between them just as Zorro grabbed her other arm.

What was this?

Coconut fever?

Ambria was infected but she had a good reason for her infection.

"I'll take that one," the voice that had sent vibrations up her spine easily doubled the effect in addition to a shot of cold fear quickly twisting into indignation. How dare he make her feel want and fear at the same time!

"No you won't!" Ambria answered.

"Hell, no, he won't!" NBA said rolling his tall frame to an upright position jumping at Zorro and giving her enough time to dart into the crowd and get the hell away from the craziness that had become the Zulu parade on Mardi Gras Day.

Yancy ducked as the tall man lunged. "DEA," he growled loud enough for the man to hear yet soft enough that he didn't start a riot.

Understanding dawned in the instant narrowing of his eyes and sudden stillness of his entire body as he tensed ready to escape. A quick jab in the tall man's midsection and a twist of his arm behind his back had the man surrendering without another moment's struggle.

Yancy cuffed and tossed the man over to Superman another undercover Drug Enforcement Agent as the Hulk calmed the few people in the crowd surrounding the immediate area. Glancing at the float he saw Jude, posed as a rider, doing his part to apprehend one of the other five involved in this drug transfer. Twisting back to where he saw the beautiful dark-skinned beauty flee with his evidence, Yancy began making his way through the crowd in her direction. It had all happened in a matter of seconds.

Scanning the area, he continued to part the crowd. As he pursued his prey Yancy knew she wouldn't be hard to find. She was wearing a pink and white cheerleader outfit. She was all legs and curvy hips. He knew that for certain. Yancy had torn his eyes from her more than a dozen times in an attempt to stay focused on the task at hand and keep his eyes on the perp. At least they got him and one of his accomplices, and hopefully all five by the end of the parade. Too bad these were the little guys in a newly developing drug ring trying to establish territory in Post-Katrina New Orleans.

A dash of pink caught his eye. She was heading down a side street carrying a gold painted coconut as it were a gift from the gods. Could she have any idea what was inside that coconut?

Sweat dripping down his face and into his eyes Yancy tossed his hat and mask pulling the string on the cape he wore he let it fall to the ground as he closed the distance between them. He understood the super hero theme for this case but whoever decided that he'd be the perfect Zorro, well, let' s just say he would have a word or two for them.

She was a mere block away from him and looking around before crossing a very busy Napoleon Avenue when she spotted him.

"Damn it!" he wanted to close on in the sexy cheerleader before revealing himself, worse yet, she as approaching a police officer, one of many who were about as abundant as bees protecting a hive at every corner. Business as usual during Mardi Gras season.

Great.

Yancy slowed his run to a jog then a walk. He pulled out his badge, held it and his other hand up in an appeasing manner.

"Stop where you are," a tall, wide cop shouted from a half a block away as his cheerleader smiled and sprinted down the next block. "You chasing women?" the cop asked.

"I'm—"

"Answer the question!" he shouted as Yancy spotted, from the corner of his eye two more of New Orleans' finest coming from his right, and a slight twist of his head indicated that another was close behind.

"Yes and no," Yancy softly answered.

"What? Trying to be smart?"

"No, I'm a DEA agent and you're letting a suspect carrying my evidence get away," Yancy handed over his badge as he watched her slide into a very old blue Corvette that started with a loud band and was out of sight by the time he proved who he was and was able to get away from the gang of cops bent on doing their job.

"Sorry man. You look suspicious and all even for a Mardi Gras, and she was one good looking woman. Sort of distracting too."

Yancy nodded. She was that, he silently agreed, so good-looking she had distracted him to a point that he hadn't been on the top of his game. All wasn't lost. He had gotten her license plate number.

"Anything I can do to help?" the officer was asking as Yancy continued to stare down the street.

"Got a car nearby?"

"At the next corner."

"How about running a plate for me?"

Chapter Two

Six-year-old Ashlyn was having a giggling fit and would have rolled straight off the hospital bed, coconut and all if Ambria hadn't quickly lifted the rail.

"What are you doing to my baby girl?" Ambria's sister Gloria came into the room just as the rail snapped into place.

"Curing her with laughter."

"Good medicine and excellent save," Gloria nodded at her sister's fists tightly holding the rail.

"What are aunties for besides granting wishes and rescuing nieces from imminent danger?"

"How about taking care of some private business?"

"Huh?"

"There's a fine somebody asking for you," Gloria said as she made it to the opposite side of the bed to plump Ashlyn's pillow, straightening her sheets and blankets all while avoiding the death grip her daughter had on her new prized possession: a gold and black trimmed Zulu coconut.

"What are you talking about?" Ambria asked tearing her eyes from Ashlyn's contented face.

Making her way back to Ambria Gloria whispered, "A guy: tall, white and f-i-i-i-i-n-ne— is asking for you. Since when do you go for white guys? Better question when have you gone for any guy lately?"

"When do I have time to go for anyone? I don't have a love life."

"Then go on out there and get one, Bri. There was a determined look in his eyes, when he asked for you. It was as if he'd die if he didn't get to talk to you."

"You're kidding, right? You *do* realize that you sound exactly like a romance novel?" Ambria hissed in her sister's ear despite a secret desire to have someone look and feel that way about her. She'd experienced that kind of look today but it had ended with a very scary chase.

"I'm obviously not a novel; I am, however, a very perceptive older sister."

"Older by fifteen months."

"That would be fifteen months more experienced in life," Gloria muttered taking a picture book off the bedside tray. It was *DJ and the Zulu Parade* the book that had begun Ashlyn's obsession with glittery coconuts.

Gloria pointedly twisted her head toward the door before reading to her daughter in a lively voice.

"Someone's here for Ambria," a nurse's head popped into the room before Ambria could get to the door.

Intrigued, and with romantic visions of a fine man with eyes only for her filling her head she stepped out of the room. Before she could look left her right was gripped by the waist and hauled against a very solid, very male body.

"Don't panic. I'm not going to hurt you," coursed down her ear canal.

"Am I supposed to believe that?" Ambria got out between unadvised, panicked, heart racing breaths.

"Yes. Now, smile at the curious nurse staring at us," he breathed into her ear, "and come with me," the rumbling voice went straight through her with a familiar "all-shook-up" feel, mixed in with a wave of self-preservation. Oh, but Ambria had no idea how she'd go about preserving herself with his hard body pressed so solidly against her.

"No-- way," she told him in a measured tone pulling together as much bravado as she could, her mind filled with scattered images of what she should do if ever confronted with such a situation. Unable to focus on any one strategy Ambria knew that the last thing she should do was to go anywhere with this man.

"You've got two choices: come with me quietly or I'll grace your wrists with a lovely pair of handcuffs." Yancy took one of her hands and pulled it to the pair of cuffs hanging from his hip. He was going about this all wrong, but the minute he saw her, all he wanted to do was pull her into his arms, so he did exactly what he wanted.

Bad move. For all he knew she was knee deep in this drug ring.

"What? Why?"

No, Yancy decided the instant his eyes connect with hers. Her confused bewilderment was too genuine. Besides, Yancy felt it in his gut. Still, that was no reason for him to throw professional ethics out the window. There were procedures and rules that had nothing to do with pulling a suspect into your arms, whispering into her ear and inhaling her sweet scent.

"Who are you?" she twisted around to get a look at him.

"Yancy DeWolf, DEA agent," he couldn't stop himself from whispering into her ear again because sometimes professional ethics had to take a back seat. The feel of her pressed against him made him pause as he thought about his next course of action. Professional? Personal? She was distracting as hell.

"Who?" she asked again.

"Yancy DeWolf," he repeated wanting her to know his name, to know him. "I'm a drug enforcement agent. If you don't want to be arrested, I suggest you cooperate."

Ambria peered into his dark eyes. "You!"

He would have thought that the all black attire he was still cloaked in would have clued her in.

"Yes, me. You didn't think I'd find you? That Corvette of yours is very distinctive. It didn't take long to figure out where you were once I spotted it." Yancy very inappropriately pulled the brown beauty closer to his side, not understanding why he simply didn't pull her down the hall, cuff and question her as standard procedure.

"Are you nuts? Of course I didn't think you'd find me. Who'd go to this much trouble for a Zulu coconut?"

"Not just any Zulu coconut." He gave her a hard look.

"They're all the same!" she said wondering why she was still talking to him instead of breaking away to make her way to the nearest police officer. But then again if she were to believe him, he was some kind of officer.

"Are they?" his eyes turned hard and dark as he stared at her.

"Well, they're painted different colors and if you would have tried to catch one yourself instead of keeping me from them you wouldn't have to act like a creepy..." finding herself babbling she trailed off, ending with, "...stalker."

"DEA agents often stalk their prey."

"I'm not prey."

"No?" he asked a very predatory expression on his face making Ambria feel as if he wanted to do something other than arrest her. Fear intensified once again along with a bit of unintentional attraction. Attraction? She needed a love life but not this desperately.

"What's going on here?" Nurse Mabel, controller of all that happened on her floor came charging down the hall.

Mr. Zorro, minus his cape and mask flashed a badge before Mable reached them. "Can you provide a private place so that I can interrogate my suspect?"

"Interrogate your suspect?" Ambria squeaked as Nurse Mabel gave her a suspicious look, as if Ambria hadn't been in and out of the hospital the last year and a half. Without a word she led them to a small, empty office.

As soon as they got through the door Ambria pulled away from Zorro, moving to the opposite side of the room. She felt like a live wire of fear, attraction and need. Need? What she needed was to get out of this room. "Be calm, be cool," she whispered to herself. She'd clear it up, whatever the "it" was.

"Where is it?" he asked.

"Where's what?"

"The coconut you stole."

"Stole? I didn't steal anything. I earned that coconut by catching it."

"So, you admit that you wanted to catch it."

"Of course I wanted to catch it. It's what people *do* at Zulu parades in New Orleans on Mardi Gras Day!"

"Why that particular coconut?" he crossed his arms, his eyes trained on her face.

"Because it was pretty and black and gold just like my niece wanted."

"Your niece?" Yancy asked beginning to allow himself to truly believe what his gut told him. The tight knot in his stomach eased. It was truly beginning to look as if she had no idea drugs had been smuggled into the coconut.

"Yes, my niece! She's stuck in this hospital and couldn't go to the parades. Ash has Sickle Cell Anemia and wanted a Zulu coconut, so, I got one for her."

And Ambria apparently, got more than she wanted. "Where is it now?" Yancy asked, his eyes narrowing in on her, giving her a warm chill of dread and again—irresistible attraction.

Talk about inappropriate reactions!

"In the hospital bed with her."

"With your niece?" he asked crossing the space between them in three strides standing almost on top of her.

"Yes."

"You need to get the coconut away from her."

"Why?" she asked already knowing but not wanting to admit what she suspected. Ambria stared into his rugged handsome face. He was as fine as the first second she saw him. Trustworthy was another adjective that had come to mind as she stared at him.

Taking a deep breath at the same moment he took in her full lips. Yancy forced his eyes back to her own. "Some coconuts were being used to smuggle drugs."

"What?" she asked, that one word seeming to be her favorite expression today.

"The one you caught was created for that purpose."

"Ashlyn!" Ambria was at the door with Yancy hot on her heels. He stopped her with a hand on her shoulder and another on the door.

"Don't go bursting in there and scaring the child half to death."

"But what if those drugs seeped through—"

"--the hard shell of a coconut?" he interrupted her with logic. "Not likely."

"But what if whatever was used to plug the coconut after filling it what that junk fell out and got on her skin. It could be seeping into her bloodstream!"

If he wasn't already certain of her innocence, the terror and concern Yancy read on her face was a sincere confirmation. "Drug dealers wouldn't store their goods without securing the container. They'd lose money. Besides we'll take it away before anything happens," he added with even more logic.

"What if it already has? If Ashlyn's lying in a layer of *cocaine or heroin*! That's even worse! And I brought it to her!"

"If, Ashlyn," Yancy took one of her hands in his own, "that's your niece's name, right?" Ambria nodded as he moved in closer, his other hand softly landing on her cheek. "If that were true, you would have noticed."

Again with the logic. But it worked. Ambria reined in the panic she had been feeling and did the next logical thing as he seemed to move in even closer bringing along comfort, need and the hottest kiss she ever experienced. It was only logical that his mouth hovered a second to heat her own, taking her lips with slow, deliberate intent. His tongue finding her own with a tantalizing "WOW!" intensity tripling the effect his mere glance had done to her during the parade and sending blood rushing to the roots of her hair simultaneously racing to her core which had become decidedly moist. The blood rush heated her toes only to continue the cycle double time as Yancy used his tongue and mouth, his amazing tongue and mouth to keep her still in his arms and take it all in.

Too soon he began to pull away. Now, that was completely illogical Ambria thought as she watched him back away in slow motion his hand lingering on her face, the tips of his fingers brushing her lips before he headed to the door with a slight shake of his head.

Too fine, Ambria thought once again as she shook her own head into enough sense to realize that someone was on the other side of the door. "DeWolf, open up. DeWolf, it's Grant."

"Alright," Yancy said his voice cracking on the "ight". His hand on the knob he turned to say, "Sorry about," he paused.

"Don't say you're sorry about kissing me," Ambria pleaded inside her head hoping it didn't show on her face.

"The interruption," he finished.

"Me too," Ambria agreed suddenly remembering what has proceeded the kiss. Just as Yancy let whoever Grant was inside, Ambria slipped passed both men and Nurse Mable intent on saving her niece from an accidental drug infusion.

"Ambria, wait!" Yancy called catching up with her, Nurse Mable not far behind and Grant reaching a hand under the cape of his Superman costume. He could not be seriously reaching for a gun.

A shot of nervous laughter burst out of Ambria. "Superman never needed a gun," she whispered to Yancy who was standing directly behind her.

"No and he doesn't need one now," he said pointedly to Grant who nodded and moved a few feet away guiding the nurse down to the other end of the hall. "Remember, keep calm," Yancy told her.

"Yep, be cool," Ambria said wondering how she was going to get the coconut away from Ashlyn.

The task was much easier than she anticipated. Ashlyn was sound asleep with the drug filled coconut resting in the crook of her arm. Poor baby had no idea what she was holding. Gloria was going to kill her.

Yancy gave her shoulder a squeeze: silent encouragement. Ambria needed it because Gloria was looking at her expectedly. Ambria motioned for her to come out into the hall. When Gloria left the room Ambria carefully pried the golden coconut from her niece's sleepy grip, immediately handing the thing to Yancy. It was all she could do not to grab some disinfectant wipes and scrub Ashlyn down. Instead she followed Gloria and Yancy out of the hospital room.

"What's going on?" Gloria asked as soon as Ambria squeezed through the door. "Why did you take Ashlyn's coconut and give it to that man?"

Ambria was speechless, still in panic mode.

"Well?" Gloria asked into the silence Ambria was having trouble filling.

"And who's the guy in the Superman costume. I know it's Mardi Gras but something more than Fat Tuesday is going on around here."

"Do you want me to break it to her?" Yancy asked.

Ambria turned to face her Zorro. He was a good guy coming to her rescue even when she had thought he was chasing her. "No, I'll handle it. It's my family, my problem."

Yancy nodded, an expression of understanding on his face which briefly turned mischievous, inappropriately so. "I guess, Lucy, you have some 'splaining to do," Yancy whispered in Ambria's ear.

"An "I Love Lucy fan"? I'm starting to like you more and more." That brief interaction melted the tension enough to give her the courage to forge on. Despite the mere fifteen months difference in age, Gloria had always seemed much older and wiser so this admission, though completely not her fault, was hard.

"We've got a situation with the coconut."

"A situation?"

Ambria nodded.

"With the coconut?" Gloria asked.

"Yes."

"That sounds weird, out with it. What's going on and again, who exactly is this guy? And that other guy?" Gloria pointed to each keeping her eyes trained on her sister for an explanation.

"Well, the situation with the coconut is that it's possibly full of some kind of substance."

Substance?" Gloria asked in a tone that said Ambria had better elaborate without her telling her she had better elaborate.

"A drug-- street drugs-- but I had no idea, which is why as soon as I found out I took the coconut from Ash," she finished not mentioning the searing kiss with Yancy in between the finding out and the taking.

"Drugs! On my baby?" Gloria's hands were on her hips. "Drugs are inside the coconut my sick little girl hugged and kissed not ten minutes ago? Who's butt should I kick and who *are* you two? Drug dealers? If you are then you'd better get the hell out of this hospital. My husband's a cop and would be right here right now if he wasn't out there helping to keep the streets safe from people like you. If he were here, he'd be helping me kick your butts."

"No, Gloria, no," Ambria was saying.

So much for letting Ambria break it to her sister Yancy thought before interjecting. "Ma'am, I know you're upset. Why don't you let me explain?"

"Go on, *explain*."

"I'm a DEA agent and one of the good guys. I'm here to protect your daughter."

"He is. I didn't know about the coconut, sis. But we took it away. No harm's
been done."

"How do you know that?"

"I'll talk to Ashlyn's doctors, have some tests run at our expense. But I'm
certain she wasn't affected.

"How did this happen?"

"I'll take over, Yancy," Ambria laid a hand on his shoulders pausing for a
second to take in the solid warmth of him.

"Bri!" Gloria said.

Ambria tore her hand and eyes from his black clad shoulder. "It started at the
Zulu Parade."

"The one you just came from?"

"Yess—"

"I'll let Ambria finish explaining," Yancy interrupted to say. While she's
doing that, it'll give me a few minutes to talk to the other agent. Then I need to speak to you." His eyes were on Ambria. His look

startled her with a reminder of their kiss but shifted to all business intent before he turned to his partner.

"What are you mixed up in, Bri?"

"I'm not sure, Glo." Ambria whispered, "I'm not sure."

Chapter Three

Whatever she was mixed up in, Ambria thought as Yancy pulled into her driveway later that evening, she was in deep. She had spent hours at a nearby police station gently though thoroughly interrogated.

"Are you sure you want to do this?" Yancy asked.

"I don't think I have a choice. I apparently caught tens of thousands of dollars' worth of drugs and somebody's out there looking for their goods and the person who took them. That would be me, possibly Gloria and unbelievably, Ashlyn."

"It's a lot to wrap your head around."

"To think that a few hours ago I thought it was Gloria who was going to kill me. She'll have to wait in line behind my brother-in-law Glen, and that's even before the drug dealers come after me."

"Glen's a cop, he understands."

"He understands, but not so well when it's his own flesh and blood involved. Imagine if your sister-in-law brought a drug infested gift—"

"—an *unintentional* drug infested gift."

"Okay, an unintentional drug infested gift—to *your* daughter."

Our daughter popped inside of Yancy's head. And the thought didn't surprise him. Completely focused on Ambria, Yancy watched as her hands moved in agitation, her face full of a dozen emotions, prompting him to still her hands with a gentle grasp within his own.

Ambria looked down at their hands marveling at the contrasts and thankful for the instant calming effect and warmth quickly rising between them. Yancy held her hands and could quite easily do what he wanted with them, with *her*. He moved forward, full-body forward, pressing his hard upper body into her, taking her nervous prattle and easily eliminating it with a killer kiss that took the calm away.

Hot, tense and needy: That's what she was feeling and, oh, what a feeling. One she was enjoying until Yancy began to ease away, right along with his warm, hard chest."Better?" he asked.

Ambria nodded preferring the heated pumping of blood to the nervous, frightened…"Oh-oh," eased pasted her lips.

"What?" Yancy asked the blue of his eye deepening.

"It came back."

"It?" he asked his eyes taking in as much a she could of their surroundings without moving his head to alert whatever had come back.

"The scared to death of getting shot and killed by a king pin drug dealer sensation," Ambria softly whispered.

"I'll get rid of it," Yancy promised.

Should she let him? Shouldn't she at least be attempting to think straight? What was she doing? Ambria, you just met the man a few hours ago, she admonished herself. *Well it had been more than a few. It was more like a lot of hours.* He was closer, making that slow lean in. *Almost an entire day, she thought.* Magnetic heat and the consequent kiss tossed away that smidgen of resistance, tossed it far-far away and soon she was experiencing nothing resembling the world as she knew it until a tap at her window pulled them apart.

"Who's that?" Yancy asked staring past her shoulder.

Ambria turned and jumped with a start despite recognizing the round face pressed against her window. "My neighbor, Ryan Adams."

"Do you know him well?" Yancy tensed, going into protector role.

"He's my Post-Katrina neighbor. I've known since I've come home after Hurricane Katrina, about two years or so."

"Not before?"

"Nope. He was here when I got back. Ryan bought the Harding place. Why are you looking at him like that? He's just my neighbor. He's got nothing to do with drugs and coconuts."

Yancy nodded, "Don't tell him or any of your neighbors anything about what happened today," he said before getting out of the car leaving a draft of cold and uncertainty.

Ryan was motioning for her to roll down the window. She opened the door instead. "You okay?" he asked his neck not only covered but overflowing with beads, the bag in his hand bulging with more beads and trinkets Ambria was certain.

"I'm fine."

"I'm just coming from my car to bring my catch inside," he lifted the hefty purple, green and gold bag. "I was getting worried about you. I didn't see your 'Vette in the driveway earlier and it's long past parade time. Then I thought you probably went to see Comus since it's the last parade of the season and that I shouldn't be worried." Ryan was darting glances at Yancy as he spoke. "Looks like I was right."

Yancy was at the passenger door by the time Ryan finished talking. "No reason to worry. I was with Ambria."

"Who are *you*?" Ryan squeaked the last word that Ambria was certain he'd meant to emphasize.

"Ambria's—" Yancy began.

"Friend!" she finished as she got out of the car, afraid to hear how Yancy would categorize them. It could be a number of ways. However, he chose could be real or not based on the situation they were caught in and the last thing she wanted was the situation to dictate their relationship or more precisely, their non-relationship.

"From college," Yancy filled in smoothly as she shut the car door and stood between them wondering at Yancy's reaction to her shy neighbor. Ryan had just started talking to her after a year and a half of distant waves.

"I thought you went to Xavier here in New Orleans?" A look of confusion touched Ryan's face.

"I get that a lot." Yancy went on with confidence as Ambria watched in awe. "Xavier's a historically black college."

"Right," Ryan said, the puzzled expression remaining.

"And I'm not black."

"You're not?" Ambria interjected enjoying the game. "And here, after all these years I thought you were one of us. Tell me that you're Creole at least, with a tiny bit of black somewhere inside you."

Yancy directed a devastating smile her way before pulling her to his side and landing a quick kiss on her lips as if he'd done it a dozen times before. He whispered, "You're such a tease," before turning his attention back to Ryan whose eyes were bugging out. "I was a pre-med major," Yancy went on to say adding a whole bunch more without her actually hearing much more. The start of his explanation was right on the mark. Xavier University in New Orleans was founded to give black students a place to gain a higher education but later became known for its rigorous pre-med program drawing a diverse population to the university. Most other courses of study were nearly one hundred percent African-America which would explain Ryan's surprise. But Yancy knowing that she went to Xavier and using a pre-med major as cover to explain their pass association wasn't what stunned her most. The ease in which he fell into the role and her instant compliance and desire to be right where he held her: flushed against his side with his fingers tracing circles across her midsection as he spoke. Too bad it wasn't all true.

Friends.

Friends, who could turn into lovers.

"Isn't that right, Bria?" Yancy's fingers stilled and pressed against her stomach for a response other than the moist rush a few inches below.

"Yeah, sure," Ambria came back to the conversation agreeing to anything as the soft sound of Yancy's voice and breath near her ear began the whole body rush thing all over again.

The name he'd called her vibrated down her ear. Why did he keep doing that? Why did he keep touching her? Kissing her?

Not that she wanted him to stop any of the above. But simply, why?

Ambria found herself being guided to her front door which she unlocked as Yancy's body surrounded her with—all of him. Ambria turned to give Ryan a fleeting wave. Her front door closed barely giving her time to see him throw a despondent one her way. Oh-oh, did Ryan have a thing for her? If so, Ambria had had absolutely no clue until two seconds ago. And then she had not a care because Yancy had wrapped his arms around her and his breath was heating her pulse as his mouth traveled from her ear to the base of her neck and back up again.

"Stay, here," Yancy told her. "I need to check the house." He pulled himself away from her berating himself for constantly giving into this need to touch or taste her when his first priority was to her safety. They shouldn't have lingered in the car, outside the house or even for the few seconds of heaven once they had gotten inside her house. His only consolation was that he knew that Grant had secured the perimeter of the house after leaving the hospital and had been watching ever since. Which meant Grant couldn't have missed the scene inside the car. Yancy had to show some control.

Coming back to the front of the house he took one look at her attempt at holding in her nervousness and fear and any thought of control had disappeared. He walked up to Bria, pulled her into his arms and continued where he left off. He kissed and pulled at the brown skin near the base of her throat nipping and warming her neck as he slowly made his way up. She shook as if chilled but the skin beneath his lips was warm, soft and, "Heaven," he whispered as he made it to her ear.

Heaven, the word lingered with a vibrating pulse as it reverberated inside her head. There were shallow breaths between them and next to nothing at all as his body held her against the door, his solid chest holding her still. Not that he needed to but...

Yancy's hands had trailed up her neck to each side of her face, her eyes opened to look into his. Ambria felt like she couldn't breathe, why couldn't she breathe? She seemed to see more than she should in his eyes.

"Beautiful," he said before taking her lips. And did he take them. Not that she had any intention of not giving them to him. But taken was the word, Ambria thought as her mouth opened beneath his and she accepted the demanding pressure of his searching tongue. Everywhere! Her lips and the soft insides of her cheek! Her mouth felt as if it had places that had never been explored or even named before?

So absorbed by what he was doing with his mouth Ambria was shocked to feel his hands on her bare skin. The cheerleader sweater had been inched up, his wide, strong hands were massaging the sides of her breasts, his thumbs were grazing her nipples, causing her pulse rate to double, her nipples to harden and throb and her lower body to press into his. He was hard, hot and so close, yet not close enough.

Ambria wrapped her arms more tightly around him only to freeze a second later when his hardness seemed to vibrate. The kiss ended with a slow caress across her lips doubling back for a nip then another as

Yancy's hands fell away from her skin leaving her breasts feeling heavy and cold. He took a deep breath and stepped back.

"Sorry," he whispered pulling his cell phone from his front pocket.

Sorry? Her entire body was sorry. Ambria stepped away to give him some privacy and her some time to pull it together. She walked to her bedroom, then her kitchen, only to wander back to her bedroom as she came down from the high of Yancy DeWolf. What a name, what a man. She sat on her bed and wondered at her reaction. Could it all be so intense because of her virgin status? After all she was the most virginal twenty-six year old she knew.

"Naw!"

Others guys she had dated had tired but had never gotten so far and so fast. Which had made saving herself easy so far. It had to be Yancy. He did something to her and that something would be intensified because he would be living with her in close quarters for-- well, indefinitely or until they caught the drug smuggling coconut stuffing bas—"

"Bria?" she heard Yancy call from somewhere in the house.

There was that shorten version of her name again. No one called her Bria. Coming from him it sounded sweet and simply right? She loved it. Too much. What was wrong with her? *You just met this man mere hours ago*, she reminded herself but it didn't seem to matter. She was going to have a very hard time behaving in her usual self preserving virginal manner. From the get go she'd been sending the wrong message.

"Bria?"

"I'm in here!" Ambria called out to him. Take a step back. "Give the right message even though it conflicts with what your body is clamoring for," she told herself. "And do it in another room," she muttered, hopping off the bed and reaching the doorway at the same time as Yancy. "Coffee?" Would you like some?" she asked, moving out of the room and away from the bed because she had no doubt that despite her intentions, she'd soon find herself flat on her back, completely naked with Yancy on top or maybe she'd be on top, her breasts rubbing against his chest. Whoa! Where were her values and morals hiding today? "Coffee!" she repeated as if coffee was her salvation. "Help me make a pot."

Without a word he followed her down the hall. Ambria knew he did because he was barely a step behind her, his warm breath caressing the back of her neck until she reached the kitchen counter, grabbed the pot and held it in front of her like a shield.

"Are you okay?"

"I'm fine. I just need the bag of coffee. It's behind you," she nodded toward the cabinet above his head.

"Okay, I'll get it for you," he said as if talking to a frighten animal. Boy was she being obviously weird.

"Grab the Community Coffee. There's nothing like coffee with chicory. That other stuff was all I could find when we evacuated for Hurricane Katrina. We ended up in Houston. I've got no idea why I even brought it with me. It's been in there for two years now," Ambria went on trying to fill the silence, afraid that if there was any it would be full of heavy breathing instead of rambling talking.

Yancy handed her the coffee without a word and sat at the round kitchen table while she filled the pot with water and then the air with even more chatter about Katrina, evacuation and moving back to New Orleans. Coffee started, she gathered mugs and various coffee additives wishing she had a bit of bourbon or Bailey's to add to her own because she had run out of steam and the quiet was making her even more nervous. What was he thinking?

Placing everything on the table including the freshly brewed pot of coffee, Ambria finally sat across from Yancy. Not knowing what to say or do she poured and lifted the black liquid to her lips wondering what to say to someone you barely knew but had recently experienced the most passionate embrace of your life with.

"Blah," Ambria gagged.

"You okay?" Yancy's eyes darken with concern.

"I don't care for black coffee."

"That's obvious." He took the cup from her. "How do you like it?"

"A lot of cream and a little sugar," Ambria stared at his hands as he poured some of her coffee into his mug to make room for more cream. They were tanned and strong and had felt so good on certain parts of her body. After preparing her coffee he handed the mug back to her

"Bria, I think we need to talk."

Boy did they need to talk. "Fix your coffee first," Ambria stalled.

"It's fine. I like my coffee the way I like my women, apparently. Black with a taste of Bria," he said taking a sip not knowing why he said what he said except that is was true.

"Just like from the movie Airplane," burst from Ambria's lips.

"Yep, it was a good movie. I changed the line a bit to suit my needs. I hope you don't mind." He saw her head shake, her ponytail swaying in response. She looked like he felt: stunned by this attraction.

"How's your coffee?" she asked taking another sip of her own.

"Black, smooth and steamy," he wanted to say but held back the double loaded comment falling back on a slow nod as a response. It was obvious that this thing between them was making her uneasy. Bria had enough to contend with. It wasn't fair that she had landed in the middle of a drug bust. And now, pursuing her the way he had, must have really thrown her for an extra loop.

"It seems that I drink my coffee the way I most recently like my men," came at him from across the table.

She laughed. Yancy joined her. For awhile they sat and drank as an easy silence began to grow between them.

"You're right," Ambria said when they both had finished a second cup.

"I am most of the time, but about what?"

"We need to talk. I think I gave you the wrong impression."

"About?"

"Me."

"That you're beautiful, sexy and—"

"I don't sleep around."

"I hope not."

"I'm not sleeping with you tonight."

"Okay."

"Okay?"

"Not tonight, but some other night," he quietly said, eyes as direct as his declaration holding hers. "Some time soon."

Ambria knew her jaw had to be somewhere on the table. Was this sexual banter? If it was, the bantering was almost as effective as his kisses. Heat suffused her face and plunged downward making her shift in the chair.

"Did I embarrass you?"

"No! Yes!" Ambria corrected. "I'm not used to all this."

"Oh!"

His eyes focused on her face which had her wondering if her blush was evident beneath her brown skin. She certainly hoped it wasn't. Ambria took another sip of her coffee and nearly sprayed it across the room when once again, he said, "Oh!" with the addition of a self-satisfied smile spread across his face.

"Oh, what?"

"You're a virgin."

It took her a second to react to his bluntness but she quickly found her tongue "Yes, I am." Ambria said with pride. She was one of a dying breed. But she was one by choice.

"Thanks."

"For what?"

"Waiting for me. Now that I understand the situation a little better, I have to apologize for coming on so strong. I couldn't help myself. You make me want to..." he trailed off.

"To what?"

"To peel every piece of clothing away from your smooth, soft skin with my teeth and use my mouth and tongue to make your entire body turn into a reddish-brown blush before easing into you and making you mine," he thought but instead the words, "I won't say," spilled out of his mouth. He hadn't missed her eyes widening in speculation. In time, he'd show her, again, and again, and then of course *again*. He could wait as long as she wanted. The moment he saw her, Yancy knew that Bria was the woman he'd been waiting for. They'd have the rest of their lives to heat the air and each other.

"Good, because we shouldn't be having this conversation. This thing between us is so completely inappropriate to the situation. It's all been inappropriate!"

"It has?"

"Let me tell you exactly how inappropriate."

"I'm sure you will."

"You bet I will," she said beginning to get all worked up again, which was probably better than getting her all worked up in the way he had been doing. Yancy plastered on a straight face as he sat back to listen. "You tell me about drugs in Ashlyn's coconut and what do I do? I kiss you."

"Actually, I believe I initiated that."

On a roll now Ambria continued. "I tell you how lousy I feel about putting my family's lives in danger, what do I do? I kiss you!"

"My turn," he told her unable to resist Yancy reached across the table to lay a hand across her lips. "We walk into your house where I'm supposed to have come to protect you and what happened? *I kiss you.* And I couldn't help kissing you just as I couldn't help lifting your sweater to feel your smooth skin under my palms," his hand skimmed across her face and rested on her neck. "Not to mention your hard nipples across my thumbs and you melting for me until we were interrupted." So much for not making her nervous.

"Exactly," she breathed, hot and blushing all over again. Grateful that Yancy eased back into his chair she muttered, "All highly inappropriate."

"But irresistibly amazing."

"True," Ambria told him seeing no sense in denying it. He could read the truth in her eyes, "but we can't do this."

"You're partly right. We can't do this *now*. We can, after this case is solved and I know you're safe. Then we can go about this *appropriately*."

Ambria nodded. "I'd like that. I'm sure you noticed, without me even having to say this, I've enjoyed your kisses."

"I noticed," he said taking his cup to the sink. The doorbell rang. "I'll get it," he told her motioning for her to stay.

Ambria heard Yancy's deep timber answered by her neighbor,

Ryan's lighter tone.

"It's Ryan," Yancy said unnecessarily.

"Ambria," Ryan rushed to say, "I bought a King Cake and knew there was no way I'd eat it all and I thought that since you had company you might want it. I already found the baby and took it out. I always thought that it was dangerous to have a plastic baby hidden in a King Cake anyway. It's a choking hazard, you know."

"Thank you," Ambria quickly interrupted to stop the flow of words coming from him. She'd never heard Ryan say so many at once. Taking the white box from him, the clear top revealed the traditional ringed cake decorated with white icing and purple, green and gold colored sugar. There was a small space indicating that a neatly sliced piece had been cut and there sat the plastic baby in the center of the ring.

"It's a filled King Cake, strawberry and cream cheese, and with the baby already out nobody has to buy the next one. Since Mardi Gras is almost over it probably doesn't matter," he ended with a faltering squeak as Yancy came toward him.

"Thanks for the cake. Bria and I have some catching up to do."

"Maybe we could all get together later?" Ryan asked.

"Sure, later," Ambria agreed not sure how to deal with the "crush discovery" of Ryan's on top of everything else. She followed the pair to the door Yancy had guided Ryan toward.

When the door closed Yancy let out a huge breath. "For the record, that guy," he pointed to the door as if Ryan was still standing there, "he's the reason for my inappropriate actions the first time we walked through that door. The other kisses were because I was trying to comfort you and for no other reason except that I couldn't help myself. And, you have to admit, they did the job of making us both feel better at the time."

"I get the wanting to make me feel better part, but what does Ryan have to do with what happened between us at that door?" Ambria asked, the wild scene replaying itself inside her head.

"He wants you."

"No!" Ambria said despite having recently come to a similar conclusion.

"Yes," Yancy came away from the door and slowly toward her. "And I had no choice but to do something to show both of us that you're mine."

"Yours?"

"Mine." he nodded before making his way back to the kitchen.

Chapter Four

"Yancy, I'm not yours! I'm not anybody's!" Ambria called to his retreating back.

"Do you want to be?" he turned backed, standing mere inches away in the next instant.

"I don't know. Maybe. After all this is over."

"That's good enough for me. As I suggested earlier, let's put it all aside until you're safe, agreed?"

"Agreed."

"Now, come with me. I want to get a better look around your house to double check security."

Instantaneously Yancy turned all business double checking her locks, windows and access points. They sat at the kitchen table once again going through her normal schedule.

"I've taken the week off," Ambria told him. She had planned to sit with Ashlyn in order to relieve her sister who would have had to report to work on Thursday and Friday. But now, they were officially under federal protection and had been moved to a hospital somewhere even she didn't know about.

"Good, I can protect you better at home then the pharmacy. Maybe this will all be over by the weekend."

"How did you know I was a pharmacist?"

At his raised eyebrows Ambria refrained from asking those kinds of questions. "It may be safer to protect me at home but would it make sense for me to sit around waiting for whoever is out there to come and get me? Shouldn't I go about my regular life?"

"What would you have done for the rest of the week?"

"Go to church since tomorrow's Ash Wednesday. Then I'd head to the hospital until Gloria came."

"No reason to now."

"True."

"So, as far as anyone knows you'll be spending a few days relaxing at home."

"More like waiting."

"And watching."

"All day long, in my house-- with you."

"Yes," Yancy nodded. "Can you handle it?"

"Of course, "Ambria told him getting up from the table. "I'll get your room ready."

Could *he* handle it? should have been the question. And he asked himself that question again and again as evening eased into the night. First as he sat across from her during a dinner of red beans and rice.

"It's a tradition for us," she had told him as she placed a bowl before him. We continued the tradition since my parents died a few years ago. Gloria or I would cook a big pot of red beans for after the parades. I cooked them yesterday and had planned to bring some to the hospital for dinner and Glen was going to meet us there after his shift. My whole family, at least what's left of it would have spent part of Mardi Gras together."

Ambria's mouth had turned down and all Yancy wanted to do was turn it upward with a gentle kiss that would have instantly cracked his fragile resolve to pull back.

Then again he wondered at his ability to handle being constantly near her as he helped her wash dishes and worse yet when he woke up in the middle of the night feeling her eyes on him. She was exotically sexy, her head covered by some silky scarf, a blanket laid across her lap as she sat in a chair on the other side of the room with her feet propped up on an ottoman.

"What are you doing here?" Yancy asked the blood pounding in his ears as he wondered, wished and prayed for the reason for her being there a match to what he wanted.

"I couldn't sleep. I was nervous."

Barely keeping the disappointed from rising from his throat in a frustrated moan Yancy lifted his head to get a better look at her and seeing the frighten expression on her face, so different from the woman who snatched coconuts from thugs and warned him with a mutter and stare, tore at his heart. Bending his elbow to rest it against is palm he searched his mind for what to say. Not knowing how to comfort her with something other than hot, heavy kisses he asked what he knew was a foolish question. "Why?"

"I thought I heard something outside."

"It was probably the wind or one of those squirrels I saw running around earlier."

"How do you know? You didn't even hear me come in."

"Of course I did. I felt you the minute you walked in. Why else do you think I didn't pull my gun on you? I thought I'd let you get comfortable before starting this late night visit."

"Good answer," Ambria shifted and pulled the covers higher hiding the deep V of the skimpy pajama top she was wearing.

"You're safe." Yancy told her wanting so much to go her and comfort her in a very inappropriate way. Instead, he stayed in bed. Tucking himself back under the covers was the best way to keep her that way. "You can stay in here if it makes you feel better."

"It's already making me feel better."

"Good night, then" Yancy said to her *and* his vivid imagination which had already had her completely naked under that blanket of hers, the mere thought causing the lower half of his body pointing like a Geiger counter in her direction.

"Could I handle anymore?" he asked himself when he woke the next morning to Ambria fast asleep, her arms flung wide, the fluffy cover on the floor and her skinny strapped pajama top twisted and exposing a round, perfect breast. A dark, brown nipple stood out against the white top. His thumbs itched to graze the hard tip. His whole hand ached to hold her. Before he gave into temptation, Yancy grunted loud enough to wake her then turned to face the wall at the opposite side of the room.

"Oh!" he heard Bria say.

The shocked, breathy sound went right through him. He wanted to really shock her. He was dying to shock her.

"Yancy!" she called. It was a gruff sleep-sexy call that had him beyond hardening easily graduating to throbbing. "Yancy!" Bria said once again with a sort of deep throat vibration causing his resolve to begin crumbling all over again and his intent shifting to pulling her into the bed with him.

He turned without a sound to find her out of the chair and standing at the door with every inch of brown skin draped by the blanket. "I thought you heard everything. Why didn't you answer?"

"I was working on keeping myself from tossing that cover you're swallowed in and pulling aside the straps to that piece of top you're wearing so I could feel my thumbs circling your nipples before my mouth had the pleasure of tasting them," Yancy couldn't stop himself from saying.

A sudden intake breath had to have made her breasts rise with the movement. Yancy had formed the picture perfect sight in his mind when Ambria's voice pulled him from it. "I shouldn't have asked."

"Maybe not, I figured if I'm not going to be able to *actually* make love to you yet, I would compromise."

"How is that a compromise?"

"I would consider making love to you with words instead of my fingers," he lifted his hand moving his fingers in a slow, erotic way; "my mouth and tongue," he continued, "a compromise."

"Words—" Ambria paused in an attempt to pull enough words out of her brain to give coherent response "—I suddenly realize, can be pretty powerful," she softly murmured.

"And I intend to use them," Yancy sat up, swinging his legs to the side of the bed.

"I'm going to get dressed for church. Be ready in an hour," she dashed down the hall before the last words reached him. Words were indeed powerful he thought noting the sudden deflation her last words had on his body. Church reminded him of his own code of ethics and his promise to Bria.

Church that morning and a trip to the grocery store were the only two things that had broken up the monotony of the day. Yancy and Ambria sat as they had most of the day: together but not. Yancy had insisted that she spend most of the day in the den with him on guard. The den was the safest place in the house. The windows were high and small and the iron security dead bolt outer door would make it difficult for anyone to get inside without making a lot of noise.

So far, reports from Grant had been that they were no closer to the ring leader than yesterday. All the agency knew for certain was that the majority of the drugs were confiscated and that one of the dealers in the crowd had gotten away and the basketball player he had captured had been bailed out, which made for an angry somebody out there who could easily identify Bria and would attempt to recoup as much of his product as possible, meaning he would be after the coconut Bria no longer had in her possession. Because the drugs were pure cocaine the street value was in the millions of dollars. Bria's coconut alone was worth close to a hundred thousand dollars worth; more than enough to make it worthwhile to find and kill her for. Yancy had seen people killed for less.

Bria's sigh reached him from across the room, followed by the slow tapping of a pencil on a pad she'd been writing on. The sound had drawn his attention back to her, not that his attention had been taken away for long. He found himself staring at her all day long. Yancy hadn't pressed her with more verbal love making and thought that it might have had something to do with the ashes that had been placed on his forehead, the symbolic beginning of Lent for all Catholics, even non-practicing Catholics like him. Then there was the sermon on penance and the offering up of sacrifices during the season of Lent. He was definitely sacrificing. Church was just a reminder of where his priorities should be.

The tapping suddenly grew louder and more rapid. Bria was as stir-crazy as he. "What are you writing?" he asked feeling safe enough to engage her in conversation.

"Nothing. I'm just doodling, you know, trying to relieve some tension. I'm not used to sitting around doing nothing but worrying about my family while I wait to be murdered."

"You could have gone into the protection program until we found him."

"For how long?"

"I couldn't answer that, Bria. "It's only been a day. My men are on it."

"I know they are, and waiting is one thing," she said the tapping suddenly beginning again. "Being here--," she paused, her pencil moving double time.

Yancy walked over and stopped the wild motion with a trailing finger across her nervous hand. "Being here?" he asked.

"With you," she told him jumping up and away at the sound of the doorbell.

"Bria, wait!" Yancy called just as she reached the door.

"I get it. Don't tell me I can't open my own front door," she turned with her hands on her hips to say. "None of this is fair. All I wanted to do was make my sick little niece happy, okay. All I want to do is right this second is to open my own front door."

"All I want to do is keep you safe," Yancy told her.

"I know that and I don't blame you for any of this. I do, however, blame you for a whole lot of other things."

"Ambria!" a voice called from the other side of the front door.

"That's Ryan," she said unnecessarily using the interruption to turn back to the door.

"What other things?" Yancy latched onto her arm wanting to confirm what he suspected he'd seen flash across her face.

"Words. You want words? Words like the one you've been tossing at me. Words that leave me hot and bothered hours after you've breathed them in my ear or scorched the air with them from across the room. My mind can't stop picturing and replaying the scene over and over again."

"Yeah, I'd like them and I'm not going to deny that I'd love to hear a few choice words from you." Yancy's hand crawled up her arm, his finger brushing her bare shoulders.

"Ambria!" I hear voices. Are you okay?" Ryan's strained tone interrupted.

Ignoring Ryan she told Yancy, "You, would." A seductively shy smile stretched her full lips. "And I think I might, but not right now. Right now I need to open the door."

Yancy made no effort to hide a growl of frustration when Ambria continued to the door. There stood Ryan, his arms full of magazines.

"Thank goodness. I was about to give up and go home."

"You opened the door a second too soon," Yancy who had positioned himself directly behind Bria, blew the words into her ear. Satisfied with the visible shiver she gave as he moved past her to stand to her other side, he possessively wrapped an arm around her waist and pulled her into his side giving Ryan grim smile.

"Come in," Bria invited Ryan the intruder.

"I hope you're not busy," Ryan threw a glance at Yancy, hesitating before stepping inside.

"Not at all," Ambria told him opening the door even wider. "What do you have there, Ryan?"

"A few of my bird magazines. I was wondering if you wouldn't mind looking through them with me. I plan on buying a new bird. Mr. T died over three months ago. The house is too quiet. I need some companionship."

"Mr. T was Ryan's cockatoo," Bria explained as if Yancy cared one way or the other.

"Mr. T," Ryan let loose a long drawn out sigh, "I miss him. Ambria, I hope you don't mind browsing through these magazines with me. I want to see what species would be the best fit for me. I don't know if I could own another cockatoo."

"Not at all," Ambria agreed wanting to help for a number of reasons: to be a good neighbor, to have a mundane and simple something to do that could channel all this nervous sexual energy she had been dealing with, and most importantly, to see Yancy squirm. He'd had her squirming from the moment she met him, it was his turn now.

Two hours later Yancy shut the door behind Ryan and gave her a loaded look before making rounds to check the locks and doors in the entire house. Not sure that she wanted to know the meaning behind his expression Ambria escaped to her bathroom to start the shower calling herself *tired* instead of *cowardly*.

"Foolish," she muttered as the spray hit her sensitive skin, wishing the sting was Yancy's hands or thumbs or both she decided as her nipples puckered at the steady stream of water sluicing over her body.

"Get out, get to bed and stop thinking about that man with the muscular chest, sexy, deep blue eyes and a mouth that delivers words *and* kisses with the same intensity as a hot, steamy August day in New Orleans.

Words! Even the ones inside her own head were making her squirm. Dried and wearing a cami and pajamas pants similar to the night before Ambria headed to her bed and almost made it before her peripheral vision caught Yancy sitting in a chair, the same chair she slept in last night, and had been moved into her bedroom. A blanket lay across his lap and his feet was propped up on the ottoman. He'd dragged it all, including himself into her room.

"What are you doing?"

"Keeping you safe."

"But you don't have to--"

"Safe and comfortable," he continued as if she hadn't spoken. "You don't need to sleep in a chair two nights in a row and you know that's where you would have ended up tonight. Don't argue," he told her before she got out another word.

"I thought you wanted to hear me talk."

"If that's the direction we're going tonight," he tossed the cover to the floor, "then talk on, I'll come a bit closer so that I can hear you better."

Realizing that she had opened her mouth before thinking Ambria held up her hand as she backed into and quickly onto her bed, pulling the covers up to her chin by the time he stood over her.

Sitting on the edge of the bed Yancy leaned over her to whisper, "Change your mind? Then how about dreaming up a few hot, bothersome words for me, *I* could use some scorching."

A few dozen immediately came to mind as she watched him walk across the room and settle himself in the chair, covering his beautiful sculpted body with a blanket. The fact that it was her fluffy pink blanket did nothing to tamper the squirminess she was feeling.

A few moments later it seemed as if he had fallen asleep. Doing the same, Ambria decided, was her best option. Pulling the covers over her head she closed her eyes and unfortunately stayed awaked, her mind actively engaged in producing hot, bothersome words.

She'd have plenty to share in the morning.

Chapter Five

Ambria didn't have the chance to do any sharing when she woke up the next morning. Yancy's sleeping chair was gone. She found him at the kitchen table, on his cell phone, in deep conversation. Something was happening.

Ambria made a pot of coffee. Preparing a mug to each of their preferences drew an inner smile that she realized appeared on her face when Yancy caught her eye while stirring her coffee. Had they gotten so close already that they were sharing smiles and memories? It seemed like too much too fast.

When she placed his mug in front of him, he pointed to his cup and skimmed a finger across her hand without interrupting his call. Yes, they had gotten that close that fast.

She had finished her coffee and had eaten a bowl of cereal and still, the call went on.

Feeling a bit of a reprieve from the expectations Yancy had thrown at her last night Ambria thought to be proactive by doing something about all the nervous pent up feelings she was having. She was going to exercise. Making her way to the den she pulled out the folding treadmill from a closet, changed into exercise gear and dug out her walking shoes and MP3 player. She was on the treadmill for a half an hour, her power walk having just begun to really make her sweat when she spotted Yancy standing in the doorway. The look on his face reminded her of the first day she met him. Was that only three days ago? He gaze was direct, focused and aware, and all of it was on her. He crossed the room and stood in front of the treadmill. He looked down at the console and pressed the stop button without a word. When Ambria's stride slowed and stopped she moved to get down but he shook his head. In the next instant Yancy was standing behind her on the treadmill. His hands rested on top of hers as she gripped the rails.

"Yancy, I'm all sweaty."

"I like you that way." His mouth was right next to her ear, the warm caress of each word having its usual effect. "Tell me."

"Tell you want?" Ambria asked, wanting and knowing there wasn't much chance of her stopping whatever was going to come next. "Tell me in your own *words* what you want to do to me?"

"No, nothing." she shook her head. *Too* close *too* fast. *Way too* intimate.

"I don't believe you," he said as a hand trailed up her left arm his legs spread so that they were on the outer edges of the machine his body moving in closer so that his hardness was pressed against her. "Do you want me to leave so that you could finish your workout?"

"No."

"Then you're ready to give me what you promised."

"Promised? What did I promise?"

"Words."

"I don't have any."

"Again, I don't believe you, but I tell you what, if you don't want to tell me what you want to do to *me* that you can tell me what you want me to do to *you*."

"What? I'm thinking that it's about as hard to understand what you just said as it is to do."

"But you did understand."

Ambria knew she couldn't deny it so she said nothing as his hand had made its way back down her arm, the other was taking a slow trip past her elbow on the opposite arm, up and across her shoulders, lingering on her neck to gently tilt her head to the side before responding. His mouth was so close, Yancy himself so close that he had to feel the shiver that shook her entire body.

"It'll be easy," his voice eased down her ear canal. "Let me give you a start," his heated breath began to warm her from the inside while his body took care of every inch of the out. "Say, 'Hold me closer'. Go on," he urged gently when all she could do was concentrate on the rush of blood and the breaths she could barely get in--let along--out. "Say it," he urged.

"Hold me closer," she rasped surprised she had been able to speak.

"Now, how about, 'Wrap your arms around me'," he continued.

Ambria felt the words fall out of her mouth because 'around her' was where she wanted his arms. Then those strong arms of his held her steady and closer than she had ever been held by a man.

Yancy's mouth moved away from her ear and grazed her neck, nipping at her skin and making her want to ask for more. "Now say, 'Touch my skin'," breezed across the column of her throat followed by a gentle suction and moist caress of his tongue.

"*Please*, touch my skin," Ambria repeated and his hands were under the stretchy material at her waist, pulling it slowing up as they spread across her belly and up her sides, the pads of his fingers heated touch points.

"Touch my skin," he said again.

"Touch me!" Ambria's head fell back, her mouth searching and finding his, her arms reaching back to hold his head close. She kissed him the way he had kissed her, with an all out assault on his mouth, lips and tongue. His hands inched higher, the heat of them hovering just above her aching nipples.

Ambria tore her mouth away from his, "Touch me there!" she demanded.

"Where?" he panted staring into her eyes, knowing exactly what she wanted.

"You know where?" she told him. How could he not know where, when she could almost feel him there already?

"How?"

"Yancy, you *know* how."

"Then tell me."

Ambria felt the flush of embarrassment but the ache of want was winning especially when he pulled her earlobe into his mouth and his palms inched toward the sides of her breasts.

"I want to feel you holding my breasts and pressing your thumbs into my nipples or I think I'm, going to scream," she found herself saying in a rush.

"You *are* going to scream," Yancy told her, "but not in frustration, think *satisfaction.*"

And then his hands were on her. The rough gentleness of his touch as he squeezed and pulled at her nipples made her lean forward to grab for the rails again. He followed pressing his hardness against her as he held her in his arms. He surrounded her with sensations too overwhelming to do anymore then ride out the explosion that came from her core and tore through her body.

"All he did was touch my breasts and I came apart. I came," Ambria thought many minutes later, finding that she had somehow turned and her face was resting against his hard chest.

"You have a very sexy scream," he told her, his hands on her hips, he shifted so that she could feel that he was still hard. And was that a throb she felt?

"Oh, my."

"Don't be embarrassed."

"I'm too relaxed to be embarrassed. This is the most relaxed I've been in--."

"--three days, I know."

"Three days," Ambria turned her head to look up at him. "I had been thinking that it had only been three days since I met you."

"Three days, a lifetime. You do know I'm going to marry you."

"You're not saying that because of what we just did?"

"No, I'm saying that because I have never met a woman who makes me want her as much as you do; who I want to protect, and know, and live with, forever. And who I enjoy making come for me."

"I still can't believe… how quickly… you did that to me. But now, what about you?"

"What about me?"

"Don't you want to?"

"With you, definitely, but later, when all this is over."

"When we're married?"

"Bria, I can't believe I'm saying this but if that's the way you want it, that's the way you'll get it."

"It's the way I've always wanted it," she reached up to kiss his neck and almost made her way to his lips when a loud static sound came into the room. The radio that had been silent for the last few days came to life. Ambria felt colder then she'd ever felt in her life when Yancy stepped away from her and reached for the radio he always kept nearby by but had yet to use.

The two-way conversation was mostly said in code with police jargon bouncing back and forth. But the stiffness in his body and a hardness that came into his face was evidence enough that the situation was coming to a head.

"What's happening?"

"A good bit."

"Gloria and Ashlyn?"

"Safe."

"Me?"

"You're with me, right?"

Ambria nodded, "And you're not only protecting me from drug dealing would be murders but also recent developments. Tell me what's happening?"

"I didn't tell you this before because I didn't want to worry you but Mr. Basketball player made bail the same day we arrested him. He's been spotted in your neighborhood."

"Oh?"

"So we have to be extra cautious. Stay with me and we'll catch him before anything happens." Yancy pulled her to his side.

"I'm counting on it." Ambria inched even closer taking in his warmth.

Suddenly a crashing sound of breaking glass reverberated inside the house. Yancy talked into the radio once again as he held her, at the same time pulling her down and under his body, using it as a shield, a second later pulling his gun from the somewhere below his calf.

"Take my cell phone, get in the closet and don't come out until I tell you to."

Ambria gave him a tight squeeze and whispered, "I gave you the words I promised, keep yours. Stay alive. Marry me."

He nodded and gently kissed her forehead before heading to the front of the house.

Ambria slipped into the closet, relieved that she had decided to exercise today otherwise there wouldn't have been room for her. She sat for what seemed liked hours listening to the silence, sharing the company of her vacuum cleaner, dust, bags of Mardi Gras beads and trinkets, and a box of party favors her butt had landed on in her hurry to get inside.

Her mind flitted from one thought to the next. Who was out there? Did Yancy have backup? Was this a trap? Was something happening to Gloria and Ashlyn? Where was her brother-in-law Glen? Why was it so quiet? *And what could she use for a weapon if she was found?*

The last thought had her quietly rummaging through her dark closet for something to protect her if the need arose. Too bad she didn't keep a flashlight in her closet, it would have been handy. Her careful search left Ambria with a bag of beads as a best defense. She tested the weight and decided that it would work best as a primitive swinging weapon. Mardi Gras got her into this, it might be the thing to get her out. Just as she settled the bag behind her shoulder in a ready stance Yancy's phone rang. Ambria dug it out of the zippered pocket of her exercise shorts and stared at the screen for a moment. Was it Yancy calling or the drug dealer who had somehow his number, captured Yancy and was calling his phone to see who would answer. Her heart stopped at the thought. No, no no, Yancy had just come into her life and he was still there alive and healthy and he was calling. "Then answer the phone, foolish," Ambria told herself as she clicked the answer button. Still, she paused and waited to hear his voice.

"Bria?" his breathing was heavy but it was his voice, deep and sexy. "Bria? Answer me. Are you okay?"

"I'm fine, how about you?"

"Wonderful now that I know you're okay."

"Did you catch him?"

"Yes, and we're taking him in for questioning. Grant's down the street. He's going to come get you. I don't want you in the house alone. You're bay window is completely smashed."

"Okay, see you soon."

"Bria, wait," he hesitated a moment before saying, "Do me a favor."

"Anything."

"Throw some clothes on. I can't have my fiancé looking so sexy around my co-workers."

"Not a problem," Ambria told him as she stepped out of the closet.

"And, Bria?"

"Yes."

"I love you."

"I love you too, Yancy."

Chapter Six

A tremendous relieve poured through Ambria as she went into her bedroom to change, but was stopped by a knock at her front door and her name being called. Grant was fast, which meant that he would see her sexy body, but he'd have to wait for her to change because Ambria had promised Yancy that she would.

The floor of her living room was covered in glass and jagged shards stuck out of the frame of her once beautiful bay window. Ryan stood on the other side looking bewildered and concerned.

"Ambria, what happened? Are you okay?"

"I'm fine. There's been some trouble."

"I see. Where's your friend?"

"Taking care of the trouble," Ambria told him not wanting to drag Ryan into any of it. Realizing that she was still carrying the bag of beads she let it ease off her shoulder but held on to it, somehow feeling comforted by the weight of it there.

"Good," Ryan said stepping into the house through the shattered window. He paused long enough to use a gloved hand to pull a jagged piece of glass from the window frame. Wondering at the reason for the gloves and even more so for pulling out the huge shard he was now holding, Ambria looked at his face to find that it had gone through a conversion. His eyes had narrowed and harden, his brows inverted and his mouth turned into a rigid line. His steps were firm and commanding and took them to her too quickly for her to react.

It was the shock that had delayed her reaction. Looking into his face Ambria realized that Ryan, sweet, nerdy Ryan was the drug kingpin. He held that jagged piece a glass in his hand with a menace she had never seen before. A finger went up one end and down to the other as he stared at her.

"You figured it out already." He told her without giving her more than a brief glance.

Ambria didn't answer trying to mesh what she knew about Ryan and what she was seeing now. Her eyes stayed glued on the glass he held in his hand as she slowly took a step back and another.

"I knew you were smart. That's why I wanted you for myself. I've been waiting, biding my time, building my clientele of users and dealers staking and claiming a wide open territory since Hurricane Katrina blew everyone else away," he arms swept wide the sharp piece of glass just missing her cheek. He went on as if he hadn't even noticed that he'd just missed cutting her. "At the same time I was creating my alto ego all with one goal in mind."

"What goal?" Ambria asked finally finding her voice. It was the only thing she could think to do because wasn't it standard procedure to keep the bad guys talking until a rescue came? In any case, Ambria thought it wise to keep him talking as she continued to back away, fear erasing the disbelief at her discovery of who Ryan actually was. Her pounding heart was a loud bass tempo to his voice that had became a muffled noise she could barely understand unless she concentrated and Ambria forced herself to concentrate. The skin beneath her workout clothes was heavy with perspiration by the time she backed into the kitchen.

"It won't work."

"What won't work?"

"Keeping me talking, let's go." He had a hand on one of her arms and the other he wrapped around her waist, the pointed part of the glass lightly touching her stomach. "Last time I missed because I don't want to scar your pretty face. Don't force me to push this into your stomach. I'd rather have you than not, but if you cause me trouble I'll have to gut you."

"You won't get any trouble from me." Bria told him wondering how she was able to keep her voice steady and her legs moving as they casually walked across her back yard to his guaranteeing that no one would see them, including Grant.

The glass press against her stomach kept her compliant as they walked through his back door. In one motion Ryan flung her away from him and into a small room under the stairs. Immediately Ambria realized that it was the pantry. Wanting to see if there was something she could use in the room she dropped the bag of beads she had forgotten that she had been holding and didn't use for defense after all. She felt around until she found a light switch. It was empty of basic food items but full of something else.

Coconuts.

There were coconuts everywhere.

"Ambria you're so resourceful. I see you found the light. I hope you like the décor seeing as you have fondness for *coconuts*!" Ryan voice rose at the end as something hit the door. Every other word had been calmly enunciated but his use f the last word showed exactly how enraged he was. Keep the bad guys talking until help comes Ambria reminded herself. Grant would go to her house, see her gone and tell Yancy. Yancy would come for her soon. If not, she would simply use the resources at her disposal she thought her eyes scanning the crates of brown coconuts stacked on the shelves.

Chapter Seven

"What do you mean Bria's not there?" Yancy yelled into his radio.

"I've searched the entire house and the perimeter, she's nowhere in sight," Grant's voice came through the radio.

"Keep looking I'll be there." Yancy felt like tossing the radio at the head of Dwayne, Mr. Basketball player, sitting the other side of the room. Instead he attached it to his belt because it was his only connection to Grant and currently his only avenue to finding Bria who had disappeared in the last ten minutes.

In three quick strides Yancy was hovering above his number one resource to finding her. "Name and address. Give them to me."

"For who, and what?" Dwayne asked with a smirk.

Yancy reacted instinctively, his right hand flying only to be caught by Jones, friend and fellow agent who had been on the case with him for that last six months. "You don't want to do that," he advised.

"Yeah, you don't want to do that," Dwayne said bravado and nervous fear had him shifting his focus from one agent to the other.

"Leave him to me. Meet Grant and find her."

Yancy nodded and was out to door, his mind so intent on doing what Jones advised that he rammed into someone talking on a cell phone.

Cell phone. Wherever Bria was, she probably still had his cell phone.

Yancy ran to the nearest phone and dialed his number hoping to hear her voice again. He had to hear her voice. He'd just found her he wouldn't lose her. Bria was his and he'd fight for her.

Ambria was gauging the weight of the coconut in her hand. They were normal everyday coconuts in their pre-decorative drug abused state. She had discovered this by shaking a few dozen in the last five minutes. The slush of the milk inside was proof enough that they had yet to be drained in readiness for refilling with whatever illegal substance Ryan had planned. She still couldn't believe it. Ryan was the kingpin dealer bringing drugs back to the streets of New Orleans.

Not having heard a sound from him in the last few minutes Ambria decided to do what she could to prepare herself. The last thing she wanted to feel was the point of glass at her stomach again and she had to think about the possibility of Ryan reappearing with a gun. That would be worse.

Pulling a handful of beads out of her bag Ambria made room for some of the coconuts which she added to the bottom of the bag. Then she went to the rear of the little room searching for an empty bag. If she surprised Ryan by knocking him in the head with a few coconuts and then swinging a bag of them at his skull maybe it would be enough to get her away from him and to help. Grant hopefully, who by now had discovered her gone and by now had informed Yancy that she wasn't where she was supposed to be. But they wouldn't know where to look if she was still stuck in a pantry. She had to get out of the pantry and out in the open.

Suddenly music filled the air. Ambria started to wonder if Ryan had gone completely mad by celebrating her capture when she also felt her leg vibrate. Realizing it was the cell phone she had forgotten slipping back in the zipped pocket of her pants. Ambria dug for it, faking a coughing fit when she heard the scrape of a chair.

"Ambria, what are you doing?" Ryan's voice came through the door.

"Just coughing, Ryan, your pantry must have more dust than coconuts," she said loud enough for whoever was on the other end of the phone to hear.

"You'll be out soon. We'll be heading to South America in a few," he told her as if he'd announced that they were going on a picnic.

"You're taking me to South America?" she squeaked in as much as surprise as to give info to her unknown caller on the other end of the line as she held the mouthpiece close holding off talking directly to the caller until Ryan had move away from the door.

"Yes, South America where we can live out our lives like two love birds. I've decided on getting a couple of love birds as pets, you know. They'll be the perfect birds to replace Mr. T. Love Birds will represent the beginning of our new life together. We'll pick them out together."

"Oh," was all Ambria could say to that though she meant "Oh, hell no, over my dead body!" reverberated inside her head as she held her tongue against voicing how she felt about Ryan's plans. Hearing steps moving away from the door Ambria inched as close to the rear wall as she could before putting her ear to the phone.

"Who's there?"

"Yancy," his grating voice was music to her ears. "Are you okay?"

"Yes."

"You're in Ryan's pantry, did I hear that right?"

"Yes. Stay put don't move. Grant's already there, he's right outside."

"Ryan's crazy. He wants to take me to somewhere in South America," Ambria told him. The click of the phone told her that he was gone but on his way.

Ambria got busy pulling a few crates of coconuts into the back corner and creating a low barricade of stacked crates with the rest. If Grant was right outside and Yancy on the way she'd delay leaving this room and being anywhere near Ryan as long as she could. Remembering the way he enjoyed taunting her with the piece of glass Ambria prayed that he would have his crazy mind set on using it as a weapon again. She could keep him at bay with the coconuts if he did. Just don't come in with a gun she thought as she turned the light off.

Mere seconds later, there was a scuffling sound and then nothing. Having gotten really good at sitting quietly Ambria waited but didn't have to wait long for the door to open. She hummed one coconut after another hitting the frame and the door and over the head of the tall man standing in the doorway who was now ducking for cover.

Tall man? Ryan wasn't tall.

"Bria, stop, it's me! Bria!" Yancy called her name a few times before she truly registered that it *was* him.

"Yancy!" dropping the coconuts in her hands she helped him move the crates and flew into his arms. "You came for me."

"I promised. How else could I marry you if I let Ryan kidnap and take you to some godforsaken place in South America?"

"Can you believe it? He had me fooled."

"He had a lot of people fooled. Dwayne, the basketball player roaming around was a diversion. He'd been waiting to get his hands on you. He didn't, did he?" Yancy started checking her body for injuries.

"He did nothing more than scare me. Yancy, I trusted him."

"I know, try not to think about Ryan. You've got me and you can trust me to be there for you. I'm yours forever, Bria, to trust and to love."

"I love you, Yancy."

"And I love you, so much that think we'd better start some wedding planning right away."

Chapter Eight

Ambria hadn't seen Yancy since the day he rescued her from Ryan. Mere hours later he'd put her on a plane to Houston with Grant as a body guard and extra precaution. She was met by Gloria, Glen and Ashlyn. Ashlyn had just been released from the hospital and they were all staying in a hotel enjoying the amenities when the call came.

Every evening at six pm Yancy called and they had *words*.

Several words.

Several, long, hot, sexy words.

Ambria smiled as the ring tone she'd designated for Yancy filled the air, time for a few more words.

Exiting the pool area, Ambria waved to her family as she headed back to her room.

"Are you alone?" Yancy asked.

"In five seconds I will be."

"What are you wearing?"

"A bathing suit."

"A one piece?"

"No, a two piece tan-kini."

"Tan-kini…" he let hang. "So much better."

"Better how?"

"Tan-kinis leave room for hands to inch under the top so fingers can reach my favorite part of your body."

"My navel?" she teased knowing full well he meant her breasts which were heavy and her nipples hardening from his suggestive tone.

"Have I ever told you what I'd like to do with your navel?"

Yancy went on to explain, the image of his tongue and mouth in action had her panting.

"I can't wait to see you," he finally said.

"When can we come home?"

"Tomorrow. Ryan's not getting out on bail. We've nailed every connection he's had and with the help of the Mexican authorities even the connections on their side of the border."

"That's wonderful news."

"I've got even more news."

"What kind?"

"It gravitates to the good arena."

"What is it?"

A knock sounded on her door.

"Hold on a second." A look though the peek hole showed no one on the other side of the door. Being extra cautious because of recent events Ambria put the safety lock on the door and looked through the crack to see more of nothing. "That's weird, no one's there. Do you think that you missed one of Ryan's connections? Could he still be out to get me?"

"There's no way we've missed anything, but *you've* missed something."

"What's that's?" Ambria asked prepared for more descriptive verbal lovemaking.

"Open the door without the safety lock and you'll see."

Understanding dawned and Ambria wasted no time in yanking the door open. Yancy stood there.

"The good news, Bria, is that I'm here." And he was. Tall, handsome and dressed all in black he stood in the doorway wearing a sexy indulgent smile but only for a second because his lips were molding hers to the shape of his as he backed her into the room.

Wrapping her arms around Yancy's warm, hard body and pulling him into her made Ambria's heart pound. His fingers were doing a roving crawl under her tan-kini making their way up when another knock sounded on the door.

Surprisingly Yancy backed away a step, then another, allowing cool air to flow between them. A mysterious look was in his eyes. "Happy to see me?" he asked.

Ambria nodded wondering at the look and the ridiculous question he already knew the answer to. He backed up a few more steps stopping when he reached the door that was vibrating with louder more insistent knocking. "Heaven knows, I'm happy to see you," he said before opening the door as if he knew who was on the other side.

Standing in the hall was Gloria, Glen and Ashlyn with Grant not far behind. Ambria smiled at her family. "Did you know about Yancy coming?" she directed the question to her sister.

"Of course," Gloria smirked.

"Then why are you interrupting us. Come back later," she told her sister pulling Yancy inside with one hand and grabbing the door with the other.

"Wait!" Gloria stopped Ambria before the door shut. "Don't tell me you haven't told her yet?" she said to Yancy."

"Told me what?"

Gloria pointedly looked at Yancy then shifted her focus to Ambria, "You've got thirty minutes to get yourself ready and in the courtyard."

"For what?"

"A promise..." Yancy took two steps toward her. "A vow..." he said two more steps closer. Our wedding..." Yancy said closing the door on her family and Grant before pulling his arms for a long hot kiss leaning back a long while later. "Tell me you still want to marry me, or am I wrong about that?"

"You're right about that. I mean the promise, vow wedding thing, but *now?*"

"About thirty minutes from now, if it's what you want."

"How?"

"I've got a licensee and a judge and Gloria took care of everything else. What do you say? Will you marry me?" Yancy asked again producing a beautiful solitaire and easing it onto the ring finger of her left hand.

Ambria leaned into him, wrapped his arms around her and breathing in his scent whispered, "Yes," into his chest, then "Yes," as a caress across his chin and "yes," directly into his mouth before her lips confirmed her answer once more.

Another knock on the door tore them apart and Gloria's urgent voice forced them to bank the fire.

"That navel thing you describe. I'm counting on it," she whispered to him as he eased away.

"Tonight," he came back to whisper in her ear. "You're going to get that and so much more," he told her before opening the door.

Exactly three hours later Ambria was back in the hotel room with her husband.

Anticipation hummed between them as the door closed. There wasn't going to be any knocks that needed to be answered tonight.

Ambria's blood hummed: passion with no restrictions.

Words thought, unvoiced, and on the edge of expression hummed at a decibel that went beyond normal sound as Yancy's eyes held hers. He would talk and he would act and he would show his new wife love making with and beyond words.

The silkily soft ivory dress she wore to the wedding was an exquisite combination of sexy inhibition, exactly like Bria. Slinky straps and soft material flowed straight and simple but hung to her body, her curvy body he thought as he pulled her back into his front when she tried to move past him and into the bathroom. The curve of her bottom aligned with his hardness. Yancy shifted against her. Slow, purposeful movements quickly elevated him to pure excitement. He knew where tonight would end and how every moment in between would be spent.

The dress she was wearing reached just below her knees and Yancy found his hands reaching down toward the edge so that he could run his fingers up her smooth, brown legs. "Should I tell you what I plan to do to you?"

"Every second."

"How about a second before it happens?"

"How about, absolutely?"

Yancy's full bodied laughter caused a friction of movement from the back of her thighs to the sensitive skin behind her ears where his warm breath blew with each heavy chuckle. "Can you feel what you do to me?"

"How can I not?"

Yancy turned her to face him and held her eyes, "I love you and I'm going prove it to you by loving every part of your body."

"Every part? Tonight?"

"We'll take it slow but eventually I'll get to each and every part, and when I'm done I've going to do it over and over again." Her husband said this while laying a gentle kiss on her forehead, the crook of her elbow, her neck and finally her fingertips.

"For the rest of our lives?"

"Forever."

"Yancy?"

"Yes, Bria."

"I love you."

"I know," he said as her hero in black went to his knees, his hands reaching up to wrap around her hips. She waited to hear the words before the actions that would lead to an unstoppable beginning. "I love your curves and I'm going to take myself around them starting down here."

"Where, Yancy? How?"

"With this," he answered raising a finger. "I'm going to trace your calf and then kiss my way up to the back of your knees and up your thighs and then…" he trailed off.

"And then?" Ambria asked.

"And then I plan to linger there for a while."

"'Oh."

"Oh is right. And do you know why?" he asked as a finger trailed up her calf, his other arm holding her bottom. "I'll tell you why," he said when Ambria, so caught up in what he was doing to her forgot to ask. "I want to feel your warmth and take in the reaction of my hands and lips on your skin," he continued as his lips followed the trail his finger had taken.

"I'm already reacting," she told him, a rush of moist heat narrowing in on one particular area of her body. Yancy looked up at her, his hands working its way up her thigh, a firm finger moving up and trailing down, his mouth blowing a concentrated breath on her stomach that tightened and ached until, still on his knees he moved behind her placing himself under her dress as his mouth tasted Bria's soft smooth skin following a meandering path to the throbbing need that was her core.

Warm fingers skimmed between her thighs opening her legs as he stood behind her once more, his entire body covering her as it always did.

"Open your legs and lean into me," Yancy whispered as his hands skimmed over her. I'm going to," he paused, "--discover you with my fingers," he finished.

Yancy discovered a great deal, mostly that the touch of his bare fingers against her was enough to pull her apart. Ambria came apart and then again as his finger got to know her very well. Coming down from that, high Ambria wanted the same for Yancy, her husband.

A bit apprehensive about her ability Ambria turned. Still within the circle of his arms she held his eyes and whispered, him, "My turn."

Yancy watched as Bria slowly dropped to her knees and reached up to his belt, her fingers dropping to caress the hard ridge just below. "I'm going to get to know you a whole lot better."

"How?" Yancy looked down at her, his face saying it all. Pausing as if she really had to think about her answer she stared at him and Yancy was certain he had grown even harder as she did.

"I want to touch you and hold you in my hands."

"Yesssss!" was all he said as her fingers went to his belt. Soon his pants were down and his boxers bulging. Ambria reached higher and inched her hands up hard thighs flexing as she got closer to his groin. She felt the heat of him before he brushed against her hand. Yancy's warmth pulled at her hand, her palms itched to hold him and she did standing as her hand caressed him. Overwhelm by the size and heat of him Ambria pressed her body into Yancy and held him as she kissed him, pulling back a second later. "I want to kiss you there."

Yancy pulled in a breath. "Only once and then we're heading to that bed," he said in a harsh breath.

Bria nodded, once again she knelt before him and gently pulled the boxers away. He sprang forward and Ambria felt her entire body aching. Aching with what she wanted to do to him and the need to feel his hands on her and his body a part of hers. Her hands wanted to caress, her breasts wanted to be held and loved. She wanted Yancy against and inside of her. It was as simple as that.

"I want you," she told him before softly pressing her lips against his hardness.

One kiss was all she was allowed when Yancy pulled her up and taking both hands backed into the bed until he fell, taking her with him so that she landed on top of him. Rolling until she was beneath him Yancy said, "I'm going to be inside of you and then we'll have the rest of the night for everything else."

"I've looking forward to both."

Without another word his hands had removed the rest of her clothes and his. Skin to skin they touched their groins met like a heated magnet and his eased into her filling her making her want more until he pushed forward pausing after he broke through her natural resistance.

Yancy paused taking in heavy breaths as he listened to her own. Unable to stop himself he nuzzled the skin at her neck and as she began to relax he whispered in her ear all the wonderful things he planned to do to her. Bria's breaths became "oh's" and soon turned into moans when his mouth, lips and tongue and fingers made good on his word.

Ambria felt hot all over, she ached again, not with that first brief pain but with the anticipation of more. Her husband was inside of her. "Yancy, I want more," she heard herself say.

"I'm going to give you more. Bria, I'm going to make love to you. And it's going to be slow and... maybe slow," were the last words he said as he moved inside of her.

Ambria moved with him their bodies in tune and climbing together.

"Oh, -- fast. Too fast." He grunted as they both exploded.

Moments later Yancy rolled to his back taking Bria with him to hold her against his chest gently settling her beside him before pulling the cover around them. "Too much word-foreplay," he whispered. "I'm sorry it should have been better."

"It couldn't have been better."

"You're just saying that because..." Yancy let trail off.

"Because I love you? Because I'm a virgin?"

"Well, yes and yes." Yancy said resting his head on his elbow his fingers caressing her cheek.

"And you're right?"

"I am? I've got my work cut out for me."

"It couldn't have been better because I love you. Making love couldn't have been better because I'm a virgin."

"Correction *was* a virgin."

"*Was* a virgin, and staying that way was something I had to fight for."

"The way I fought for you?"

"The way you hunted me down, cornered me, protected and fought for me."

"Like I said, the way I fought for you, just as I always will. I'm hoping I won't have to fight for a chance to show you that making love can be even better than better?"

"That's something you won't have to fight for," Bria told her husband as he leaned down to whisper a few choice words before his lips followed suit demonstrating to his wife once again how much he loved her.

About The Author

Pamela Leigh Starr, a wife and mother of three, works to aid teachers in creating readers, and hopefully future fans, as a national staff trainer for an educational publishing company. Ms. Starr traces the budding of her love for writing back to her very first creation, entitled *The Terrifying Night*, an approximately 20-page comedic thriller illustrated by a fellow seventh-grade classmate. Long after the writing of *The Terrifying Night*, Ms. Starr found the courage to develop love stories that were thrilling and romantic and continues to do so. She has fallen in love with presenting the never-ending cycle of two people meeting, opening their hearts and finding their way to love.

Champion
by
Eve Vaughn

Chapter One

That low-down, spineless, good for nothing, deadbeat, mama's boy! Reese clutched her steering wheel until her knuckles nearly lost all color: no small feat considering the deep chocolate hue of her skin. DeMarcus had frustrated, irritated and downright pissed her off in the course of their tumultuous relationship and even rockier breakup. But he'd never pushed her to the point of near homicide.

Reese Green was tired of being the bigger person, tired of trying to get DeMarcus to take responsibility for his son and especially tired of dealing with his overbearing mother who didn't know when to mind her own business.

Allowing Jeremiah to attend his father's family reunion had seemed like a good idea. When DeMarcus suggested their son attend, Reese thought perhaps her ex was turning over a new leaf and wanted to spend time with his child. She should have known better. Turns out his mother thought it would look bad if Jeremiah didn't show up. To know that they'd only invited him to save face was beyond enough.

She'd never gone to court for a formal agreement on child support payments as long as he spent time with their son, but he couldn't even do that. Now she was seriously reconsidering that particular course of action. But still, she knew how much Jeremiah missed his dad no matter how sorry he was.

Reese checked her face in the mirror to wipe away all signs of tears when she parked. The last thing she needed was to let her son see her cry. He was a sensitive kid and didn't need the emotional burden of her problems.

She reached to the backseat and gave her son a gentle shake. "Baby, wake up. We're home."

Jeremiah stretched, releasing a yawn. Once he was alert, instead of the ready smile he usually wore he looked on the verge of tears. It tore at her heart.

Once they were inside, he turned to her, his expression forlorn. "I think I'm ready for bed."

"But it's only six-thirty. I thought we'd watch Transformers on

DVD and eat ice cream."

Jeremiah shook his head. "I'm kind of tired."

It wasn't like him to turn down his favorite movie and junk food, but she didn't press the issue. When he was ready to talk he would. "Okay, baby. I'll be upstairs to check in when you're all washed up."

He nodded and turned to go, his gait awkward because of his leg braces. Once he was out of earshot, Reese indulged in the tears she'd been holding back since her altercation with her ex and his family. Her heart broke over their treatment of Jeremiah and deep down she knew it would never change because they had a problem with her. DeMarcus's mother in hated her guts and never made a secret of it.

From the time she and DeMarcus began dating in her junior year in high school, Nona Stevens made it clear Reese wasn't good enough for her only son. And not once did DeMarcus stand up for her. Yet, like a fool, she stood by her man believing one day he'd stand up to his mother and defend her, but it never happen. When she got pregnant, it only made things worse. Finally, she walked away from a man who never put anyone above himself, his selfish ambitions and his mother.

She hated that he ignored their son and often looked at him with contempt.

Her phone rang interrupting her musings. "Hello?"

"May I speak with Ms. Green?" the voice on the other end asked.

"Speaking."

"This is Jennifer from the Montgomery County Big Brother's Big Sister's Program. I was calling in reference to the application you'd filled out on behalf of Jeremiah a few months back."

"Oh, yes. I didn't think I'd hear back from you guys for a while after you told me how long the wait list was for a big brother." Because Jeremiah saw so little of his father she thought enrolling him in the popular outreach program would provide her son with a positive male role model. But after meeting with the match specialist she was informed that some little boys had been on the wait list for months because there was a shortage of eligible men volunteering for the program.

"We've have surge in volunteers lately. And I'm please to inform you that we've found a match for Jeremiah. Are you still interested in having your son participate?"

"Yes. I'd have to meet them first, though."

"Of course. We do thorough background checks on all volunteers, but we want to make sure the Big and Little will get along so we'd like to set up a meeting between Jeremiah and his new big brother with you and I present to see how they interact. If all goes well, then I'll brief you on our guidelines and you and the Big can work out a schedule for when it's convenient for him to spend time with Jeremiah."

"That sounds great. What time can we meet?"

"Mr. Austin says he's available anytime this week after six. We could come over to your place, that way Jeremiah will be on his home turf. But let me tell you a little bit about him first. His name is J.T. Thirty-three years old, he's recently moved back from California and he's opened up a business in the city. He's really excited to meet Jeremiah."

He sounded responsible which is the kind of guy Jeremiah needed in his life. And the fact that he volunteered to spend time with a child in need spoke volumes about J.T. Austin's character. Reese hoped this worked out. "Sounds great. I'm available six-thirty on Tuesday."

"Fantastic. I'll contact Mr. Austin and I'll call you back by Monday to confirm our appointment."

Reese was giddy by the end of the conversation. Excited to share her news with Jeremiah, she rushed upstairs. She tapped on his bedroom door before entering.

Jeremiah was sprawled on the bed looking through his baseball cards. He loved sports, but because of his disability didn't get to participate as he wanted to. She didn't give up hope that one day he would, however.

"Hey, baby. Are you okay in here?"

He gave her one of his ready smiles although this time something was missing. That twinkle that usually lurked within their golden depths was absent. It tore her to pieces to see him this way. "Hi, Mom. I'm just organizing my cards."

"I see." Reese walked into the room and took a seat on the edge of his twin-sized bed.

Jeremiah rolled over and sat up. "Mom, can I ask you a question?"

"Sure, honey. You can ask me anything."

"Why doesn't Dad want me around? I don't know why I have to keep going back over there. All he does is ignore me. And I don't like the way Grandma talks about you."

Reese knew the time would come when her son would question her relationship with his father and grandmother. She'd hoped it wouldn't be this soon. "It's complicated. Your father, grandmother and I have had problems in the past. But you have to realize, no matter what, we all love you."

"Dad doesn't act like it. Grandma is nice sometimes, except when she says mean things about you. She says I'm the way I am because of you."

As much as Reese wanted to call that old battle axe out she didn't want to upset Jeremiah any further. "Your father is just one of those people who get along better with people his own age. He loves you."

"I think he's ashamed of me. Because of these." He eyed his braces with disdain.

"You won't always have to wear them. The doctor believes your legs will eventually be strong enough to go without them."

"I hope so. I hate them." He pouted.

Reese leaned over and gave him a quick hug. "I know, sweetie. Hopefully the news I have will cheer you up?"

"You got tickets to the Summer Slam?" Jeremiah loved watching wrestling and when he found out an event was coming to town he'd begged her nonstop to get tickets.

"Baby, you know I'm really not a fan of violence."

"But Mom, it's not really violent. They're entertainers."

"Well, I'm glad you at least realize wrestling is fake. Unfortunately, they're a little out of my price range but I promise to save up for the next time. Anyway, what I wanted to tell you was that Big Brothers Big Sisters has finally found a match for you. Remember when we went to the office together and you told the nice lady the kind of big brother you wanted?"

"That was such a long time ago."

"Well, she did warn us that the wait list was long for little brothers waiting for big brothers. We'll be meeting him on Tuesday. What do you think?"

"I don't know, Mom. What if he doesn't like me? What if he sees my braces and doesn't want to be my big brother?"

"Baby, don't say that. I'm sure he won't care. And if he does, he's a jerk and you're better off without him. I have a good feeling about this. I'm sure the two of you will get along just great."

"Promise?"

On her budget and there were very few material things she could give him besides the necessities. This was one promised she hoped she'd be able to keep. "I promise."

Chapter Two

J.T. glanced at his watch. "Shit." It was already six thirty and he was already late. He hadn't lived in the Philly area for so long, he'd forgotten how crazy it could get sometimes.

He pulled out his cell phone and called the case worker to let her know he was running a little late. He'd wanted to make a good first impression and there was very little chance of that now. He'd hung back at the gym a little longer than he should have, but not wanting to meet his new little brother and his mother in his sweaty state, he'd run home to shower and change because he'd forgotten a change to bring a change of clothes.

By the time he pulled into parking lot, he was a half hour late. He was nervous when he knocked on the door. He hoped his little brother liked him.

His breath caught in his throat when the door opened. A woman with the biggest, darkest eyes with lashes that went on for days opened the door. Her lips were full and generous and she had the most delicious looking milk chocolate skin. Her hair was short, hugging her head like a silk cap. It suited her. In a word she had to be one of the most gorgeous creatures he'd ever laid eyes on.

J.T. was so stunned however, he didn't notice the apparent displeasure on her face, or the slight narrowing of her eyes?

"May I help you?"

"Huh?" The husky timbre of her voice caught him by surprise.

"Are you a salesman because I'm not interested." She attempted to close the door.

Finally snapping out of his trance, he placed his hand against the door to prevent her from closing it. "I'm here to meet Jeremiah. I was sent from Big Brothers. I'm sorry I'm late."

"You're J.T.?"

He smiled. "In the flesh ma'am."

"You're white."

This was awkward. "Uh, will that be a problem?"

"Well, I was expecting...well, never mind, I guess we can sort it out with the case manager. You might as well come in since you came this far." She stepped back and opened the door to let him in.

It wasn't quite the welcome he'd expected and judging from the little lady's scowl, he doubted very much she wanted him here. Did she have something against white people? It was a shame if she did. He could easily picture a pretty little thing like her in his arms and in his bed.

Feeling his temperature rise, and his cock stir, he took a deep breath to settle down his raging hormones before following her inside. Once inside the small living room immediately recognized, Jennifer the woman he'd dealt with in the organization. She stood, beaming. "J.T. I'm so pleased you could make it."

"Sorry, I'm late. I didn't anticipate traffic being this bad."

She waved her hand. "Don't worry about it. I was having a nice conversation with Ms. Green and Jeremiah."

J.T. scanned the room but saw no child in site. "Where is he?"

"He's in the bathroom, not that it matters. Actually Jennifer, I don't think this is going to work out. I didn't realize…maybe I should have been more specific about the requirements, but—"

"What she's trying to say," J.T. interrupted, "is she wanted a black big brother for her son." He didn't know whether to be pissed or feel sorry for her.

Jennifer reddened. "Oh, dear. I didn't think it would be a problem. We matched J.T. and Jeremiah based on their common interests and we thought they'd fit together quite well. Wouldn't you at least like the two of them to meet first before making a decision?"

Ms. Green shook her head. "I don't think that would be a good idea. I'm sorry to have wasted your time, Jennifer. I would really like for Jeremiah to remain on the wait list if at all possible for a more appropriate choice."

That was it. J.T. was officially annoyed. Beautiful or not, this woman had some serious issues and needed to be told a few home truths. "Perhaps you're, right, *Ms. Green*, I don't think this will work out either. I certainly wasn't expecting someone like her either."

Dark eyes narrowed and hands flew to curvaceous hips. "What the hell is that supposed to mean? Someone like me?"

"Already you've made up your mind that your son and me won't make a good match because of what I look like instead of the kind of person I am. I'm not a fan of bigots and I hope your son is not as small minded as his mother."

Her mouth fell open giving her the look of a fish on a hook.

"Hey, Mom, is he here yet? I thought I heard the doorbell and…" Jeremiah entered the living room, his sentence trailing off when his gaze latched on to J.T.'s.

The look of recognition and admiration was clear in the child's eyes. He'd seen that expression in a number of his fans' eyes. It was gratifying at least to know the kid didn't seem to have the same hang ups as his mother.

J.T. walked over to the child and held out his hand. "You must be

Jeremiah, it's finally nice to meet you."

The child stared at him with wide-eyed wonder, taking the offered hand and shaking it enthusiastically. "You're J.T. Austin. You were the champion!"

"You know this guy?" Ms. Green looked at him questioningly.

"Do I? He's the greatest MMA fighter ever. This is the coolest things ever. Just wait until I tell all the kids at school about you! This will be so awesome!"

J.T. wished the situation was different because he liked this kid right away. He was the kind of person who knew whether he liked someone or not from the start and he was usually right in most of his accessions. "Just plain J.T. will do. It's nice meeting you, but I think it's probably time for me to get going. I wish we could have gotten to know each other better." It was obvious the kid wouldn't have a problem with him being his big brother, but as Jennifer had pointed out to him during one of their previous conversations, there were plenty of little boys waiting for Big Brothers. He didn't need the hassle of a mother who clearly didn't want him around.

Jeremiah held on to his hand. "You're leaving now? I thought you were going to stay for a while."

J.T. gently tugged his hand out of the kid's grip. "I wish I could, but I'm not sure if a match between us is going to happen."

"Why?" And then as if he'd reached an epiphany, sadness entered his eyes. "Oh, it's because of these? That's okay. I understand." He looked down at his legs drawing J.T.'s attention to them. For the first time he noticed metal braces extending from the inside of his pants over his shoes. That explained the awkward gait he'd noticed when Jeremiah entered the room.

J.T.'s heart went out to the child who was obviously sensitive about his condition. He shot a glare toward the child's mother who'd put him in this position.

Ms. Green finally spoke up. "That's not it at all, baby. I just think it would be better if you had a Big Brother more like you."

"I don't care if J.T. doesn't have braces on his legs," Jeremiah argued.

Bless his heart. J.T. wanted to bend over and give the child a hug. It was a shame there were people in the world like his mother who'd one day shatter his childhood naïveté with her own prejudice views. "I'm sorry, son. I'd very much like to get to know you better, but that decision isn't mine to make. But I can leave you my number and maybe your mom could bring you to my gym one day and I'll show you around."

"That's very nice of you, Mr. Austin," she said stiffly before smiling at her son. "You see honey, if you'd like we can visit J.T. and in the meantime, Jennifer will work on finding you a more suitable Big Brother."

Jeremiah's gleamed suspiciously with the sheen of unshed tears. "If I can't have J.T. as my Big Brother, I don't want to be in the stupid program anymore." He turned around and fled the room not quite running but moving very quickly.

J.T. had been in the ring more times he could remember, some opponents who he respected tremendously and some not so much. But never before had he wanted to throttle someone as much as he did Jeremiah's mother. "Are you happy now?

Chapter Three

The second her son hobbled out of the room, Reese knew she'd made a big mistake. She could have definitely handled the situation better. Two pair of accusing eyes turned in her direction, and she wanted the floor to swallow her whole. She hadn't meant to come off as such a bonehead but it was the impression she'd given and ended up hurting her son because of it.

"No. I'm not happy and I apologize if you think I'm some kind of bigot, but that isn't the case."

Jennifer stood up, her lips pursed. "Well Ms. Green, seeing as your son was on the wait list for so long, I didn't think race really mattered, but I'll be sure to note that on his worksheet, but I will give you a word on warning that there's no telling how long it will take to find another match. I can't guarantee the next Big Brother available will go to your son."

J.T. walked over to the woman and put his hand on her shoulder. "Jennifer, do you think I might be able to talk to Ms. Green in private?"

The case worked batted her eye lashes at him. Reese had a feeling J.T. got that reaction a lot from women. "If you think it will help. May I use your restroom, Ms. Green?"

Reese nodded. "Sure, it's down the hall, second door on your left."

Once they were left alone, she could barely meet his gaze. "I know what you must be thinking, but I have nothing against white people. Honestly, I don't but-"

"You just don't want me spending time with your son? Look, Ms. Green, the reason why I joined this program was because when I was a kid someone reached out to me. Had my mentor not stepped in when he did, I think my life would have turned out a whole lot worse. I've always wanted to give back and in turn be a mentor for a child that needs me. I don't care what color the child was, and I'm sorry my race is a problem for you."

When put like that, her objection did seem silly, but it didn't allay all her concerns. "Please, call me Reese. Maybe my words didn't come out right, but please try to understand where I'm coming from. The reason I signed my son up for the program in the first place is because his father is more interested in chasing a pipe dream than spending time with his son. And on the rare occasions Jeremiah sees his father, it doesn't turn out well. My son needs a strong male influence in his life that I can't provide. A strong black male influence. I commend you for wanting to mentor a child, but what could you teach my son about what he'll face growing up as man of color?"

"You're right, Reese. I may not know what it's like to be a black man and I can't teach him that, but I can be a positive role model in which he can take guidance from. My mentor was a black man by the way and he taught me it wasn't what was on the person's outside, but the inside that counts. It seems like Jeremiah doesn't mind what color I am and isn't this supposed to be about what he wants? I don't know you or your situation, but for some reason that kid is letting his disability hold him back in more ways than those braces are."

Reese's cheeks flamed. "You're right, you don't know anything about my situation and you certainly don't know Jeremiah."

He sighed. "It's not an accusation. I'm just saying there's something deeper going on here. Why did he think I'd shun him because of his legs?"

Reese crossed her arms over her chest not wanting to discuss her son with this man a second longer.

"Please Reese." Something in her voice had her raising her head to meet his gaze.

Her breath caught in her throat. She hadn't realized how green his eyes were. Oh, she'd noticed he was a good looking man...for a white boy, but those eyes were like a deep jade that seemed to into the deepest depths within her. He was tall, well over six feet, lean, but the jeans and t-shirt he wore did nothing to disguise the lean corded muscles beneath.

Closely cropped dark blond hair hugged his scalp, highlighting a face that looked to be chiseled from stone by a master artist. His lids hung lower; bedroom eyes. His lips were full and well shaped. What saved him from being a pretty boy however, was his nose. I looked slightly off center with a slight bump at the top as if it had been broken more than once, and hadn't been set right. Yet it worked for him. Jeremiah had mention something about him being in MMA, whatever that meant.

Something told her this man was dangerous and she should keep her distance. She thought there were plenty of cute white guys, but she'd never been interested in one in a romantic sense. Why this guy was any different, she didn't know, but she didn't like the way her heart quickened or the warmth that spread to her core. Not one bit. She had to get rid of this guy and quick.

"You just wouldn't understand. I just think it's best if you left, J.T."

"And break Jeremiah's heart? He wants me around. Why don't you? Maybe it isn't the white thing at all. You felt it too didn't you?"

Reese took a step back with a gasp. "I don't know what you mean." Even to her that came out a bit too quick.

A slow smile curved his sensual lips. "Okay, Reese, I won't press for now. But I really wish you'd tell me why Jeremiah feels the way he does about his disability. What is his condition if you don't mind me asking."

She did mind, but something told her he wouldn't go away unless she told him something. With a sigh, she walked over to the couch and sat down. "He has cerebral palsy. Thankfully it's on the mild end of the spectrum, but he had several surgeries when he was little and he has to wear the leg braces until his legs are strong enough. In the meantime, Jeremiah can't do a lot of thing other boys his age can, he can't run as fast, play sports like he'd like to and his father...well, he's not as supportive as he could be. So my son is very sensitive about his condition. He gets teased sometimes at school and as his mother, I try to do the best I can, but there's only so much I can do. It's one of the reason I enrolled him in the program in the first place. There's only so much I can do as his mother. I meant no offense to you earlier, I just believed, well you know."

"That Jeremiah would be better off with a black man?"

"Yes. I'm sorry I came off as a bigot."

"Apology accepted. I guess I can understand where you're coming from, but won't you at least give us a chance? I mean Jeremiah seems like a great kid and I would love to spend time with him, with your permission."

J.T. seemed like a nice enough guy, but there again was that underlying current that ran between them she couldn't shake. "I don't know."

"Give us a trial period. If after that month you and Jeremiah aren't completely happy about us spending time together then I'll back off. Please Reese, I can be the man your son needs."

She wanted to protest, but he'd framed his words in a way that if she said no, she'd look unreasonable. He was a sly one he bore watching but did she have in her to break her son's heart.

"Okay, you have a month."

J.T. smiled, revealing even white teeth, giving him a devilishly handsome appeal. "You won't regret this."

And that's exactly what she was afraid of.

Chapter Four

The month passed by before he knew it. Although the Big Brothers Big Sister program, encouraged matches to meet at least twice a month, J.T. made the time to see Jeremiah at least once a week. He usually came by on a Sunday to pick Jeremiah up and spent the greater part of the day with him. In that short time, he fell in love with the kid.

Jeremiah was smart, funny and had a lot of heart. It was obvious the child loved his mother from the way he talked about her. He was a sensitive child who was aware of things that maybe some kids shouldn't be. On one of their first outings, J.T. had taken Jeremiah out for lunch and had told him to order anything off the menu he wanted.

Jeremiah scoured the menu until he'd chosen, his little finger, going down the price list until it rested on one of the cheapest things on it. J.T.'s heart went out to him. There was a time when he was that little boy, having grown up in a single family home, where every penny mattered. Except when he was younger, he hadn't been so conscious of cost. Jeremiah was just one of those people who noticed things more and tried to make things better for other people. The child was polite, said please and thank you, and was genuinely enthused about the time they spent together. He was a credit to his mother.

Jeremiah slept in the back seat as J.T. parked his truck in one of the spaces in front of Reese's townhouse. Careful not to wake his little brother up, He unbuckled him and lifted him out of his seat. The kid was small for his age and it was no trouble at all for him to carry him to the front door.

Reese answered on the first ring. "Hi, J.T. did you two enjoy the baseball game? Jeremiah talked about it all week long."

"We had an awesome time. We ate hotdogs and popcorn and drank root beer. I even caught a foul ball. At the end of the game we got to go to the locker room and met some of the team who signed the ball."

Reese smiled. "He must have loved that."

His heart flip flopped. She was already pretty, but when she smiled, she was gorgeous. Many nights he lay in bed dying to touch her pretty brown skin, to kiss her, to have him beneath her. He sported a raging hard on whenever she entered his thoughts. Something had to give sooner or later or he would explode.

Still he needed to tread lightly. Other than their initial meeting, she'd given him no indication that she was attracted to him.

"He did. That's why we're a little later getting back than I said. I hope you don't mind."

"It's okay. It's summertime, so he doesn't have school tomorrow. He looks exhausted, poor baby. Would you mind terribly if you carried him to his room. I'll show you where it is. You can just lay him on the bed, and I'll undress him later."

"Not a problem. Lead the way."

Once Jeremiah was put to bed, J.T. followed her back to the living. He couldn't help notice the swell of her ass in her tight shorts that should have been outlawed on a body like hers. Shaped like an apple it was round and firm. His cock jumped to attention. Shit, not here. Quickly his hands flew to the front of his pants so she wouldn't notice.

She turned around. "I uh, believe our month trial period has come to an end?"

"Uh, yeah." J.T. turned his body so she wouldn't see his dick straining against his pants.

Reese crinkled her nose. "Are you okay?"

"Yeah, I'm fine. My uh, leg feel asleep." He groaned inwardly. As excuses went that one was pretty damn lame.

"Standing up?"

"It does that sometimes. Ring injury."

"Oh, I see. Would you like to have a seat? I can fix you a glass of sweet tea I just made."

"That sounds great."

"One sweet tea coming up."

He was relieved to see her retreating back. Taking a seat he adjusted himself so that the erection wouldn't be so noticeable. The woman did things to his equilibrium. Reese had absolutely no idea what she did to him. This past month had been torture, seeing her and not being able to touch. It had been a long time since he'd been this interested in a woman.

It wasn't like he didn't have his share of groupies when he fought professionally, but those women only wanted him because of his fame, not for the person he was. He had no problem using them for sex when he had a scratch he needed to itch, but he was beyond that now. The fake people and the hangers on was one of the reasons he got out of the business.

He was ready for the next stage in his life but at the time of his retirement from the ring he hadn't been sure what that was. Now, from having spent time with Jeremiah and his delectable mother, J.T. knew family was what he longed for the most. To be a part of a circle of love that no outside force could penetrate.

It wasn't that he'd known them all that long, just a few weeks, but in that time he realized he didn't need another year or even another month to know he wanted to be a part of their lives. Jeremiah was a great kid. There was no question about Reese's beauty, but I was her quiet inner strength that drew him to her, making J.T. want to be a better man.

He'd fight to stay in her life. No matter what it took.

Chapter Five

Reese tried for the tenth time to get her breathing under control. What the hell was wrong with her? He was just a man. Hadn't she sworn off men a long time ago to focus on her child and career? She wasn't even sure she liked him. Well…that wasn't exactly true. How could she not like J.T. with his easy going smile that curled his lips at the corner. And Jeremiah couldn't stop singing his praises. Anyone who had as much patience with children as J.T. obviously had, had to be a good person right?

But what she didn't like was how she reacted when she was near him. The scent of his cologne had her scouring through department stores to see what brand it was. She supposed she could have asked him as any normal person would have done, but she didn't want him to think she was interested. She couldn't afford to get involved with anyone. Her heart had been well and truly shattered after DeMarcus had stomped all over it.

No, she would not react to him and she'd pretend that her pulse didn't race when he zoned those green eyes of his on her, or how broad his chest and shoulders were, and how she wanted to run her fingers along his rippling biceps. She would especially ignore how her panties got wet when he spoke in a deep baritone that would have made Barry White jealous.

Taking one more deep breath she took the glass of tea to the living room. Hopefully he wouldn't stick around much longer. The sooner he was gone, the sooner, she could get under the shower and use the very special massager.

A welcoming smile was plastered on his face, giving his rugged features a boyish appeal. The lamplight shone on his closely cropped blond head making it shimmer like gold. She paused in mid step, nearly falling over from the sight of that smile.

Get a grip girl, she silently chided herself before walking over to the couch. Pasting a smile on her face, she handed him the glass of tea and took a seat on the other side of the sofa, careful to leave enough space between them so they wouldn't touch.

"Thank you." He took a sip. "Mmm. Good stuff."

She cleared her throat. "I owe you an apology."

His dark blond brows flew together in his confusion. "What exactly would you be apologizing for?"

Reese moistened her suddenly dry lips. "For how I reacted to you the first time we met."

J.T. chuckled, a rich throaty sound that sent tremors of longing through her body. "Oh. I thought we'd gotten past that."

"Well, I didn't think it would be right to not say something now in light of the month trial period being over. Seeing as that you and my son get on so well, and basically it's always J.T. this and J.T. says that, and from seeing how well you treat him, it would be cruel of me to separate the two of you. So if you'd like to continue seeing J.T. you have my full support."

"Of course I'd love to continue spending time with him. He's my buddy."

"Good to hear. I guess I should explain why I was so adverse to you when we met."

"You don't need to."

"But I want to. Please listen."

"Okay."

She threaded her fingers through her hair and sighed in an attempt to find the words. No one except her sister and the parties involved knew about her struggles but here she was opening up to a man she'd only known a month. "I guess you've figured out I'm a single mother." Damn that sounded stupid. She giggled nervously.

J.T. placed his glass on the coffee table and reached over to place a hand on her knee. "Take your time."

His soothing voice relaxed her, bringing a smile to Reese's lips. "Thank you. Uh, basically, I met Jeremiah's father when I was still in high school. I was only sixteen and he was twenty-one. He was one of the first guys to show any real affection to me."

"A beautiful woman like you? I find that hard to believe."

"Don't get me wrong. I was hit on, but by boys who only wanted one thing. DeMarcus was different. He was so full of dreams and ambition. He wanted to be a rapper and I thought he was special and in turn I felt special because of the attention he showered on me. Right after high school, we moved in together and I worked two jobs to support us while he pursued his dream."

J.T.'s eyes narrowed. "And you were what? Eighteen? This grown man let you support him?"

She winced. He sounded like her sister Kim. "Basically. It sounds bad when put like that."

He snorted. "Yeah."

"Well, at the time it didn't matter because I was in love. But living with him became hard when I realize he had another woman who would always come before me."

"He cheated on you?"

She nodded. "I didn't find out about those other women until much later in the relationship, but the other woman I was referring to is his mother. She hated me from day one. I wasn't good enough for her baby. She would come into my home and disrespect me. And if I said anything to DeMarcus about it, he'd get angry and storm off, sometimes not coming back for days. When he'd return I was just so grateful to have him back, I basically just took him and her flack until the next blow up. I was twenty when I found out I was pregnant. Needless to say, it was the beginning of the end. His mother accused me of sleeping around, even had some of his cousins say they saw me with some other guy. She told DeMarcus the baby wasn't his. My pregnancy was a nightmare, I was sick all the time and he was less than supportive being out all hours of the night and coming home drunk. Jeremiah was the spitting image of his father, but that wasn't good enough for his mother. Basically when she still casted doubt on my son's paternity, I expected my man to stand up for me. And he never did. That's when I knew that's how things would always be with him. I realized I was better off raising my son on my own. DeMarcus never spent a lot of time with his son and when Jeremiah was diagnosed with Cerebral Palsy, he spent even less time with him. Jeremiah is really sensitive about his condition in case you haven't noticed and it doesn't help that his father treats him with so little regard. I've tried to get DeMarcus involved with our son, but he's not really that interested. That's where I was coming from. I thought…"

"A father substitute?"

"Not really. Just someone he could look up to."

"And you didn't think he could look up to a white man?"

"It wasn't that, I wanted someone who would understand the struggles of a black man and teach him the things I can't. Honestly I didn't think they'd pair him with a white big brother. I know that sounds silly but there you have it. It wasn't you. I just made a lot of assumptions and ended up looking like a fool."

"I see. Well, to tell you a little about myself, I've struggled too. It was me and my mom, so I know what it's like. After she died when I was ten, I was bounced from one foster home to the next, some bad, some even worse. But I do know about struggles. And I may not be able to teach Jeremiah everything; I will do my absolute best to be the mentor he needs."

She believed him. It felt like a big weight had been lifted from her chest to clear the air between the two of them. They'd glossed over the subject in that initial meeting, but nothing had truly been resolved. Reese found herself starting to relax. "Thank you."

"You're welcome." He smiled. That smile should have been outlawed.

"So are you going to finish that tea or not? The ice is melting."

With a grin, J.T. picked up the glass and brought it to his lips and took several gulps, his Adam's apple bobbing up and down as he swallowed. Reese couldn't take her eyes off of him. "Ahhh!" He grinned, placing the glass on the coffee table. "Now that was some might fine iced tea. I haven't had anything like that since I was in Carolina. What does a city girl like you know about making sweet tea?"

This seemed like a safe enough subject: neutral enough for her to not blurt out something embarrassing. "My sister and I used to spend our summers down south with my grandmother. I loved it, the wide open spaces and plenty of cousins and distant relatives around our age to play with. But my absolute favorite thing was helping Sugar Mama in the kitchen."

"Sugar Mama?"

A smile touched her lips as she remembered the six foot tall matron with cast iron grey hair and dark eyes that could stare down a Marine drill sergeant. But she always had a ready smile on her face and her home was full of warmth and love. "That's what my sister and I called her. She didn't want to be called grandma because that title was for old ladies."

"She sounds like a pistol."

"Oh she was. I remember spending hours in the kitchen helping her prepare a meal, preserving fruit and learning her secrets. I will probably never be as good a cook as she was, but I don't think I'm half bad."

"I love southern cooking, not that I was allowed to eat much of it because of a rigorous training regimen, but all bets are off now. I'd like to try your cooking sometime."

She raised a brow. "You would."

"Yes."

"Well, I usually make a big Sunday dinner once a month when my sister brings her husband and kids over it happens to be next week. If you'd like to come, you're more than welcome. I'm sure Jeremiah would be thrilled."

His lips twisted and something flashed in his eyes, but it faded so quickly she was unable to get a good read on what that emotion was. "And what about you? Would you be thrilled to have me over for dinner?"

"I'd be happy to have you join us for dinner. Jeremy—"

"That isn't what I meant."

"I-I'm not sure I follow."

His lips tilted to a half grin half smirk as he scotched closer until their thighs touched. "Oh, I think you do. You feel it too don't you?"

Her face burnt with embarrassment and she thanked God her skin was dark enough that a blush wouldn't be so noticeable. "Look, it's getting late and I think you should go."

"Not yet. Not until you tell me you don't feel what I'm feeling."

Her gaze darted from left to right, seeking an escape although she had a feeling that if she tried to get away, he'd catch her.

J.T. leaned closer and she knew he was going to kiss her.

"Don't."

"I have to." And with that, he pressed his lips against hers.

Chapter Six

He only wanted one taste—just one taste to determine the softness of her inviting lips. And Dear God, they were. The initial contact with their mouths was just a simple brushing over their lips. But that wasn't enough for him. With a groan, he pulled her against his chest and brought his mouth back down in hers with a savage need so strong it surprised even him.

He couldn't remember ever being this turned on by a kiss. J.T. slid his tongue along the seam of her lip. "Open up for me, sweetheart." Threading his fingers through her hair, he grabbed a clump and yanked back, causing her to gasp. Taking advantage of her parted lips he slip his tongue inside her mouth. And man was she sweet. His cock pressed inside the rough material of his jeans, begging to be free. She was like nothing he'd ever experienced. Reese was sugar and spice, with a touch of honey and ambrosia. A man could get high from the taste of her.

Reese's hands that had been splayed against his chest were now clenched with a fistful of shit in each of them. She pulled him closer as she moaned into his mouth. Pure heaven.

He wanted to touch her, and explore the soft contours of her body. Too many nights he'd lain away as he dreamt of her and could hardly believe she was finally in his arms. The press of her full breasts against his chest had his senses reeling. He wanted more. Needed it.

Easing her back to the couch, he positioned them until they were lying down with Reese beneath him. He was careful not to break the tight seal of their lips. By now she returned his kiss with equal enthusiasm, her tongue dueling with his in a battle for supremacy.

Tearing his mouth away from hers to catch his breath he was grazed the side of her neck to with his teeth before sucking the flesh into his mouth.

Reese, dug her fingers through his hair. "J.T." she moaned. The sound of his name on her lips was like music to his ears. Planting kissing along her neck and collar bone, he slid a little downer down the length of her body. He fumbled with her button up top, anxious to get a glimpse of the body that had featured heavily in his wet dreams.

J.T. pulled her shirt open to reveal a lacy black bra. It was the kind that fastened in the back. Too impatient to reach around, he slipped his hand inside the cups and lifted the warm brown globes from them. His breath caught in his throat. He'd never seen a more beautiful sight; her milk chocolate breasts were crowned with large silver dollar nipples the color of blackberries. His mouth watered in anticipation as licked one inviting tip reveling in the sensation of it coming to live beneath his tongue.

"Oh, J.T." Reese dug her fingers through his hair, holding his head against his breast. It was all the incentive he needed to take the burgeoning peak fully into his mouth. He sucked the hard little nubbin, hollowing his cheeks.

Reese writhed beneath him, bucking her pelvis against his erection. She was driving him insane with lust. Transferring his attention to the other nipple, he gave it the same treatment as the first one. He licked laved and suckled until she practically purred. J.T. loved how responsive she was. It was such a natural and honest response that made him want to rip the rest of her clothes off and bury himself deep inside her damp heat.

But he knew that he could only go so far with her and any minute, he'd had to put an end to this or else he would end up taking her. He didn't want their first time to be on a couch in a rushed frenzy like a couple of teenagers. He wanted it to make it special for her. J.T. suspected that her self-esteem was still damaged from her broken relationship. He wanted her to know that she wasn't just a fling for him. Reese was the type of woman who deserved flowers and romance which he fully intended to give to her.

So with great reluctance, he pulled away, his breathing raged.

She stared at him with dark, passion-glazed eyes, confusion marring her lovely face. "J.T.?"

He couldn't resist the temptation of dropping one last kiss on each nipple before pulling her bra cups back over her breasts. "There's nothing I want more than to make love to you, but you're not ready yet. You deserve commitment and I'm willing to give it to you, but you have to be willing to accept it first."

She opened her mouth and then closed it before attempting to speak again. "This is too soon. Too fast."

He slowly buttoned up her top, letting his fingers drift across bare skin as she went along. "Exactly, which is why I'm backing off, but I thought I should declare my intentions now so you have fair warning. I want you. And after this there's no denying you want me too.

Reese wiggled from beneath him and landed on the floor. She was on her feet in an instant. "You can't just go around telling a woman you want her like that. You and me? I don't think we'd work."

"I think what just happened says otherwise."

"It was a fluke, besides, wouldn't it be a conflict of interest getting involved with me when your focus should be on my son?"

"I don't see why I can't spend time with Jeremiah and devote time to you as well."

She threw her hands up in the air. This is crazy. I can't be in a relationship with you."

He raised a brow. "Because I'm white?"

"No. It's because I can't be in a relationship with anyone. They're too much work and at the end of the day, someone ends up getting hurt. And I get the feeling that someone would be me."

Seeing the vulnerability and uncertainty in her eyes tugged at his heart. He was on his feet and had her in his arms in the next moment. Taking her chin between his finger and thumb, he tilted her head back, forcing her to meet his gaze. "Reese, I could never hurt you."

"That's what you say now. And anyway, I just don't have time for any entanglements, with you or anyone else. Besides, I have Jeremiah to think about."

"You can't always use him as an excuse. Eventually he'll grow up and got out on his own. What then? Do you want to look back on your life and wonder what if?"

Reese scowled and placed her hands against his chest in an attempt to push him away. "I don't have to listen to this."

J.T. tightened his grip on her arms, not even to hurt, but to keep her immobile. "What are you so afraid of, Reese? I think you're afraid that you may actually want to find out what this thing is between us and you don't want to admit it."

She opened her mouth but immediately clamped her lips shut. The brief widening of her dark eyes told him he'd hit the nail on the head.

"That's it isn't it?"

She exhaled sharply. "Okay. I'm attracted to you. So what? It'll pass."

"Not if I have anything to do with it."

"You have no choice."

"Like hell I don't. We're attracted to each other and when we kiss…it's explosive. You can't deny that as much as you can stop breathing. Reese, I can't guarantee what will happen to us down the line, but I think what we have is worth fighting for and if you're not willing to take a chance I think you may regret it. Please, give me a chance. One date is all I ask. This Friday."

Her dark gaze roamed his face as if she were trying to test his sincerity. J.T. took her hand in his and placed it against his chest. "Feel that. See how my heart races when I'm around you? And If I touched you there, I bet yours would be beating as the same pace of mine."

Her tongue shot out to slide over her lips. "I don't know what to say."

"Say yes."

"Yes."

Chapter Seven

Reese couldn't remember being this nervous in her life. What the hell should she wear? J.T. never mentioned what type of date it would be so she was torn between a little black dress, and some dressy jeans accompanied with a frilly blouse. After standing in her closet for nearly an hour, Reese finally settled on a nice pair of black slacks and a sleeveless silk top. Thankfully she didn't have to fuss much over her hair too much because of the length. Slicking it back with gel, she placed place a couple of crystal barrettes in her hair as accents.

She kept only used a hint of make up having been blessed with a smooth complexion. Once she was done her toilette, she studied herself in the mirror. Not bad. Her thoughts drifted to J.T. What would he think of how she looked? Would he liked it or think she was too overdressed or maybe underdressed.

Her hands shook in anticipation of seeing him again. She felt like an awkward teenager about to embark on her first date instead of a mature twenty-eight year old single mother. Her stomach rumbled with nerves and she couldn't stop fidgeting. He'd be here any minute now.

Not for the first time Reese wondered what she'd been thinking of saying yes to J.T. in the first place? The only thing she knew about him was what Jeremiah shared with her. And the fact that he was somewhat of a celebrity was a bit daunting although one would never know from the way he carried himself. He didn't seem like the arrogant bully type she expected someone like him to be. Yet he'd lived the glamorous life when he'd been on top. Reese had performed a search on the internet and learned he was originally from Kensington in Philadelphia and had gotten into boxing as a teenager. Shortly after, he trained Brazilian Jiu Jitsu and Shoalin Kempo Karate earning third degree black belts in both disciplines. He'd won several amateur competitions before making his official debut in a professional mixed martial arts match. From then on he dominated the sport. In addition to making himself a huge name in the mixed martial arts world, "The Champion" had garnered several endorsements and made several television appearances as well garnering a few small roles in major motion pictures.

Reading his bio was intimidating to say the least and several times throughout the week she debated calling him and cancelling their date. Dealing with him on the level of her son's big brother, but as J.T. Austin the celebrity she had no clue how to carry on.

In the middle of debating her dilemma, the bell rang. Damn. Well, it was too late to turn back now. She was committed to this one date. It wasn't often she had a night out. Maybe nothing would come out of this and they could chalk it down to an interesting experience when all was said and done, but when she answered the door, all coherent thought flew out the window.

Dressed in pair of sinfully tight black jeans and a button down shirt with the first couple buttons to open to reveal the strong column of his throat and a hint of hard chest, he looked like walking talking sex on two legs. The scent of his cologne drifted to her nostrils and she literally wanted to swoon. He smelled so good. Looked so good and for the life of her she couldn't move even if she wanted to.

J.T. grinned. "You look, beautiful Reese. Are you going to let me in or would you rather we just leave now?"

Realizing how rude she must appear standing in the doorway like an idiot, she offered him a sheepish grin. "Oh, I'm so sorry. Won't you please come in?" She stepped back enough to allow him inside her home.

For the first time, she noticed he carried a huge bouquet of multi-colored roses. "For you."

"They're lovely. No one has ever given me flowers before."

"Then you're long overdue for receiving some."

"Let me go put these in water and I'll be ready to go. Would you like something to drink?"

"No thanks. I'll wait here."

Reese slowly backed away, nearly tripping over a rut in the rug. She righted herself and sped to the kitchen. Breath, she told herself. You can get through this. Quickly she located a vase and filled it with water. She placed the flowers inside and arranged them to her liking, buying herself the time she needed to calm down her racing pulse.

When she returned to the living room with vase, J.T. smiled. Her heart did a flip flop, but she quickly pushed away the feeling of excitement racing through her veins. "Ready to go?"

"I've been ready since you agreed to go out with me. Did I tell you how lovely you look tonight yet?"

Heat crept to her cheeks. "You did, but I don't mind hearing it again."

"You look beautiful."

"Flattery will get you everywhere?"

He cocked a dark blond brow. "Oh yeah? And might I add you will be the best looking woman in the restaurant tonight. Does that get me a kiss?"

Reese chuckled, surprised that she was so at ease with him. "Don't push your luck, buddy."

"Hey, you can't blame a guy for trying." He held out the crock of his arm to her. "Shall we?"

She smiled at him, and took the offered arm. Here goes nothing.

* * *

"I can't believe you did that!" Her sides ached. Reese couldn't remember a time when she'd laughed so hard. She didn't realize J.T. was so funny. He regaled her with stories of some his life in California which she found fascinating.

They had gone to a new restaurant that was apparently the talk of the time. Though it claimed to be a casual dining type place, when they walked in, men were in suits and women wore fancy cocktail dresses. The snooty maitre d' had looked down his thin nose at them. One look at the menu and they mutually decided to go elsewhere. J.T. ended up taking her to his favorite Italian restaurant on South Street. The atmosphere was much more relaxed and the food was divine and after the main course, they shared a serving of tiramisu as they talked and laughed.

"Well when you're on the road as much as I was, you get close to the other guys and when we all get together it's a frat house mentality, especially if you get some alcohol in us."

"Yeah, but streaking a group of people coming from church. You probably gave some little old lady a heart attack."

J.T. snickered. "Not one of my finer moments, but I was dared and I had a bit of a rep for not turning down a dare. Of course that was ten years okay when I had more muscles than sense."

"Now it's your turn. Tell me about the wildest thing you've ever done?"

"I plead the fifth."

"Hey, I told you. It's only fair you return the favor."

"Okay, but it seems pretty tame compared to streaking in front of church people."

"Shoot."

"Okay, when I was a teenager and worked at a fast food restaurant, I snatched the toupee off my boss's head."

J.T. chuckled. "Now somehow I never expected something like that of you. "Why'd you do it?"

"He was one of those micromanaging types who liked to breath over everyone's shoulders. It was always his way or no way. He harassed us, talked down to us, and if you got on his bad side, he gave you the worse shifts. He was awful. One day I wasn't feeling well and I asked if I could go home. He told me I'd have to suck it up and deal with it. I wasn't in the mood to put up with his B.S. so I snatched his toupee off and he told him to kiss my black ass."

"Wow, he must have been pretty ticked."

"That's putting it mildly. He ordered me off the premises and threatened to call the police. I became an instant hero among my former co-workers."

"I'll bet. Do you know what ever happened to him?"

"Not sure. I didn't really keep in contact with the other co-workers after I left and I never stepped foot inside again. But I can imagine him still being there. He lived for that place. Anyway, that's probably the craziest thing I've done. Other than that I've always been the one to do all the right things, get the good grades and basically keep my nose clean. My sister Kim on the other hand was the loud, troublemaker. Our mother's hair was cast iron gray before she reached fifty, mainly because Kim was the cause."

"Are you close with your mother?"

A wave of sadness washed over her as she remembered her mother and how loving she'd been. "No. I lost her shortly after my seventeenth birthday. She was a heavy smoker and got throat cancer which eventually moved to her lungs. The illness claimed her pretty quickly, but in a way it was a blessing because she would have been in a lot of pain otherwise. Thankfully, I had Kim to lean on."

"And your father?"

"He hadn't been in our lives since my parents divorced. Last I heard he was down south somewhere. Occasionally I'll get a Christmas or birthday card from him, but that's about it. Being that I didn't grow up with a father, I think that's probably why I tried to make things work with DeMarcus when I found out I was pregnant instead of cutting my loses like I should have."

"It's certainly understandable. Our stories are similar in that my father walked out on my mom and I when I was eight. No explanation or anything, one day he just left and never looked back. My mom tried her hardest to keep it together, but I don't think she ever really recovered from his desertion. She didn't smile or laugh or even get angry anymore. It was as if she'd stopped living. A year and a half later she was hit by a Septa bus. They say she walked out in the middle of the street because she wasn't paying attention. In retrospect, I think she wanted to die."

Reese reached across the table and took his hand in hers. "I'm sorry."

"Don't be. I think the events in my life have helped shape who I am now. Granted, I didn't have the stellar experience in foster care and I was just an angry kid in general. I was always starting fights and lashing out. One day I let my mouth write a check my ass couldn't cash. Mind you, I'm not a lightweight, but this kid half my size beat the shit out of me. I had it coming though. It was then this guy in the neighborhood took me aside and basically told me something that I really needed to hear. Tyrone told me when I was mature enough to handle it, he'd show me how to channel my anger more constructively."

"Is this the mentor you told me about before?"

"Yep. He still runs the boxing club in the neighborhood. He was the one who got me into boxing and probably saved my life in the process."

"So how did you get involved in mixed martial arts?"

He scooped up the last bit of tiramisu and washed it down with a gulp of wine before continuing. "Martial arts always fascinated me. I loved watching old Kung Fu movies. While I liked boxing, I wanted to learn more. I convinced the owner of one of the local dojo's to give me free lessons in exchange for some help around his place. MMA came a little later. I got into that accidentally. A friend and I were just looking to make some fast cash and signed up for one of those amateur bouts. I ended up winning and got a taste for it. The rest as they say is history."

Reese smirked, "And then the fame and fortune came."

"I can't complain about the money, but the fame I could take of leave. I'm not a Hollywood type of guy and if it weren't for an extremely persistent agent, I probably never would have taken any movie or television roles. Half the stuff I endorsed I'd never even tried and it was just getting crazy."

"Is that why you retired?"

"That was a big part of it, but for a long time I sensed something was missing and I could never figure out what it was. All I know is that I no longer got that rush when I got into the cage. Mixed Martial arts is one of those things that take a lot of heart which I didn't have anymore."

"And how have you settled in to retirement?"

"I like it. My gym has been a success so far and I have a competent general manager who oversees the operational side of it so I don't have to be as hands on. It frees me up to do things I enjoy, like volunteering and spending time with people I care about."

His words seemed to hold a wealth of meaning she wasn't sure she wanted to delve into. Sure, she was having a good time with him tonight. Actually she was having a great time, but afterwards, after tonight then what? She quickly changed the subject to what she hoped was neutral territory. "You said you didn't know what you were looking for when you got tired of fighting. Did you ever find what you were looking for?"

He ran his tongue across his sensually full lips as if he were a wolf eyeing a particularly tasty morsel. "I believe I have." His direct blue gaze looked at her as if he was seeing into her soul, making Reese squirm in her seat. If she was a conceited woman she'd think he was talking about her.

"I see." She took her glass and swallowed its remaining contents.

J.T. smirked. "Chicken."

"What's that supposed to mean?"

"I think you know what I'm talking about."

She couldn't meet his gaze, turning her head away from him. "I don't."

"Liar. But we'll play it your way. For now."

Chapter Eight

"What's wrong with you boy? You seem mighty jittery today. And you're not focused." Tyrone eyed J.T. with his shrewd gaze.

J.T. swung at the body bag again, but his mentor, Tyrone, was right. He wasn't focused and couldn't stop thinking about his date the night before and Sunday dinner with Reese and her family. After his date with Reese, he realized his instincts about her had been right from the beginning. She was the one. And he believed his feelings were reciprocated even though she still held a part of himself back from him. That worried him.

What would he need to do to break through her reserve? From the way Reese had spoke of how close she was with her sister Kim, he knew this meal could either make or break what he was trying to build with them. Damn, he wanted to meet the bastard that made Reese so unsure of herself as a woman. She was beautiful, desirable, possessed an innate sweetness and she had a touch of vulnerability that made him want to protect her.

J.T. sighed, giving up all attempts to continue the sparing exercise. "I guess you can put it down to nerves, I guess."

"Oh yeah? What you got to be nervous about? Heard that fancy gym of yours was doing well. Doesn't hurt that it's being run by a bona fide celebrity." Tyrone gave him a playful wink.

"Cut it out with that celebrity mess. I'm still the same Jonas Todd who you used to chew out quite frequently."

The older man chuckled. "Not quite the same, but you didn't turn out so bad. So what's the matter?"

Tyrone was a father to him who he could tell anything to, but he'd never talked about matters of the heart with him before. It was hard to put into words what he felt for Reese and he wasn't sure if it was even right to read anymore into what they had until she herself confirmed it.

"Whatever is on your mind, you know you can tell me, son."

"Well, it's about a woman."

The older man's brow shot up, but he didn't say anything, instead he nodded his head as if signaling J.T. to continue.

"We had our first date last night and everything went well. I took her out to my favorite spot to eat and then to a jazz club to hear to some live music. We had a great time. I think we really made a connection."

"So what's the problem?"

"I really like her, but I sense she's scared to open up to me because of her past. Even though we had a great time, I got the feeling she was holding a part of herself back from me, it's almost as if she's scared to open up to me. I understand her ex did a number on her, but I don't know how to break through."

"Sometimes you have give a seed a little extra sunshine and water before it can sprout."

Tyrone was known for his euphemisms, most of which didn't make a lick of sense, and but this one hit home.

"So you think I just need to give her some time? I can do that if I didn't think she'd try to eventually push me away. It's like I can see the cogs spinning in her head as if she's trying to come up with reasons why we shouldn't be together."

"Then you should counter them with reasons why you should."

"I guess you're right, but I'm worried that if I push too hard I'll frighten her away. I really think we made some progress last night, but I'm still uncertain how to go on."

"Give her the time she needs boy, but let her know that you'll be there for her. Be her friend and take and listen to her needs. She'll appreciate you for it."

"That's pretty wise of you. When did you become such an expert on love?"

"The Missus have got me watching Dr. Phil now. By the way she wants to know when you're coming over for dinner."

"Well, if I have my way, I'll be spending a lot of time with Reese, so let's play it by ear. Tell Miss Myra that I miss her cooking."

"Well you don't have to come by just to eat. You could just come by for a visit sometime. Or are you too Hollywood to come to the old neighborhood?"

"Don't start you start with that. And if I'm not mistaken, I am in the old neighborhood."

"You know what I mean. You come to boxing club, but you don't go anywhere else, visit old friends, that kind of thing."

"Mainly because most of the so called friends I used to hang with are either dead or in jail. Come on, cut me some slack."

"I suppose you're right. You do help me around here a lot. The youth program you started up here is keeping a lot of the young fellas off the street and I don't have to tell you how a lot of them look up to you. I don't say this much, but I'm very proud of you. You turned out to a be a fine young man and if that lady you like doesn't see that then that's her lose."

Tyrone wasn't one to be over complimentary with anyone, giving his praise sparingly, so to hearing this from someone he respected so much touched J.T. "Thanks, Tyrone." Something compelled him to reach over and give the older man a hug.

Though the older man returned his hug, he seemed slightly uncomfortable with this public display of affection. "Well, don't let it go to your head or anything. To me, you'll always be that punk kid that got his ass whipped by little Jimmy Smith."

J.T. chuckled. "Ouch. You'll never let me live that down will you."

Tyrone's dark eyes twinkled with humor. "Not a chance. Now, are we going to stand around here yammering or are we going to finish this workout. I'm an old man, my time is precious."

J.T. shook his head. Good old Tyrone. Talking to his mentor always seemed to put things into perspective. Some of the nerves that had plagued him only a few minutes ago, seemed to drain away. His confidence was boosted and he fully intended to charm the socks off of Reese's sister and win Reese's heart in the end. This was a fight he didn't intend losing.

Chapter Nine

"Girl, if you keep looking at that clock as if you expect it to speed up time," Kim chuckled, pulling the baked macaroni and cheese from the oven.

"Am I? I didn't notice." Reese stirred the greens even though it wasn't really necessary. She just needed to give her hands something to do. J.T. would be here any minute and while this was supposed to be an informal gathering, with family, but she couldn't shake the feeling that how this day went would determined where things were headed for her and J.T.

"I guess not because you've been stirring those greens for the past ten minutes. You're going to tear them to shreds if you keep going on like that."

"Oh." Reese replaced the lid with a sigh. "I guess I just want things to go well today. I know you were never crazy about DeMarcus. And I really want you to like J.T."

Kim raised a brow. "I didn't like DeMarcus because he was a twenty-year old bum still living with his mother with no ambition other than to chase the pipe dream of being a rapper. You were only sixteen years old when he attached himself to you like a parasite. And the fact that he ignores his own son while he still cleaves to his mama's breast makes him even less than a man in my opinion. Sis, I know what you tried so hard to make it work with him. He was your first love and I have to admit, the jackass had his charming moments. He had your nose wide open. I think you stayed with him when things started going bad because you were hanging on to the good memories you had at the beginning of your relationship. I know how those things work. Before I married Frank, I had dated my share of losers, believe me. Don't be afraid to let J.T. in because of what that turd did to you."

"I don't know, Kim. J.T. is so different. I mean he's from the area but he's been traveled all over the world, probably met women much prettier than me and someone like him seems like he should be with someone who isn't me."

"But he wants to be with you. And you really shouldn't count yourself out. You're a good looking woman and you have your head on straight. You have a lot to offer a guy. I haven't even met this guy and I'm halfway there to liking him already. The way Jeremiah talks about him, he sounds like a good guy."

"He is. It's just—" The door bell rang at that moment interrupting her flow of thought. "That's probably him. He's a little early, but that's okay."

"Go answer the door. I'll keep an eye out on the food." Kim gave her an encouraging smile.

Reese's took off her apron and slung it over one of the kitchen table chairs. She walked passed her brother-in-law Frank who was so engrossed in the football game in the screen before him he probably hadn't heard the door.

When she made it to the door, Reese smoothed down her hair to make sure it was still in order. Pasting a smile on her face, she opened the door, it immediately fell when she saw who stood on the other end. Her mouth fell open and then closed. What the hell was he doing here?

The cocky smirk she used to think was sexy tilted DeMarcus's full lips. His hair was corn rowed in an intricate pattern that probably took hours. He wore a pair of jeans that sagged to his hips, and an open button down shirt over a white wife beater t-shirt and a large gold chair with a medallion almost as large as his head. He was thirty-three years old but still dressed like a teenager. With his smooth dark chocolate skin and bedroom eyes, he could have been quite handsome if he didn't insist on looking like a thug. It had to be one of the saddest sights she'd ever seen. Again she had to ask herself what in the world had she ever seen in this man.

"Are you going to let me in, or do I have to stand out here all day?"

"What are you doing over here, DeMarcus? Shouldn't you be hiding behind your mama's skirt right now."

His eyes narrowed slightly, but he maintained that smirk. "Leave Mama, out of this. She's been nothing but gracious to you."

Reese snorted. "If gracious means calling me ghetto trash in front of our son, then I'd hate to see her when she's disrespecting me. Again, I'll ask: what are you here for?"

"First of all, if you hadn't come to the picnic acting like you were all high and mighty, mama wouldn't have said anything."

"How was I acting high and mighty? By voicing my concerns because Jeremiah wasn't allowed to participate in the games with the rest of the children."

"He's a cripple. It's not like he could have done much. You make it sound like we were abusing him or something."

Reese tried desperately to hold on to the last bit of temper she had in her reserve. No one pushed her buttons like DeMarcus did. "He does have some limitations, but he's far more capable of doing things any normal kid can and I'm tired of you and your mother treating him like he can't. It doesn't help that you barely have anything to do with him. I haven't asked you for a dime of support, all I required was that you spend time with him, but you can't even do that."

"Well that's why I've come. I want to see my son and to have Sunday dinner with you."

"Like hell you are! You can't just show up whenever you feel like it and not see your son again for God knows how long. I refuse to play this game with you."

"Hold up. You were just complaining that I don't spend time with the boy and now you're complaining that I'm here. Is it really any wonder why the hell I don't come around that much."

It was on the tip of her tongue to tell him he didn't come around because he was sorry son of a bitch, but she bit her tongue when Frank called out, "Is everything alright? Do you need any help?"

DeMarcus used Reese's temporary distraction to sidle past her and get inside the house. "Everything is cool. I was just coming for dinner. I was invited after all."

Reese's hands flew to her hips. "I never—"

DeMarcus cocked a brow. "Oh, you never told me that I'm welcome to join you for Sunday dinners with the family so I can spend time with my son? You said it's an open invitation every third Sunday of the month. You're not going back on your word are you?"

Damn. He had her. But she'd issued that invitation a few years back when she'd bought her house and started the Sunday dinner tradition. He hadn't come a single time.

"Okay, I guess I did invite you. But why now after all this time? What do you want?" She knew him well enough to realize he probably wanted something in return."

"Look, I haven't always been around for little man like I should, but I want to change that."

She searched his face for signs of sincerity. He was a blank slate making her wonder what he was up to.

If she sent him away, it might upset Jeremiah, but if she allowed him to stay, it would make J.T. uncomfortable. She didn't have time to ponder on a decision before the doorbell rang. This time she knew it had to be J.T. Damn. What would he say to see her ex here?

She opened the door with a lot less enthusiasm as she had before, her stomach twisting in knots as she thought of everything that could go wrong.

J.T. stood on the other side of the door in a pair of khaki slacks a black crew neck top. It was a little on the preppy side, but she suspected he dressed that way to impress her family. His conservative gear however did nothing to hide the corded muscles of his thick arms, and thighs. He looked good enough to eat. And as always, smelled so good.

He bent down and gave her a kiss on the cheek. "Hey sweetheart.

You look nice. I know I'm a little early, but I wanted to see if you needed any help."

DeMarcus was temporarily forgotten. It was just her and J.T. "You're my guest. All that's required of you is that you relax. My brother in law is watching the football game on the television. Why don't you come inside and I'll get you something cold to drink."

"Sounds good." He stepped in. "Where's my little buddy?"

She liked the way he immediately asked for Jeremiah's whereabouts, showing a genuine concern for her son. "He's in the den playing video games with his friends. He'll be thrilled that you've come. He's been talking about it none stop since I told him you'd be joining us for dinner. His cousins are pretty jazzed to meet you too. Apparently they're fans."

Frank walked over and held out his hand to J.T. "J.T. Austin? Get the hell out of here, Reese, you didn't tell us we'd be dining with a celebrity. I've seen some of your fights. It's an honor to meet you." Her brother in law was a man of few words and not easily impressed but he was gushing over J.T. as if he were the second coming of Jesus.

Reese raised a brow. "I didn't realize you wanted Ultimate Fighting, Frank."

"The boys watch. I supervise."

J.T. smiled at Frank and shook his hand. "Please to meet you."

"What brings you to the Philly area?" Frank inquired.

"I'm from Kensington actually so when I retired I wanted to come back here to settle down. I started my own business in the city."

"And how did you come to meet, Reese?"

Reese was slightly embarrassed that Frank was asking so many questions as if he'd stepped into the role of father.

J.T. didn't seem to mind however. "I'm Jeremiah's big brother through the Big Brother's Big Sisters program."

"Oh, yes. I believe my wife may have mentioned this. So do you plan on going back to the ring?"

J.T. shook his head. "I'm pretty happy with the way things are going for me now."

"J.T.!" Jeremiah, called to his friend as he entered to room. He was across the room as quickly as his little legs could carry him. He barreled into J.T.'s side to give him a hug.

J.T. bent over to return the hug. "Hey, buddy how's it going?"

"Great. Me and my cousins are playing Tekken. Do you want to come play with us?"

"Sure. Why don't you go ahead and wait for me and I'll be in shortly. I just need to talk to you mother for a minute."

The child nodded eagerly. "Okay. But hurry up though. My cousin is talking a bunch of trash. I bet the two of us could take him."

J.T. chuckled, ruffling Jeremiah's hair. "We'll see kiddo."

The boy would have walked back to the den but he halted, noticing his father for the first time. "Dad?" Even he sounded incredulous that his father was there.

Reese held her breath, not sure how this was going to go.

DeMarcus was currently glaring a hole into J.T. his lips pursed. He tore his eyes away from the other man long enough to look down at his son. "Hey, little man. Are you glad to see me?"

Jeremiah, hesitated for a moment. "Uh, yeah. I didn't know you were coming."

"Well, I wanted to see my boy."

Reese could smell bullshit a mile away and wondered why DeMarcus was laying it on so thick.

Kim came out of the kitchen at that moment to announce dinner was ready. Reese squeezed the bridge of her nose. She had a sinking premonition this dinner would be a disaster.

Chapter Ten

J.T. was going to rip that bastards head off. The only thing that was keeping him from doing it was because there were four children at the table and he didn't think Reese would appreciate it. What probably could have been a pleasant meal, had turned tense and agonizing. Everyone seemed to be on edge except for the fucker who caused it.

Things started out fine. Reese, sister was charming if not a bit on the protective side asking him several questions including his intentions for her sister. He didn't mind though. It was obvious she cared for Reese. Frank asked him a few questions of his own, but other than that the conversation was friendly. Reese's three nephews seemed to be in awe of him as Jeremiah had been when they first met. J.T. answered all their questions as best as he could. Jeremiah on the other hand seemed subdued and even when he J.T. tried to draw him into the conversation the little boy only gave him one word answers. It soon became clear why he seemed to shut down.

DeMarcus.

J.T. knew the type, a man who liked to talk a big game but couldn't back it up. Not only did he talk a lot, he was the type who liked to put other people down to make himself feel better because he was a loser. Throughout the meal he made barbed comments about Reese's cooking and how it wasn't as good as his mother's and how uptight she was.

J.T. could tell Kim and Frank seemed to be as annoyed with him as he was. Reese however, seemed to take his comments in stride but any fool could see that his remarks made mother and son uncomfortable. When he could no longer take it, J.T. spoke up. "So, DeMarcus, I've heard so much about you. How's the rap career going." He knew it was low, but he was tired of this guy's bullshit.

Unfortunately the other man was too stupid to know when he was being made fun of.

"I'm talking to some producers about laying down some tracks. I have a few labels interested in me, but I want to make sure I land the best deal. You know anything about rap, white boy?"

"It's J.T. and yes, I enjoy rap. So what do you do in the meantime while you're in pursuit of this dream?"

Kim snickered and Frank cleared his throat loudly. He could hear Reece groan.

DeMarcus still didn't seem to have a clue that he looked like a big tool. "I write songs, it takes up most of my time."

"I see. So you're currently unemployed then?"

Kim snickered even harder catching DeMarcus's attention. As if a light bulb went off over his head, he swung an angry gaze toward J.T. "What the hell are you saying?"

"I'm not trying to say anything. I'm merely asking a question."

"What I do is none of your fucking business. Who the fuck invited you here in the first place?"

"Watch your mouth, DeMarcus," Kim scolded.

"DeMarcus, please," Reese pleaded.

Out of the corner of his eye, J.T. could see Jeremiah sliding deeper into his chair as if he was trying to disappear. As must as he wanted to take it to this dipshit, J.T. knew he had to back off.

"If I've offended you, I apologize."

DeMarcus however wasn't mollified. In fact he seemed even more incensed. He turned his angry gaze toward Reese. "What the hell is he doing here anyway? You messing with white boys now? Black men no longer good enough for you."

"That's none of your business, DeMarcus. And if you can't be civil at my dinner table you know where the door is."

"Why should I be the one to leave?"

J.T. couldn't hold his tongue if he tried. "Maybe because you're the one who's making everyone uncomfortable."

DeMarcus pushed away from the table and stood abruptly. "Who the hell you talking to? I will fuck you up."

J.T. cut his gaze toward Jeremiah who has sunk even deeper into his seat and then to Reese who's mouth hung open. "That's enough. You were asked nicely to refrain from the profanity." He stood up and walked toward the door. "Perhaps we can go outside and discuss this like adults so everyone else can finish their meal in peace?"

"Are you threatening me? You think you gonna do something?"

"Talk."

"What we got to talk about? I suggest you keep your damn mouth shut and stay out of business that has nothing to do with you. You may be fucking Reese now, but I'm still that kid's father."

The collective gasp around the table was the final straw. J.T. had had enough. Standing abruptly, he faced the other man. He towered over DeMarcus by a good six inches. "You have ten seconds to apologize to Reese, your son and everyone else at this table for your foul manner or I will personally throw you out."

"Fuck you!"

Some people just didn't know when to quit. In one swift movement he grabbed the other man by the collar and dragged him toward the door. DeMarcus was no lightweight, but with the element of surprise on his side he was about to get his adversary outside with little effort.

J.T. stepped outside as well and closed the door behind him.

Seeming to recover quickly from his ejection, DeMarcus charged toward him swinging wildly which J.T. managed to side step. He had no plans of throwing punches. Fighting the other guy was pointless. His opponent came at him again swinging for J.T.'s head.

He dodged the blow again and then another. For each punch thrown his way he managed to avoid and after a while it was becoming obvious the other man was tiring himself out.

"Fight me like a man, white boy? What's the matter are you scared?" DeMarcus panted heavily as if this was the most exercise he'd had a in a long time.

"I don't want to fight you, DeMarcus. We're too old for this bullshit and your son is inside. Is this the kind of example you want to set for him?"

DeMarcus's eyes narrowed. "Don't tell me how the hell I should act around my son. If anything he needs to learn how to be a man." He swung again.

J.T. moved to the side. "Acting uncouth and then threatening to beat the shit of out me is doing that?"

"He's got to know you can't take any crap or this world will swallow you whole. Seeing as I have to start spending time with the boy now or else his mother will start asking for child support payments, I don't want him being no sissy."

J.T. couldn't believe his ears. He's already figured DeMarcus was a worthless piece of shit, but this took the cake. Narrowing his eyes, he spoke with more calm than he felt. "Are you saying you only want to spend time with your son now, because you don't want to make child support payments?"

"I'm about to hit it big and I don't want Reese coming after my bankroll. My mama said that's what all the hood rats are like. You make a little extra dough and they always have their hands out."

"And you don't think you should help her out financially for raising your son on her own?" J.T. was absolutely incredulous. He simply couldn't believe there was someone in the world this damn slimy.

"I never wanted the kid anyway and look at him. He's useless with those things on his legs. But I'm trying to be a good father, despite everything."

"Good father? On what planet? Bizarro world?"

DeMarcus sneered and threw a punch in J.T.'s direction. This time J.T. was waiting for him, catching DeMarcus's fist and then grappling the man in a chokehold with one arm and twisting DeMarcus's arm behind his back with the other.

"Let me go, motherfucker!" DeMarcus squirmed but cried out in pain when J.T. tightened the hold he had on his arm.

"Listen jackass, if I ever hear you say one negative things about Reese and Jeremiah again, I will tear your fucking head off. Jeremiah is a great kid and if you took your head out of your mama's ass for more than a few seconds you would see that. He's smart, funny and has a lot of heart. Any man would be proud to call him son. As for Reese, she's the mother of your son and therefore deserves your respect. And if you were any kind of man you wouldn't talk to her the way you did in there, especially in the presence of her son and other children. The next time you see, Jeremiah, you better act like you want to be there instead of it being a chore. Got it?"

DeMarcus tightened his lips mutinously.

J.T. twisted his arm harder. "I said do you got it?"

DeMarcus cried out in obvious pain. "Yeah, I got it. Just let me go, will ya?"

J.T. released the man with a hard shove sending his adversary to the ground. When it looked like the fool would get up and try to charge him again, he shook his head. "I wouldn't if I were you. I hold two black belts and though I'm retired from the ring, I'm not adverse to using my skills on you. And I'll warn you right now. I don't fight fair."

The other man looked as if he was debating on whether to make a move but thought against it. Instead, he pulled up his sagging pants and walked toward his vehicle, but not before he shot J.T. one last hateful glare.

Something told J.T. that DeMarcus wouldn't be around for a while if he decided to show his face again.

Chapter Eleven

"Mom how come you get to hang out with J.T. tonight? I want to stay home with you guys," Jeremiah whined.

"Your aunt will be here any minute now, and she has a fun weekend lined up for you boys. Aren't you excited about going to the movies, eating junk food and staying up as late as you want? Besides, J.T. promised to pick you up on Sunday and take you out for ice cream."

The child sighed. "I guess that okay. Mom, can I ask you something?"

"Sure, baby."

"Are you and J.T. gonna get married?"

That question took her by surprise but she should have known it would come sooner or later. She and J.T. had been dating for six months now and things couldn't be going better. He was considerate, funny, charming an excellent conversationalist, not to mention he made her toes curls with just a look from his smoldering green eyes.

Even with their busy schedules he made time to spend with her and Jeremiah separately and sometimes together. It had been time since she'd let someone into her heart and it felt nice. Since he'd come into their lives, Jeremiah had blossomed and was more accepting of his condition. J.T. was even teaching him some karate which Jeremiah seemed to be a natural at. He never asked about his father anymore, didn't even seem to miss him.

After that disastrous Sunday dinner, DeMarcus stayed away for the most part, showing up every blue moon, surprisingly however, he was cordial and was on his best behavior. J.T. had never shared what he and DeMarcus had talked about when they were outside, but it must have spooked DeMarcus really good because every time J.T. was over when her ex came around, DeMarcus looked like he saw a ghost.

Reese no longer felt bitter toward her ex. In fact she felt sorry for him. He was a man in his mid-thirties who didn't have the talent or the drive to achieve what he still wanted most. He lived with a mother who did everything for him and hindered any possibility for a mature adult relationship with any woman. He was a man boy who would never grow up. Her son was better off without him in his life, but she would never make that decision for him and keep him and DeMarcus apart. Ultimately it would be up to Jeremiah if he wanted to continue having a relationship with his father when he got older. And Reese intended to support him no matter what he decided.

Enrolling Jeremiah in the Big Brother Big Sisters program was the best decision she'd ever made. Not only did J.T. enrich his life and taught him self-worth, he taught her how to love again.

"What brought this on?"

"Well, you guys are mushy with each other, like Aunt Kim and Uncle Frank are."

"Well we haven't discussed it and if it ever gets to that point it may not be for a while."

"Oh." He seemed a bit disappointed.

"Why? What do you think of the idea."

"I wouldn't mind having him around all the time. He's cool and he makes you smile. He would treat you way better than Dad. And…I love him." If her son was nothing else he was certainly observant.

It warmed her heart to hear such a glowing endorsement. Kim and her brood seemed to think J.T. was the best thing since sliced bread although the opinion that matter the most to her was her sons.

She knelt down in front of him and gave her son a hug. "Thanks baby. I'm glad you do. I love him too."

"So does that mean you'll get married?"

Reese chuckled. "Slow down, honey. If it happens it happens. You can't rush these things." She stood up and stroked the top of his head.

Reese glanced at the clock anxious for Kim to arrive. Tonight was going to be a special night. She was going to make love to J.T. He didn't know it yet but she fully intended to have him in her bed by the end of the night. The sexy kisses and heavy petting had been the reason many pairs of the silk panties she favored were ruined. She couldn't be in the same room with him without getting wet.

He was a perfect gentleman though, always telling her, he would only make love with her when she was ready and dammit, she was more than ready.

Relief flooded her chest when the doorbell rang. Jeremiah got to the door before her. He opened it up. "J.T.!"

He leaned down to give Jeremiah a hug. "Hey, kiddo. I see you're already packed up and ready to go."

"Yep. Aunt Kim is taking us to see that new 3-D movie with the talking kung fu squirrels."

J.T. grimaced. "Sounds entertaining."

Reese laughed at his expression. "That's what I said. I'm glad Kim is the one who has to suffer through it."

"It's supposed to be a good movie, Mom," Jeremiah protested.

Reese chuckled. "I'll take your word for it." She walked over to J.T. and raised tilted her head back to receive his kiss. It was only recently that the two of them had openly showed affection with each other with

Jeremiah when she was sure it wouldn't bother him.

"Hey, sweetheart." J.T. dipped his head and brushed his lips against hers and then fastened his mouth more firmly over hers.

Reese returned his kiss with enthusiasm threading her fingers though his hair and opening her mouth beneath his persistent tongue.

"Hey you two, get a room." Kim walked through the still open front door.

J.T. and Reese moved apart from each other as if they were two kids who were caught with their hands in the cookie jar.

"Hey, Kim." J.T. nodded in her direction.

"Hey yourself. I guess I don't need to ask what you two will be up to tonight." She gave him a meaningful smirk. Well, I'm not going to dally. The boys are waiting in the car and the movie starts in a hour and you know it's take me forever to find a parking space and get them popcorn and candy. Ready to go, Jeremiah?"

"Yep." He grabbed his overnight bag and ran to his mother and hugged her goodbye and then did the same with J.T.

"You kids be good tonight." Kim wiggled her eyebrows negating her words.

Once Kim and Jeremiah was gone, Reese went into J.T.'s arms. "Alone at last. So where were we?"

He grinned. "I think we were here." He caught her bottom lip between his teeth and nibbled playfully tugging and nipping at the tender flesh. His bit down, but quickly ran his tongue over the spot he bit to sooth the little hurt.

Reese went up in flames. She wrapped her arms around his waist, pushing herself against the solid wall of his body. Someone hard and thick pressed against her belly and it only made her tingle even more to know he was just as aroused from this kiss as she was. She threaded her fingers through his hair, opening her mouth beneath his to let him in.

Their tongues touched and mated, swirling around each other in sensual dance of lust. Reese couldn't get enough of him. He tasted of mint. The warmth of his moan in her mouth had her body throbbing all over.

J.T. cupped her bottom and brought her closer to him, rubbing his erection against her stomach. She gyrated against him, wanting to get closer still. Her hands flew to his shirt and frantic fingers undid the first three buttons before he pulled away.

"Whoa, baby. Slow down, I just got here," he chuckled.

She looked up at him, barely able to think coherently. "I want you." Reese cupped the back of his head and tried to bring it back down to his mouth but J.T. shook his head.

"No, Reese, not yet honey. We need to slow things down unless you want me to carry you upstairs and rip your clothe off."

She grinned. "That sounds promising."

He cocked a brow. "Are you sure?"

"Yes. I've never been more sure of anything in my life. I want you, J.T."

He caught her chin between his thumb and forefinger while his stroked her cheek with his other hand. "If I make love you, Reese there's no turning back."

"I understand."

"Do you? Because when I don't plan on ever letting you go. I want a real commitment."

"Aren't we already exclusive?"

"That's not what I meant. I'm talking about the forever kind of commitment."

Her breath caught in her throat. "Are you asking what I think you are?"

His mouth twisted to a half smile. "What do you think I'm asking?"

"Are you asking me to marry you?"

"No. I'm telling you we'll be married. I want to be there for you and Jeremiah."

If she wasn't already crazy about him, she'd be annoyed at his assumption, but Reese was too deliriously happy to care. "I see. Do I have a choice in the matter?"

"Nope."

She threw her arms around his neck with a wide grin. "Well in that case, what are we waiting for?" Standing on the tip of her toes, she snaked her tongue out and ran it along the seam of his lips.

"You little tease," he growled. Bending slightly, he lifted her in his arms and raced to the stairs, taking them two at a time as he went.

J.T. laid her down on the bed gently and stood over her, his hungry gaze slid across every inch of her body, making Reese shiver in anticipation. "You're so beautiful."

Quickly he finished unbuttoning his shirt and tearing it off. His pants and boxes followed leaving him naked. She gasped at the sight of him. He was male perfection personified. He was all corded muscled and hard flesh. A toned torso led to rippled abs and lean hips. His shaft jutted forward hard and proud. His length was slightly above average and but the girth. Sweet Jesus he could probably put a hurting on her.

Reese began to undress, but J.T. pounced on the bed and grabbed her hand. "No. Let me." He grabbed the hem of her shirt and lifted it over her head and tossed it away. She shivered as the cool air hit her skin. J.T. kissed her shoulders and the tops of her breasts that peeked out from her black lace bra.

He then undid her pants and pulled them down his her hips and legs before discarding them as well. He caught her heel in his palm and ran his tongue over her foot and up her ankle. Reese never realized how something like this could feel so good. He took his time worshiping her foot before turning his attention the other one, giving it the same treatment.

Slowly, he moved up her thighs and gently nudged this apart. He planted light kisses on their inside kissing every bit of skin except where she wanted it the most. He was driving her insane and she had a feeling he was doing it on purpose.

Reese bucked her hips, pressing silently begging for more.

He laughed. "Easy, baby. We have all night." He tongued her navel and then made a wet trail to the valley of her breasts. Reaching around her back, he unclipped her bra to reveal her breasts.

J.T. brushed his thumbs over her nipples that hardened instantly at the contact. A burst of flame shot through her. Damn. If he continued on this way she was she was going to climax without him being inside her.

"You are so gorgeous. You know that?"

She smiled, cupping her breasts in her palms, offering them to him. "So you keep saying. Are you going to do something about it?"

Lowering his head, he latched on to one turgid peak and pulled it between his teeth, nipping and sucking it. He suckled hard and deep as he rolled her other nipped between his thumb and forefinger.

Reese writhed beneath him, her core aching for more. She dug her hands through his hair as he laved the sensitive peak until she couldn't stand it anymore. She was so close to the edge, she could hardly breathe. Reese didn't know one could climax just from having their breasts played with, but she knew if he continued she would. J.T. turned his attention to her other breast giving it the same treatment until she clawed at his back.

"Please, J.T. I need you. Don't make me wait, please." She was on fire and only J.T. could provide what she needed to ease the ache within.

Finally when Reese didn't think she could take anymore, he slid down, and yanked her panties off before settling between her thighs. Hooking his arms beneath her body, he pulled her to him. There were no soft kisses of caresses. He dove in face first, devouring her. He attacked her core like a starving man. Reese bucked her hips against him mashing her sex against his face. She grabbed his hair and held on to him which only seemed to make J.T. lick and suck her heated flesh with more urgency.

When he slipped two fingers inside her channel, tunneling in and out of her, she lost it. Her climax came hard and swift, but he wasn't finished with her yet. He continued to run his tongue over every inch of her nether region until tears of pleasure course down her cheeks. Only when he pulled a second orgasm out of her, did he lift his head.

He moved over her body and covered her mouth with his, swallowing her moans. The taste on her on his tongue was heady to say the least. Finally when their lips parted enabling them to catch their breaths, he nudged her thighs further apart. "Are you ready baby?"

She nodded, lifting her hips to receive him. He position the tip at her entrance before gently easing into her, inch after delicious inch. Reese had never felt so full and stretched and the feeling was phenomenal.

"I love you," he whispered against her neck.

She wrapped her arms around him. "I love you, too. More than I thought it possible to love anyone."

Their mouths joined once again as they moved together, slowly at first to catch their rhythm and then picking up.

J.T. slid in and out of her and she met him thrust for thrust, reveling in the sensation of making love with the man who held her heart.

When her release came, it was explosive, coursing through every single nerve ending in her body. She shook uncontrollably. She tightened her muscles around J.T. which send him barreling over the edge with her.

Collapsing on top of her, he wrapped his arms tightly around her and gave her another hungry kiss. "Mmm. That was...wow."

Reese chuckled. "I'll say. Let's do it again, champ."

About the Author

Eve Vaughn has enjoyed creating characters and making up stories from an early age. As a child she was always getting into mischief, so when she lost her television privileges (which was often), writing was her outlet. Her stories have gotten quite a bit spicier since then! Eve likes to read, bake, make crafts, travel, and spending time with her family. She lives in the Philadelphia area with her husband and pet turtle. She loves to hear from her fans, so feel free to contact her at EveVaughn10@aol.com. Visit her website at www.evevaughn.com or join her yahoo group at www.evevaughnsbooks@yahoogroups.com

Made in the USA
Lexington, KY
23 September 2010